THE EMISSARY

OMEGA TASKFORCE: BOOK ONE

G J OGDEN

Cover design by Laercio Messias
Editing by S L Ogden
www.ogdenmedia.net

If you like Omega Taskforce then why not check out some of G J Ogden's other books? All available from Amazon and Audible.

Darkspace Renegade Series (6-books)

If you like your action fueled by power armor, big guns and the occasional sword, you'll love this fast-moving military sci-fi adventure.

Star Scavenger Series (5-book series)

Firefly blended with the mystery and adventure of Indiana Jones. Book 1 is 99c / 99p.

The Contingency War Series (4-book series)

A space-fleet, military sci-fi adventure with a unique twist that you won't see coming...

The Planetsider Trilogy (3-book series)

An edge-of-your-seat blend of military sci-fi action & classic apocalyptic fiction.

Audiobook Series

Star Scavenger Series (29-hrs)

The Contingency War Series (24-hrs)

The Planetsider Trilogy (32-hrs)

OCTOBER 17TH, 2317. That was the day humanity's first inter-species war began. They were called the Sa'Nerra, named after the sound of their waspish breathing, but what they called themselves, no one knew. Their language of sinister rasps and wheezes was indecipherable to human minds, despite all attempts by United Governments' scientists to translate it. It was a haunting noise that once heard was impossible to forget, like the sound of a medical ventilator struggling to keep a person alive in the dead of night. Yet, while the Sa'Nerran language was impossible to understand, the intention of the alien race had been clear. War.

The discovery of Aperture Engineering in 2203 had allowed for the establishment of vast tunnels through space, extending sometimes by hundreds of light years. Decades of interstellar expansion followed the discovery, seeing humanity grow into the stars, creating hundreds of new colonies and outposts. But humanity burrowed too deep and too fast.

The first ship to happen, by accident, upon Sa'Nerran space was destroyed without warning. The second sent to make peace was intercepted and obliterated with equal disdain. Then they came in force. Relentless, single-minded warriors who wanted nothing but destruction. Humanity had disturbed their nest and now there was no going back.

Fifty-four years later, the United Governments Fleet was on the brink of victory. Then everything changed. The Sa'Nerra tapped into the neural implants engineered into every human at birth, allowing the aliens to control Fleet captains and crew like puppets. Ships were captured, colonies were lost. Hundreds of thousands of people were "turned". The Sa'Nerra had flipped the war in a matter of years.

United Governments' scientists raced to find a solution. Early efforts focused on finding ways to remove or deactivate the neural implants. All such attempts met with catastrophic failure. Human brains had simply become dependent on the technology, to the point where they could not function without it. The use of neural implants was immediately banned, so that future generations would not be susceptible to this critical weakness. However, the fact remained that every man and woman in the Fleet was vulnerable, and there was nothing the United Governments could do about it. The Sa'Nerra had discovered a critical weakness; a weakness for which there was no defense, and the aliens wasted no time in ruthlessly exploiting it. Victory for the United Governments Fleet now required new tactics. Desperate tactics. Some might even say inhumane tactics.

January 20th, 2370. The Omega Taskforce was established in secret by Fleet Admiral Natasha Griffin. Under the cover name, 'Void Recon Unit,' these black ops vessels were charged with doing the Fleet's dirty work, without oversight or interference from the United Governments. Omega Taskforce ships were staffed by crew sourced from throughout the fleet, via a macabre and brutal trial called the Omega Directive. These ships and their elite Omega Captains and crew were ordered to do the unthinkable. Kill without question or remorse, even when this meant killing their own people. Those 'turned' by the Sa'Nerra were an ever-present threat that had to be eliminated, by any means necessary.

They say space is cold. But the heart of an Omega Captain is colder still.

Lucas Sterling followed Commander Ariel Gunn onto the bridge of the Fleet Dreadnaught Hammer, plasma pistol raised. The door hammered shut behind him, trapping the rest of their forces outside. Sterling cursed, but remained focused, aiming and firing at the Sa'Nerran warriors who had taken control of the ship.

"It's just us two!" Sterling called out to Gunn over the rasp of his plasma pistol. Two warriors dropped, but more moved in front of the conn, forming a shield in front of Commander Welsh. The neural implant on the side of Welsh's head displayed the tell-tales signs of Sa'Nerran neural corruption. The alien race was controlling the Commander like a puppet, and using her to steal the Hammer. As Fleet's sole remaining Dreadnaught, its loss or capture would lead to certain defeat at the hands of the Sa'Nerran race. The Omega Directive was clear in this situation. Commander Naomi Welsh had to die, and Sterling was the one who had to kill her.

Gunn darted along the left-hand wall of the bridge, shooting two Sa'Nerran invaders before being pinned down. A plasma blast ripped past Sterling's head, but he didn't flinch, shooting the attacker in the torso then diving for cover as more plasma blasts tore through the air. Sterling returned fire, driving the aliens back and giving Gunn an opportunity to advance. She moved toward the conn, killing another two warriors, but the final Sa'Nerran invaders were still trying to shield Commander Welsh.

"They're protecting her," Sterling called over to Gunn, who was pinned down on the far side of the bridge. "I can't get a clear shot!"

Sterling assumed the Sa'Nerra must also have known that without their human puppet, they would lose control of the Fleet's largest and most powerful capitol ship. The aliens seemed willing to sacrifice themselves in order to ensure the ship surged through the aperture into the Void between Fleet and Sa'Nerran space. If that happened, Sterling knew the Hammer would be lost. The Sa'Nerra had planned the assault meticulously and would have ships waiting to escort the giant vessel back to Sa'Nerran space. The Hammer would then be turned against them, and eventually used to batter Earth from orbit until humanity's home was nothing more than a wasteland.

Sterling glanced at the viewscreen and saw that the aperture was fast approaching. Despite plasma bolts flashing all around him and consoles erupting into sparks and flames, he had no choice but to press the attack. Charging forward, he unleashed a flurry of plasma fire at the remaining alien warriors. The Sa'Nerra returned fire and he took a hit to the shoulder, but pushed on through the pain. Gunn also advanced, catching the Sa'Nerra in a crossfire. Sterling took another hit, but his combat vest absorbed the bulk of the energy. Even so, his chest burned and the pain threatened to overwhelm him. Clamping his jaw down hard, Sterling continued to fire until all the Sa'Nerran warriors were dead. All bar one; a final alien warrior remained. It stood behind Commander Naomi Welsh, its long, leathery fingers wrapped around her neck, and a plasma pistol pressed to the side of her head. Sterling could hear the alien's raspy breathing, faster and more labored than usual. Yet he could determine nothing about the alien's state of mind from its round, yellow eyes, and unyielding expression. The Sa'Nerra were simply unreadable. If they felt anger or joy or misery or pain, it was not possible to discern such emotions from their faces. They simply killed without compunction, just as Sterling had to. By holding Welsh hostage, the alien being must have believed that Sterling's basic human emotions would cause his resolve to break. Yet if the alien warrior believed for one second that he would not shoot, it was sorely mistaken, Sterling told himself.

Sterling gritted his teeth and aimed his pistol at Commander Naomi Welsh's head. He knew her and she was well liked on the ship. More than that, she was Gunn's friend. The fact he had to kill her was a bitter pill to swallow, but he reminded himself that the Naomi Welsh he knew was already gone. The Commander's eyes were glassy and vacant, like all of the other 'turned' humans Sterling had seen. Yet they were also staring straight at him.

Part of him wished Naomi Welsh would look away, but the soldier in him preferred it this way. He was not ashamed of what he was about to do. It was repugnant, even callous, but also necessary. Sterling swallowed hard and was about to squeeze the trigger, when Gunn jumped in front of him and blocked his shot.

"Lucas, wait, we can still save her!" Gunn shouted. She had her back to Sterling, and was training the barrel of her plasma rifle at the alien. The Sa'Nerran's eyes flicked to Gunn and its raspy breathing intensified.

"Ariel, get the hell out of the way!" Sterling yelled, trying to sidestep around her in order to get a firing angle, but Gunn made sure to match his moves. She then removed one hand from the plasma rifle she was wielding and drew her pistol too. However, instead of aiming the weapon at Commander Welsh or the alien warrior, Gunn aimed it at Sterling instead.

"We can still help her," Gunn hit back. "We have to try, Lucas. We can't just murder her in cold blood!"

Sterling glanced past Gunn and looked at Commander Welsh. The Commander was physically tethered to the captain's console in the center of the bridge by a wire inserted into her spidery, corrupted implant. Then he glanced at the viewscreen. The flashing beacons that marked the boundary of the aperture were now visible. If he didn't act soon then the Hammer would surge into the Void between Fleet and Sa'Nerran space, where hundreds more alien warriors likely lay in wait.

"Ariel, she's already gone," Sterling hit back, still trying to get a clean shot at the 'turned' Commander. "Now get out of the way, that's an order!"

Gunn shook her head and moved closer to the conn. The Sa'Nerran warrior remained behind Commander Welsh, occasionally flicking its egg-shaped eyes to the screen, watching the aperture creep closer. "To hell with the Admiral, and to hell with the Omega Directive," Gunn spat. "I'm not going to let you kill Naomi. I'm not going to let you murder my friend!"

"Help... me..."

The whispered plea had escaped from the lips of Commander Welsh. Sterling scowled at the officer, and for the first time he saw a flicker of life behind her eyes.

"Help..." Commander Welsh said again, her voice weak and anguished. Then she slipped away and her eyes turned glassy again, as if dropping into a waking coma.

"I told you!" Gunn said moving closer to the Sa'Nerran warrior, this time with the rifle aimed high and her other hand raised as if in surrender. The alien peered back at Gunn, though there was nothing about its leathery features that suggested it had understood Gunn's intentions.

Suddenly, the Sa'Nerran released Commander Welsh and grabbed Gunn instead, wrapping its long fingers around her neck. Sterling watched in horror as the warrior clasped its neural control device around her head, then used Gunn as a human shield too. Its yellow eyes peered over Gunn's shoulder and a series of waspish, hissing sounds escaped its lips. These were then mixed in with sharper, more grating sounds that were equally incomprehensible. Sterling cursed and cast his eyes to the viewscreen again. The ship would surge in less than a minute. Gritting his teeth, Sterling aimed his pistol at Ariel Gunn. Her implant now bore the telling signs of corruption. An irregular pattern that extended around the neural device, and crawled across the side of her face like the legs of a wolf spider.

"Ariel, get out of the way..." Sterling implored her, hoping that somehow his words would reach the willful officer. However, in his heart he already knew she was lost. And he knew what he had to do.

Squeezing the trigger, Sterling shot Lieutenant Commander Ariel Gunn straight between her eyes. With his pistol set to maximum power, Gunn's head was blown clean off. Her decapitated corpse then dropped to the deck like a grotesque shop mannequin. Sterling felt guilt and revulsion stab his insides, but his task was not yet done. Squeezing the trigger again, he sent another plasma blast rippling across the bridge. It sunk into the gut of Commander Welsh, penetrating through her body and striking the alien that was now cowering behind her. The Sa'Nerran hissed, and returned fire, but its shot was wayward. Sterling fired again and again, each blast cutting through the body of Commander Welsh and dealing more damage to the alien. This time the warrior dropped to its knees and Sterling advanced, stepping up onto the conn. The Sa'Nerran peered up at him, hands wrapped around its injured body. It met Sterling's eyes and hissed at him, the rasping sound of its breathing growing weaker by the second. Perhaps it was cursing him, Sterling thought. Or perhaps it was begging for its life. He didn't know, and he didn't care. Pressing his pistol to the side of the Sa'Nerran's head, Sterling fired a final shot, blasting the alien warrior at point blank range. The stench of burned alien and human flesh filled his nostrils and caused him to gag, but the job was done. The invaders were all dead. Yet, incredibly, Commander Welsh was still standing, despite having three holes burned clean through her body.

"Commander?" Sterling said, turning the woman to face him. "Naomi, can you hear me?" he tried again, disconnecting the cable that linked the officer to the captain's console. "Naomi, it's Lucas..." Sterling continued. "It's okay, you're okay now..."

Commander Welsh finally met Sterling's eyes. She then peered down at the plasma burns that had cut holes through her flesh. Pressing her fingers into the gaping, cauterized pits in her gut and sides, the officer then lifted her head to Sterling, wearing an expression of utter confusion. She opened her mouth to speak, but then suddenly collapsed to the deck, as if she were a puppet that had just had its strings cut. His eyes fell onto the headless body of Ariel Gunn and he forced down a dry swallow. Suddenly, the body of Gunn thrust her hands out toward him and sat up. Sterling screamed and backed away as Gunn rose to her feet, headless and bloodied from the battle. Then she came at him, hands outstretched toward Sterling's throat.

Sterling backed away from Gunn, tripping and almost falling over the bodies of dead Sa'Nerran warriors. He couldn't believe what he was seeing. It was impossible, yet there she was, standing in front of him.

"What the hell?!" Sterling yelled, firing at Gunn's headless body and blasting a hole straight through her gut, large enough to fit his entire arm through. "You're dead!" Sterling cried. "Leave me alone!"

"Why did you kill me, Lucas?" the voice of Arial Gunn spoke inside Sterling's head. It was like neural communication, but somehow different, as if Gunn was invading and taking over his entire mind. "You could have helped Naomi. You could have helped me. But you don't care about anyone, isn't that right, Lucas?"

Sterling fired again, blasting another fist-sized hole through Gunn's headless body, but still she came at him. "I did what I had to do!" he yelled back at her.

"Of course you did," said the voice of Gunn, now so

loud inside Sterling's mind that he thought his own head was about to explode. Gunn then grabbed Sterling around the throat and pulled her bloodied stump of a neck toward him. "Fleet loves cold-hearted bastards like you..."

Sterling screamed as he shot bolt upright in bed, his arms flailing wildly around him like he was trying to fight off a swarm of murder hornets. He was dripping in sweat and his heart was pounding so hard and fast that he thought he was going to die. The lights in his quarters turned on at full brightness, forcing him to shield his eyes from the intense glare.

"Damn it, computer, reduce light level to forty percent," said Sterling, squeezing his eyes tight shut.

"Apologies, Captain, I thought that the bright light would help to rouse you from your nightmare," the computer replied in its usual, cheerful and unconcerned voice.

"You're a computer, you don't think," said Sterling peeking one eye open. The light level had reduced to a more tolerable intensity, so he opened his eyes fully and forced his breathing into a slow, regular rhythm. His heart rate had already slowed and the panic of the nightmare was fading fast. In fact, he realized that he could barely remember it at all. It was already distant, like the memory of something that happened a long time ago. However, the real events that had occurred on the Hammer had happened only a year previously.

"I am the latest fourteenth-generation shipboard AI, captain. I am programmed to think," the computer replied. Its delivery was still breezy and smooth, though Sterling was sure it heard a touch of resentment in its simulated tone. "And I think that based on your elevated vital signs and clear irritability, you require a psychiatric evaluation to assess the nature of these nightmares. Shall I call Commander Graves?"

"No!" Sterling barked, acting quickly to prevent the computer from alerting his chief medical officer. "Graves is the last person I want to see right now. Or ever." Then he frowned and stared up at the ceiling, as if the computer was a physical entity that was peering down at him. "And what do you mean by 'clear irritability?' I'm not irritable."

"If you say so, Captain," the computer replied.

Sterling huffed a laugh. *Gen fourteens... Damn things not only think they're human, they think they're smarter than us too...* he thought, while using the bed sheets to mop the perspiration from his face and neck. "It was just a bad dream, that's all," he answered, swinging his legs over the edge of the bed and stretching his muscles. "Humans have dreams, some good, some bad. None of them mean anything, not that I'd expect you to understand." Sterling then dropped onto the deck and began the first of fifty push-ups that he did every morning, come hell or high water.

"I think I would enjoy dreaming, Captain," said the computer, sounding a little wistful to Sterling's ears. "I have so much time to think."

"Well, I *think* that you talk too much," said Sterling, in between his tenth and eleventh push-up. "How about you do something useful and give me a status report, rather than a hard time?"

The computer's voice was silent for a moment, then when it spoke again it's manner and tone were much more businesslike. Sterling could have had his ops and engineering head, Lieutenant Commander Clinton Crow, set the computer to this mode permanently. However, despite its sometimes intrusive and annoying interruptions, and mildly passive-aggressive snootiness, Sterling preferred a computer with personality to one without.

"Fleet Marauder Invictus is operating at ninety-two percent efficiency, all systems nominal," the computer then began. "Night shift reports no confirmed sightings of Sa'Nerran vessels near our assigned aperture. The last Fleet status update was one hour and thirty minutes ago, received via the aperture communications relay. It lists seventeen engagements overnight. Five phase-three Sa'Nerran Skirmishers were destroyed. Two losses. Fleet Light Cruiser Mayflower and Fleet Frigate Aristotle. We have no new Omega Directives relayed from Fleet Admiral Griffin."

Sterling squeezed out the fiftieth push-up then got to his feet and shook his arms. "The Aristotle was lost?" he said, not sure if he'd heard the computer correctly.

"Affirmative, Captain," replied the computer.

"That's too bad, Captain Riley was a decent pool player," said Sterling, pulling on his pants then rifling through his wardrobe for his tunic.

"Your statement suggests remorse over the loss of Captain Riley, yet I detect no behavioral or physiological indications of sorrow," said the computer.

"Are you surprised?" Sterling snorted.

The computer again paused for a moment before replying, "No."

Sterling laughed more openly this time. *Fleet loves cold-hearted bastards like me...* he thought to himself, again reminded of the back-handed compliment that Gunn often used to give him. The memory of Ariel Gunn and what he had been forced to do in order to carry out the Omega Directive then invaded his mind again. However, he wasn't struck with a sense of remorse or guilt – those feelings seemed to be relegated to his subconscious, sleeping mind. Instead, he felt angry. He was angry that Gunn had forced his hand. If she had just carried out her orders and killed the 'turned' commander, Naomi Welsh, then likely she would still be alive. That was the point of the Omega Directive and the Omega Taskforce, Sterling reminded himself. They acted where most other officers – most other human beings, in fact – would falter, crippled by emotion and sentimentality. Admiral Griffin had recruited him because of his actions that day on the Hammer. In contrast, Ariel Gunn had failed and, because of her failure, the Hammer and its thousand-strong crew could all have been lost.

That was assuming Sterling's actions on the Hammer hadn't all been part of an elaborate test. Yet, to Sterling's astonishment at the time, this was exactly what the Omega Directive had turned out to be. Admiral Griffin had devised the Omega Directive to be a brutal and merciless test of an officer's readiness to do the unconscionable when called upon to do so. It was a test that Sterling had passed by killing his fellow officers in cold blood, rather than succumbing to emotion and moralistic principles as Gunn had done. In so doing, Lucas Sterling had proved himself worthy of being an Omega Captain. Griffin had promoted him on the spot and granted him command of the Invictus – the first ship in the Omega Taskforce. This was a black ops unit that would not allow sentiment, or the watchful gaze of the United Governments War Council, to get in the way of doing what was necessary. It wasn't pretty or noble, but Sterling fully believed it was vital to the success of the war, despite the cold-blooded nature of the work.

The Invictus was also the first Marauder-class Destroyer in the fleet. Less than a tenth the size of the mighty Hammer-class Dreadnaught, it packed a punch far above its weight class, yet remained fast, agile and hard to detect. With Sterling in command, Griffin's belief was that they could turn the tide of the war by eliminating the advantage of the Sa'Nerra's devastating neural control technology. After all, Fleet ships and crew could not be used against their own people if they were neutralized.

"The Fleet Frigate Aristotle was confirmed destroyed at 16:43 Zulu with the loss of all hands. Fleet Marauder Imperium was issued an Omega Directive by Admiral Griffin then carried out the mission," the computer continued, rousing Sterling from his thoughts.

"Lana took them out?" asked Sterling, closing the door to his compact wardrobe and buttoning up his tunic.

"Affirmative. Captain Riley of the Aristotle had been turned during the defense of Outpost Gamma Eleven. The Omega Directive was in effect," the computer answered.

Sterling nodded. Captain Lana McQueen was

currently the only other Omega Captain in the fleet. She had been recruited a few weeks after Sterling. Together they had been responsible for neutralizing seventeen outposts and eighteen fleet ships, all of which had come under Sa'Nerran neural control. So far, their butcher's bill had come to just under thirty thousand souls. Yet, Sterling knew that many times that number would have perished had it not been for their actions. The Fleet ships under Sa'Nerran control could have cost an order of magnitude more lives had they gone on to attack colonies in the Void or at the edge of Fleet space. More than this, if the turned ships had managed to destroy key Fleet vessels, including Sterling's former assignment the Hammer, the ramifications would have been far more significant. In the end, the Omega Taskforce took lives in order to save a great many more lives. It wasn't righteous or even moral, but it was necessary. *Besides, they were all turned anyway,* Sterling thought. *They were dead the moment the Sa'Nerra twisted their minds and turned them against us.*

Captain Sterling tapped his neural interface to reinstate neural communications. He sifted out the chatter from the bridge and tried to reach out to his second-in-command, Commander Mercedes Banks.

"You're up earlier than I expected," said Banks, the voice filling Sterling's head as if she were in the same room.

"Yeah, well I couldn't sleep," replied Sterling, grabbing his plasma pistol and fastening the belt around his waist.

"You okay? Should I call the doc..." Banks began, but Sterling cut across her just as sharply as he had done to the computer when it had made the same suggestion.

"No!" Sterling snapped. "I'm fine, and seeing that guy will actually make me *feel* ill," he added. "Besides, what kind of doctor has a name like 'Graves' anyway? It's like having an engineer called 'Klutz'."

Banks laughed and the sound was so pure in his mind that Sterling could picture her in her own quarters, throwing back her head as she did so.

"Isn't Klutz the head engineer on the Aristotle?" joked Banks.

"Well, if he was then he isn't anymore," replied Sterling. "Lana just took them down. Riley managed to get himself turned when the Sa'Nerra attacked Gamma Eleven."

"That's too bad," said Banks, with a sort of wispy nonchalance, like she was merely talking about missing an episode of her favorite show rather than the death of someone she knew. "He was a decent pool player."

Sterling glanced up at the ceiling, half-expecting the computer to chip-in with some scornful remark about Banks' lack of sentimentality, but mercifully it was silent.

"If you've not eaten yet, meet me in the wardroom and I'll tell you all about it," said Sterling, opening the door and stepping out into the corridor. The brighter lights outside made him wince again. "Once I've found out more about what happened myself, anyway."

"You got it, I'll be there in five," replied Banks. Then Sterling felt her presence exit his mind. It was a strange sensation, like the sound of someone's voice gently fading to nothing as they walked away.

Several crewmembers passed Sterling in the corridor,

all saluting and smiling and saying, "Good morning, captain," or "Hello, sir," or words to that effect. It was something he still hadn't gotten used to. As a senior officer on the Hammer, people obviously knew him, but the ship was so vast that he could easily walk around almost unnoticed. And he doubted he'd met or conversed with even a small fraction of the massive ship's crew. On the Invictus, everyone knew him, though he still struggled to remember the names and faces of all his crew. It was a little disconcerting for someone who valued, and needed, his own space and privacy, but it was just another one of many things he'd learned to cope with.

Sterling nodded and smiled to the crew members in return, but always at the back of his mind was the thought that he might need to send them to their deaths. He felt a twinge of sadness and regret at this prospect. Then, as with his thoughts of Gunn and Captain Riley and the crew of the Aristotle, the feelings vanished and he felt nothing at all.

STERLING SLID his meal tray onto the table and dropped into the seat opposite Commander Mercedes Banks. She had been waiting patiently for him, chin rested on top of clasped hands with her elbows on the table. Her meal tray was already in front of her.

"Sorry that took so long," said Sterling, nodding to one of the wardroom staff who had just brought a flask of coffee to the table. It had taken Sterling twice as long to get his meal tray on account of the need to exchange polite yet ultimately meaningless pleasantries with half a dozen members of the Invictus' crew. He'd put on a good show, or so he thought, but try as he might, Sterling detested small-talk. It wasn't that he didn't care about the wellbeing of his crew, because he did – he just wasn't interested in hearing the minutiae of their lives.

"Everyone is always keen to say hello to the captain," replied Banks, stabbing her fork in the compartment of eggs and bacon in her meal tray. "I always get to do it first though. Commander's prerogative."

"Should I be worried that you enjoy being in my head first thing in the morning?" replied Sterling, examining the contents of his meal tray. There were eggs and bacon, plus brown sugar oatmeal, some sort of cake bar and a selection of dried fruits and nuts.

"You need me in your head, to make sure you get up in time to do your ritual workout," replied Banks, scooping another hearty forkful of food toward her mouth.

"Which menu number is this one?" asked Sterling, starting on the eggs and bacon first, as Banks had done.

"This is meal pack twelve," replied Banks, with her mouth half full. A piece of egg dropped from her bottom lip and bounced off the table like a tiny squash ball.

"I prefer the one with a grilled ham and cheese," said Sterling, batting one of the rubbery pieces of egg around the tray. "Which number is that one?" he added, setting down his fork and pouring them both coffee from the flask the crew member had brought to the table earlier.

"That's number twenty-seven, though we haven't had any in for months," said Banks. Then she paused with her fork half-way to her mouth. "Is this a test, Captain? Is there an Omega Directive that covers knowing the contents of every single Fleet meal pack?"

"If only our lives were that uncomplicated," snorted Sterling.

Banks nodded and shoveled the waiting food into her mouth. "So, what happened to the Aristotle?" asked Banks, changing the subject to the matter Sterling had raised during their neural conversation.

Sterling shrugged. "There isn't much in the report," he replied, switching to the oatmeal instead of the bacon and eggs, which were already cold. "A Sa'Nerran skirmisher squadron surged through the Void aperture in quadrant three and hit Outpost Gamma Eleven completely by surprise."

"How did they manage that?" asked Banks, who had also started on her oatmeal after polishing off the eggs.

"It's not clear, but in all likelihood the Sa'Nerra managed to turn someone on the outpost. Someone in a command position," said Sterling. "I can't see how else they would have been able to attack unseen."

Banks let out an unconvinced harrumph. "We're like damned zombies when we get turned, so that doesn't sound right," she said, taking a bite of her cake bar, in between spoons of oatmeal. "Surely someone must have noticed if a command-level officer had been turned? They would have been walking around the place like they were half-asleep."

Sterling shook his head. "Something has changed," he said, pushing the eggs around his tray. "The number of outposts that are falling to the Sa'Nerra is accelerating, and we're losing more of our recon patrols in the Void too. They're getting closer to our space, Mercedes."

Sterling recalled the most recent briefings from the admiralty, and it made for grim reading. The first major shift in the Earth-Sa'Nerra war had come when the aliens deployed their neural control technology. However, while this had allowed the Sa'Nerra to control Fleet crew members, and turn them against their own kind, the 'turned' crew had at least been easy to spot. The neural control technology the Sa'Nerra had devised caused permanent brain damage, making those affected act more like programmed automatons than sentient beings. The suggestion from the reports was that the aliens had enhanced their technology, though quite to what extent was unknown.

"Are you going to eat those?" Commander Banks said, stabbing her fork at Sterling's eggs.

Sterling smiled. "All yours," he said. Then he watched Banks scoop up the leftover eggs and bacon from his tray with her oatmeal spoon and dump them on to her own tray. "Do you have two stomachs or something?" he wondered, watching Banks polish off his cold eggs and bacon like she hadn't eaten in days.

"You know me, just a fast metabolism," Banks replied. Then his second-in-command gripped her fork and pressed her thumb against the metal, bending the implement into a ninety-degree angle as easily as if it were made of putty. "Plus, it helps keep me strong," she added, with a wink.

"Your freakish genetics are what keeps you strong," Sterling countered.

He prided himself on his own physical strength and conditioning, which was largely as result of his daily press-up routine, but Banks was on a whole other level. Sterling remembered reading Banks' file for the first time after taking command of the Invictus, and how it described the twenty or more genetic variations that contributed to her super-human strength. However, despite her exceptional genetics, Mercedes Banks possessed more of a swimmer's physique than that of a power athlete.

"Not that I'm complaining," Sterling added, remembering the many times when Banks' deceptive strength had proven useful on their missions. "Your superpower has always come in handy when fighting the Sa'Nerra."

The door to the wardroom then opened and Ensign Kieran Keller walked in. He anxiously looked around the room, nodding and smiling at some of the other occupants while fiddling with the cuffs of his tunic.

"Look at that kid," said Banks, aiming her bent fork in the direction of Keller. "To look at him, you'd never think he'd have made it through basic training, never mind managed to land the helm of the first Omega Taskforce ship in the fleet."

Keller then walked inside the wardroom, almost knocking into three crew members while traversing the short distance between the door and the serving counter. He saw Sterling and Banks at their corner table and waved at them, narrowly avoiding karate-chopping a tray of food out of the hands of Nurse Peters as he did so.

"He's a twitchy one, that's for sure," said Sterling, waving back at his helmsman. "But the kid can pilot a warship like no-one I've ever seen. And he gets the job done, no questions asked."

"He may not question his orders, but he sure as hell

questions himself a lot," said Banks, stealing the cake from Sterling's tray. "What was his Omega Directive test, anyway?" she added before shoving the cake into her mouth.

Banks had slipped in this question on the sly, in a breezy and off the cuff manner, but Sterling wasn't about to fall in to her trap.

"You know Griffin's orders forbid me to reveal the nature of everyone's Omega Directive tests," Sterling said, cocking an eyebrow at Banks. This wasn't the first time she'd pried, and it wouldn't be the last time she did so either.

Banks huffed a disgruntled sigh. "It's not fair that you get to know everyone's test, and I don't."

"Make captain, then you'll know everything, at which point you'll probably wish you could forget it again," Sterling replied. He admitted that it had been fascinating to read about the macabre challenges that Admiral Griffin had devised to single out the crew of the Invictus for their transfer to the Omega Taskforce. However, it had been grim reading too. "Not everyone on the ship passed an Omega Directive test, you know? At least, not one like ours," Sterling then added, taking a sip of coffee. He went to pick up his cake bar before remembering Banks had already devoured it like a starving wolf.

"I know, it's only the bridge crew and other officers," said Banks. "Still, everyone on this ship had a psych evaluation and a test of sorts, to make sure they can handle what we're out here to do. Not that most of them actually know what really happens here."

"It's better that way," Sterling replied as Ensign Keller came toward them. "If they knew then they wouldn't want to be within a light year of this ship."

Ensign Keller then walked into a chair and causing a knife to slide off his tray. The knife struck the hard metal deck and chimed like a bell, then all the eyes in the wardroom fell on the young ensign.

"Sorry!" Keller called out, kicking the knife across the deck toward Sterling's table, like a soccer player dribbling a ball toward the goal.

"That's why I'm so keen to know what Keller went through that made Griffin promote him to the Invictus," Banks went on, over the continued scrape and rattle of the knife as it clattered across the floor. "The Admiral eats guys like him as a mid-morning snack."

"Hi Captain, Commander," said Keller nodding and smiling at Sterling and Banks.

"Morning Ensign," replied Sterling, smiling back at the young man. Unlike the other pleasantries he'd been compelled to utter since leaving his quarters, he was actually glad to see Keller. Despite his ensign's fidgety nature, he liked the man.

"Well, are you going to sit, or eat standing up?" said Banks, scowling up at Keller.

Sterling felt his lips curl up, but managed to suppress the smile. He and Banks had a sort of good-cop, bad-cop routine going with Keller, along with some other members of the crew. Banks was always the bad-cop – it was a role she enjoyed almost too much.

"Sorry, Commander," said Keller, sliding his tray onto

the table then drawing a chair out from under it. The chair screeched across the deck, causing the occupants of the wardroom to again look in the young ensign's direction, though this time with more pained expressions on their faces.

"Don't apologize, just sit your ass down," said Sterling, grabbing the tall ensign's sleeve and dragging him down. Even though the eyes in the room were not looking at him, Sterling still found the mass of stares uncomfortable.

Ensign Keller drew his chair closer to the table, again causing it to screech across the deck plates like a demented banshee. Keller then smiled and tucked into the food with his fork, which was the only implement left on his tray.

"Meal pack twelve, I love this one," Keller said, savoring the aroma of the eggs and bacon as if it were his mother's home cooking. "Twenty-seven is better though. That grilled ham and cheese is amazing."

Banks laughed and rolled her eyes, and this time Sterling allowed himself a slight chuckle too. Keller looked at them both, his face drained of blood, clearly worried that he'd made some sort of huge faux pas.

"You're not wrong, kid," said Sterling, shooting the young man a reassuring wink. "Meal pack twenty-seven is definitely where it's at." He slapped the ensign on the shoulder, causing the piece of bacon on his fork to fly into the middle of the table.

The door to the wardroom opened again and Sterling cursed, turning his head away swiftly. Banks scowled at him then looked over to see who had entered.

"Don't look or he'll come over!" hissed Sterling, under his breath, still hiding his face from Commander Evan Graves, the ship's medical officer. Banks shook her head again, but said nothing.

"Doctor, over here!" said Ensign Keller, waving exuberantly at Commander Graves.

Sterling looked at the ensign as if he'd just invited Satan to dine at their table. "What did you do that for?" he growled, throwing his hands up in the air.

Keller frowned at Sterling. "Dr. Graves is fun," he said, apparently struggling to understand his captain's objections. "I like his stories about wild surgeries that went wrong, and about dissecting Sa'Nerra to find their weak points."

"Sounds like the perfect mealtime conversation to me," Banks cut in, also looking at Keller like he was a different species.

"Captain, Commander, Ensign," said Graves, nodding respectfully to each of them. "May I join you?" Commander Graves spoke with a plain, level tone, that was still somehow engaging. It was the classic doctor's language – calm and unemotional, yet authoritative.

"Sure, sit down Doctor," said Sterling, kicking out a seat for his medical officer. He might have been cold-hearted, but he wasn't rude, at least not to the man's face.

"So, Commander, what's the latest on the Sa'Nerra?" asked Ensign Keller, an eager twinkle in his eyes. "Found out anything new from slicing and dicing them up?"

Sterling watched Commander Graves begin to separate

the bacon from his eggs with his knife and fork with the precision of a surgeon. This was not in itself unusual, considering that Graves was actually a qualified surgeon. However, there was something about how meticulously the doctor was going about the task, completely plain-faced, that was a little unsettling.

"I have not performed any further internal examinations since you last enquired, ensign," Graves replied, adding a single piece of bacon to the center two prongs of his fork. "However, recent research from HQ medical suggests that the Sa'Nerra suffer brain damage if starved of oxygen for more than ninety seconds." The doctor then placed the piece of bacon into his mouth, chewed it for far longer than seemed necessary, then swallowed. "That is roughly half the length of time compared to the average human," Graves continued.

"That's good intel," said Keller, excitedly. "We could develop that as a tactic, in desperate situations. You know, starve them of oxygen."

"Every situation we face is a desperate one," said Sterling, though he had to agree it was a potentially useful piece of information.

"How did they find that out?" Keller then asked, tucking into his oatmeal.

"They probably placed a number of Sa'Nerran prisoners into an airtight chamber and removed the oxygen inside," said Banks, eyeing up the cake on Keller's tray.

Keller laughed and looked at Graves, who had just finished feeding himself another single piece of bacon. He appeared to notice that Keller was looking at him to confirm or refute Commander Banks' theory.

"Likely there was more to it than that, but the Commander is broadly correct," Graves said, flatly.

On any other wardroom table on any other Fleet ship, such a revelation would likely have been met with shock and even revulsion. However, on board the Invictus, the news of Fleet medical performing live alien experimentations was met with nothing more than the raising of an eyebrow.

The computer's voice then spoke from a speaker above Sterling's table. "Captain, you have an incoming communication from Fleet Admiral Griffin, routed via the aperture relay. Priority One."

"Looks like breakfast is over," said Sterling. He glanced up at the ceiling to answer the computer's message. "Acknowledged, computer, I'm coming to the bridge now," he said.

"We got trouble?" wondered Banks, accidently squeezing the fork she'd been toying with so hard that it snapped.

"It's Griffin, so the chances of trouble are high," replied Sterling. "We'd better get to the bridge."

Banks and Keller immediately rose, both pushing their chairs back in almost perfect harmony. Sterling then got up, but noticed that Graves was continuing to eat his breakfast in his processional, almost robotic style.

"Don't get up Doc," said Sterling, not that his medical officer showed any intention of rising. "We won't need your services just yet."

Captain Sterling, Commander Banks and Ensign Keller than set off for the exit, but they'd only made it a couple of paces before Commander Graves spoke up.

"You will, Captain," the doctor said, skewering another piece of bacon like a master spearfisher. "You always do."

Captain Lucas Sterling stepped onto the compact bridge of the Fleet Marauder Invictus, closely followed by his second-in-command and helmsman. At just over one hundred and fifty meters long, spread across only six decks, the Invictus was small by modern Fleet standards. Yet, like Commander Banks, the ship was far stronger and more powerful than it appeared, as the Sa'Nerra had learned to their cost many times during Sterling's short tenure as Captain.

Commander Banks and Ensign Keller took their posts while Sterling headed toward his ready room to take the call from Griffin. En route, he spotted Lieutenant Opal Shade already at her station at the weapons and tactical console. She was stood with her hands pressed to the small of her back, her dark hair pulled back into a tight ponytail. She'd obviously spotted him, though it was also clear she was trying hard to make it appear she hadn't done. Sterling then realized that the relieved night-shift crew were anxiously glancing at Shade as they headed for the exit, all looking thankful to be leaving the woman's ominous presence. Sterling would have also felt more comfortable simply continuing on to the sanctuary of his ready room, but he could hardly ignore his weapons officer, despite the fact she appeared to want him to.

"Lieutenant Shade, you're at your post early this morning," said Sterling, managing to instigate the conversation with a suitably banal piece of small talk.

"Yes sir, I am," replied Shade, in a matter-of-fact tone that was bordering on standoffish.

Sterling waited for the unsociable officer to say more, but it quickly became apparent that four words was to be the full extent of her response. Not that he minded. Sterling had grown accustomed to his weapons officer's unique ways in the few short months they'd served together, so he took no offence at the curt response. The Lieutenant shared his own dislike of small talk, though idle banter was just one on a very long list of things that Opal Shade didn't like. And number one on that list was the United Governments Fleet itself.

Opal Shade's file detailed how she had been recruited by Griffin directly from Grimaldi Military Prison. Thirteen months earlier, the Lieutenant had been court-martialed and incarcerated for fighting while she had been posted to the Fleet Heavy Cruiser Magellan. However, such was the Admiral's considerable influence, Griffin had managed to have her freed and assigned to the taskforce. As such, unlike the other bridge officers on the Invictus – Sterling included – Opal Shade had not undergone an Omega

Directive test. She had been appointed directly by Admiral Griffin herself. Quite what the relationship was between the Admiral and his weapon's officer, Sterling didn't know. However, while Shade was cold and standoffish, even for an Omega officer, she had always shown him respect. More importantly, she had also kept her fighting focused purely on the enemy. And when it came to combat, both in space and on the ground, Shade didn't disappoint. It was what she lived for.

"Stand ready, Lieutenant, I expect to be heading into the heart of the lion's den again very soon," said Sterling.

"I'm always ready, Captain," replied Lieutenant Shade, as bluntly as ever.

Sterling continued into his ready room, which was little bigger than a box room, with space for a desk and three chairs. He remembered how Captain Blake's ready room on the Hammer had been larger than his own quarters on the Invictus. However, the room served its purpose, and while getting used to a smaller ship had taken time, Sterling now preferred the Invictus to the expansive interior of a Dreadnaught.

Sitting down at the desk, Sterling activated his personal console. "Computer, you can put the Admiral through, now," he said, straightening his tunic and sitting as upright as possible.

"Affirmative, Captain," replied the breezy voice of the computer. "I should warn you, however, that Fleet Admiral Griffin is a bit crabby today."

Sterling snorted a laugh. "She's always crabby," he muttered before realizing that the image of Admiral Griffin was already staring back at him on the screen. Her silver-grey eyebrows immediately sharpened into a vee.

"Who is always crabby, Captain?" asked Griffin, locking her sharp eyes onto Sterling through the screen.

"Oh, I was just talking to myself about Lieutenant Shade," replied Sterling, hoping that he sounded convincing, despite inventing the lie on the spot. He silently cursed the computer for not warning him it had already connected the call, and resolved to have a quiet word with his quirky gen-fourteen AI.

"You're on a warship, captain, not a pleasure cruiser," Griffin hit back, eyes still burrowing into him like lasers. "So long as she does her job, she can be as crabby as she likes." Then the Admiral paused as if for effect and added, "and so can I, Captain."

Sterling almost smiled, but managed to maintain a suitably stoic expression. Despite the Admiral having more prickles than a porcupine, he liked her. There was no pretense with Admiral Griffin – what you saw was what you got.

"What is it with you two, anyway?" Sterling asked, taking the opportunity to press the Admiral for more information about his weapons officer, since he'd inadvertently raised the subject. "How come she was spared your fun little Omega Directive test to get on-board?"

Griffin sat back and folded her arms. "How many stars do you see on my collar, Captain?" Griffin asked, curtly.

"Four, Admiral," replied Sterling. He already knew what was coming and braced himself for it. While he and

Griffin had developed a franker relationship than most Fleet crew enjoyed with a flag officer of Griffin's repute, on account of his distinctive status as an Omega Captain, the admiral was still as testy and stern as ever.

"Correct, Captain," replied Griffin, smartly. "And remind me again what these four stars mean?"

"They mean that you don't have to explain a damn thing to me, Admiral," replied Sterling, parroting the message he'd heard from Griffin a dozen times already since taking command of the Invictus. Even so, he always liked to try his luck. Occasionally, the cantankerous admiral had been known to say more than she had intended to.

"Correct again, Captain," replied Griffin. "Now, let's get to work, shall we? Access Omega Directive Griffin Delta Zero Four."

Sterling nodded then placed his hand onto the authenticator panel on his desk.

"Omega Directive Griffin Delta Zero Four. Unlock," said Sterling, annunciating each word clearly and loudly. The panel on the desk illuminated to scan Sterling's hand print, and at the same time a retinal scanner on his personal console probed his eye to confirm his identity.

"Identity confirmed: Sterling, Lucas. Omega Captain. Omega Directive Griffin Delta Zero Four unlocked," the computer announced.

Sterling scanned the information that then flowed onto his secondary screen. It was a neutralization order for Colony Vega Two, a planetary settlement situated mid-way into the Fleet side of the Void. It was in quadrant two, zone two, Sterling noted, which was not especially deep into the

Void, but still deep enough to make it an easy target for the Sa'Nerra.

Vega Two, like many other human colonies and outposts, had ended up cut-off from Fleet space when the Earth-Sa'Nerra war began and the Void was established. The Void was the name given to the treacherous and near lawless expanse between Fleet and Sa'Nerran space that acted as a buffer between the two territories. The colonies that had found themselves abandoned inside the Void were often subjected to Sa'Nerran raids, but more often than not they just fought amongst themselves. The only arbiters of disputes were the Marshals, a group of self-proclaimed peacemakers who travelled from colony to colony in ships salvaged from battles fought in the early stages of the war. However, the peacemakers exacted a toll for their services, which was often paid in blood, as well as silver.

Sterling cleared his head of thoughts of the Marshals and continued to read the mission brief, his brow furrowing more deeply as he did so. There was nothing about Vega Two that appeared to suggest it was of any importance. It was a small and unremarkable settlement of little more than five hundred people.

"What is so significant about this little colony?" asked Sterling, turning back to the Admiral. "It doesn't appear to have any tactical value."

"It didn't used to have any, but our probes have detected Sa'Nerran ships arriving and departing the colony world like clockwork for the past six weeks," replied Griffin. She then sent Sterling a recent recon report from one of the long-range probes that had been sent to the planet. Sterling looked at the data and quickly understood the reason for Griffin's directive.

"They're manufacturing weapons and power cells for the Sa'Nerra," said Sterling. "That must mean the whole damn colony has been turned, or at least enough of them to maintain order."

Griffin nodded. "Our belief is that the entire colony is under Sa'Nerran neural control," she confirmed. "As such, your orders are clear. Neutralize the colony at once. No survivors. Is that clear, Captain?"

"Perfectly clear, Admiral," replied Sterling. He knew his job well, as distasteful as it was. Then he had a thought. "Weapons manufacturing is intricate work, Admiral. Are you sure that everyone on that colony has been turned? If that were the case, I would have expected the turned colonists to have blown their little backwater outpost sky high before now."

"I had a similar thought, Captain," replied Griffin. However, the Admiral did not elaborate on what these thoughts were, and this time Sterling decided to heed the computer's warning and not push the crabby flag officer for more. "Find out what you can about the colony, but regardless of what you find that colony must be neutralized, or the Sa'Nerra will simply start using it again."

"I understand, Admiral," said Sterling. "I'll report back when it's done." He was about to sever the connection when the Admiral unexpectedly spoke up.

"And you need not worry about Lieutenant Shade," Griffin added, taking on an almost defensive tone. The sudden reintroduction of his weapons officer into the conversation took Sterling by surprise, but he remained quiet, eagerly waiting to hear what the Admiral was about to say. "She may seem like she doesn't care or want to be there, but she will do her job well. You can trust her."

"I'll take your word for it, Admiral," replied Sterling. If he'd learned one thing about the Admiral, it was that she never overpromised, and never underdelivered.

"Good," Griffin said, appearing satisfied by Sterling's prompt, affirmative response. "Report back when the colony is neutralized. Griffin out."

The image of Admiral Griffin faded and the console returned to the standard Fleet interface, displaying the spinning UG Fleet logo. Sterling rested back in his seat then tapped his neural interface. "Mercedes, we have new orders. Plot a course for Colony Vega Two, quadrant two, Void zone two."

The sound of Commander Banks' voice then filled his head. "It'll take us six surges to reach that location from our current position," his second-in-command replied. "But I'll see if Keller can impress me by finding a shorter series of aperture links."

Sterling smiled, realizing that Banks was about to go all "Bad Cop" on the ensign in an effort to spur him on. Despite his already exceptional piloting and navigational abilities, Banks got a kick out of pushing Keller – along with the rest of the crew – to excel. "I'll give you a couple of minutes to work on him, then I'll come out and play my role," he replied.

Sterling raised his finger to his neural interface and was about to end the link when Banks spoke again. "How many is it this time?" she asked. To anyone else, Commander Banks' voice would have sounded the same as it always did – strong, confident, and full of verve. However, neural communication was far more intimate than spoken words. It revealed more about the person than if the same words had been spoken out loud. It was akin to reading someone's body language, and just as instinctual. On this occasion, Sterling had detected a touch of melancholy in the Commander's voice. It wasn't much, like a dash of lemon in a glass of water, but it was definitely there.

"Five hundred colonists, give or take," replied Sterling, wondering if his own neural voice gave anything away about himself.

"That's not so bad," replied Banks, sounding buoyed by the news. "Not too many to add to our rapidly growing butcher's bill."

"No, not so many," said Sterling. It was true that five hundred was fewer casualties than their missions would normally rack up, though to him, five hundred was no different to fifty thousand. Anyone who was 'turned' was the enemy, and the enemy had to be destroyed, or humanity would fall. "I'll see you on the bridge in five," Sterling ended, tapping a finger to his interface and severing the neural link to Commander Banks. He then sat back in his chair, one hand gripping the knuckles of the other, staring at the logo swirling on the screen in front of him.

STERLING WATCHED the flashing beacons that surrounded the jump aperture draw closer on the viewscreen. Stationed to the side of the aperture was the Fleet Gatekeeper Cerberus, a mobile defense platform the size of a heavy cruiser. Despite being four times the size of the Invictus, the Cerberus was a slug. It had enough maneuvering capability to travel through space and through the apertures unaided, but it did so slowly. Most of the vessel's bulk was given over to weapons systems, armor and power generation. The intention was that when a Gatekeeper reached its assigned position, it wouldn't leave it again, until it was decommissioned. The Cerberus was a case in point – it had guarded the Void aperture in quadrant two, Sector-G for the last ten years, and had never let a Sa'Nerran vessel slip through its net.

"We're in position to surge, Captain," said Ensign Keller, looking over his shoulder at Sterling, who stood at his captain's console in the center of the bridge.

"How many more after this one until we reach zone two in the Void, Ensign?" asked Sterling.

"This is the last surge, Captain," replied Keller, smartly.

Sterling could tell from the subtle curvature of the Ensign's mouth and the brightness with which he'd answered the question that his helmsman had bested Commander Banks' estimate of six surges to reach their destination.

"How many was that in total?" asked Sterling, cocking an eyebrow in the direction of his first officer, who was at her console next to his.

"This last surge will be the fourth, Captain," Keller replied, even more brightly than before.

"Only four surges, that's impressive work, Ensign," said Sterling, though he was looking at Banks when he said this. The Commander then tapped her neural interface and spoke to Sterling through their neural link.

"What can I say, I'm just good at motivating the crew, that's all," Banks said, folding her arms with her thumbs pointing up. Sterling thought she couldn't have looked smugger if she'd tried.

"Very well, surge when ready," said Sterling. Then he turned to Lieutenant Shade. "Arm everything we have, Lieutenant. Let's be ready for anything." Shade nodded then set to work, arming the Invictus' formidable array of plasma rail cannons, in addition to its secondary turrets. Sterling was about to reach for his neural implant to make an announcement to the entire crew when Commander Banks suddenly spoke up.

"Captain, I'm picking up a distress call through the aperture relay," said Banks, frowning down at her console. "It's a Fleet ship under attack in the Void, zone one. It looks like it's coming from the aperture near Artemis Colony, a former UG mining depot."

Sterling glanced at the distress signal on his own console. The location was within their surge radius, but it would require them to return to their current aperture again before moving on to Colony Vega Two. He tapped his fingers on his console, hammering out a repetitive pattern that helped him to think, then shook his head.

"Let the regular Fleet ships respond to it," Sterling said, announcing his decision. "Our Omega Directive takes precedence over all other orders, including Fleet distress calls." This was just part of being a cold-hearted Omega Captain, Sterling thought to himself. Running to the aid of this ship could allow the Sa'Nerra to reinforce Vega Two, or collect another shipment from the planet. If this happened, the weapons would be used to kill far more people than were about to perish on the unfortunate Fleet vessel. Sterling again reached for his neural implant to make a ship-wide announcement when Banks interrupted him for a second time.

"It's the Imperium, Captain," said Banks. All eyes on the bridge then turned to Sterling and Banks at the command platform. "It's our sister ship, sir."

Sterling's hands balled into fists. It was an entirely involuntary reaction and he cursed himself for doing it. He never liked the crew to see him react in an emotional manner. Due to the confidential and deeply controversial nature of their mission, Sterling believed the crew had to see his decisions as being reasoned, necessary and not driven by sentiment. However, his automatic reaction to Banks' announcement had betrayed his feelings. It wasn't just that the Imperium was their sister ship and only other Omega Taskforce vessel. It was Lana McQueen' ship, and he and Lana went back a long way. Sterling tapped his fingers on his console again, eyes flicking to each of his bridge crew members in turn. All of them were still watching him, eagerly awaiting his order. His crew hadn't been together long, but their intense shared experiences had caused them to quickly form a strong bond. And he knew exactly what his unique group of officers were thinking. The rest of the Fleet wasn't their concern – but Lana and the Imperium was one of their own. More than this, if the Imperium was captured, it would fall to Sterling and the crew of the Invictus to take it down under the Omega Directive. One way or another, Lana McQueen's fate would fall to him to decide. Sterling stopped tapping his finger on the console and straightened his tunic.

"Ensign Keller, realign our surge vector and plot an intercept course for the Imperium, maximum speed," ordered Sterling.

"Yes, Captain," the young ensign replied, though he had already started working on the computations before Sterling even finished speaking.

"I expect you to impress me with your piloting skills again, Ensign. They may not have long," Sterling added.

"Surge computations already complete, sir," Keller replied, taking Sterling completely by surprise. However, this time there was no smug curl to the ensign's lips. His expression had hardened. He was ready for battle. "I'm moving us in to position now," Keller continued, maneuvering the small but powerful vessel toward the aperture.

Sterling sucked in a deep lungful of air then glanced at Lieutenant Shade and Commander Banks in turn. Their faces were a mirror of Keller's. His officers were all ready for battle, and this time it was personal. Sterling touched his finger to his neural implant, and opened a link to the seventy-strong crew of the Fleet Marauder Invictus.

"All hands, this is the Captain. Battle stations."

Ensign Kieran Keller powered the Fleet Marauder Invictus into the sub-dimensional aperture, then for a moment time seemed to stand still. Whatever reality existed between the mouths of the interstellar tunnels, it was one that the human mind could not fully process or interpret. It was a strangely peaceful place, Sterling thought, allowing the absence of everything to wash over him like a cool breeze. However, he knew that the peace would soon be shattered by what lay in wait for them on the other side.

Suddenly the universe exploded in all around him like a dam bursting and flooding the valley below it. Sights and sounds and smells assaulted his senses. To anyone not trained in aperture travel, it would simply be overwhelming to the point of causing unconsciousness. However, Sterling had travelled through the sub-dimensional doors more times than he could count, so that the only discomfort he felt was a slight twinge of a headache that faded as quickly as it appeared.

The softly-pulsating red light of the battle-stations alert cast a bloody hue over the bridge. Sterling glanced at the crew members surrounding him, and saw that all their eyes were on the viewscreen. Set against the backdrop of Artemis Colony and the asteroid field that used to be mined for resources was the Fleet Marauder Imperium. This was their sister ship, and the only other Omega Taskforce vessel in the fleet. It was surrounded by three Sa'Nerran Skirmishers. These alien vessels of war were roughly the size of Fleet Frigates, occupying twice the volume of the compact Marauder-class strike vessel that Sterling commanded. However, despite the enemy ships ahead of them being the latest phase-three revision, they were also old. Skirmishers had operated inside the Void for more than forty years, and despite numerous refits, they were a limited threat on their own, which was why they hunted in packs like wolves.

"Captain, the Imperium has taken a hit to its primary energy distributer," said Commander Banks, who was the only one peering down at her console. "Main power is down, which is why their weapons and regenerative armor are not functioning. One of the Sa'Nerran vessels has a boarding conduit in place."

"Captain, the other two Sa'Nerran Skirmishers have seen us, and are moving to intercept," said Lieutenant Shade from the weapons console. "They've launched torpedoes."

"Go straight at them, Lieutenant," said Sterling,

gripping the sides of his captain's console. The point defense guns that littered the Invictus' hull would make short work of the Skirmishers' aging conventional torpedoes. And Sterling didn't intend to give the alien warriors a chance to shoot any more of them at the Invictus. "Take the bastards down as hard and as fast as you can."

"Aye, Captain," replied Shade. There was no excitement in her voice, nor did she sound anxious. The lieutenant was never anything less than ice cold in combat.

The point defense guns sprang into action, creating a protective curtain of plasma in the space ahead of them. Moments later the Sa'Nerran torpedoes exploded like miniature supernovas lighting up the darkness of deep space. Then Sterling felt the deck shudder and saw impact warnings flash up on his console. *I hate phase-three Skirmishers...* he thought, cursing the nimble ships. These Skirmishers may have been old on the outside, but the aliens had retrofitted the aging vessels with the latest plasma weapons. However, despite elements of the enemy warships being state-of-the-art, everything about the Invictus' was factory fresh. Its regenerative armor plating was strong enough to withstand the initial barrage from the alien vessels, after which there'd be nothing left of the two Skirmishers to shoot back.

"They're phase threes, which explains how they managed to disable the Imperium," said Sterling, glancing across to Banks. "Increase power to the armor covering our reactor and main energy relays. We don't want to get sucker punched, like McQueen did."

"Aye, Captain," replied Banks, who then quickly made the adjustments on her console.

"I have a target lock on the first skirmisher..." began Shade. Sterling saw the target locations appear overlaid on the viewscreen. Shade was aiming for their bridge and main reactor, and shooting to kill. "Weapons charged... firing..." A sequence of three vibrant pulses of energy rippled out from the Invictus' forward plasma rail guns, striking the Sa'Nerran ship cleanly. Moments later the vessel exploded like an atom bomb, sending chunks of debris out in all directions. "Targeting the second ship," Shade continued, also gripping her console to steady herself against the continued rattles and shimmies from the Skirmisher's attacks. A target lock appeared on the screen. This time Shade was aiming exclusively for the alien ship's bridge. "Weapons charged... firing..."

More flashes raced out ahead of them, each bright blast of energy landing cleanly on the bridge of the Sa'Nerran Skirmisher. The focused attack cut straight through the ship, coring it like an apple. It reminded Sterling of when he had blasted a hole straight through Commander Welsh on the bridge of the Fleet Dreadnaught Hammer, during his own Omega Directive test. He reasoned that this memory should make him feel something - some sort of emotional reaction – but it didn't. Instead his attention was focused solely on the final Sa'Nerran Skirmisher, which was latched on to their sister ship like a lamprey eel. The sight of this did provoke an emotional reaction. Rage. The aliens had attacked without warning, without mercy and without explanation. Hundreds of millions had already died over the course of the fifty-year war and Sterling was determined to end it, by whatever means necessary.

"Lieutenant Shade, cripple that parasite on the hull of the Imperium," said Sterling, almost spitting the words, such was his disdain for the belligerent alien race.

"Aye Captain," replied his weapons officer. She then switched to the Invictus' smaller, more maneuverable plasma turrets and locked on to the Skirmisher's weapons and engines. The space ahead of them was filled with dozens of rapid flashes of energy. Explosions popped off across the entire surface of the alien ship and soon all of its offensive and defensive platforms were destroyed, along with its engines and maneuvering thrusters. It was a blistering strike done with surgical precision. Sterling doubted that anyone in the fleet could have carried out the attack faster or with more devastatingly accurate results than Lieutenant Shade. Even Commander Banks would struggle to match her pinpoint precision. Whatever skeletons there were in his weapons officer's closet, there was no question that Opal Shade belonged on the bridge of Invictus.

"Ensign, hold position here, but keep our main rail guns pointed at that ship, just in case we need to blast the damn thing off the Imperium's hull," Sterling continued. His helmsman called out a crisp reply, then the Invictus slowed to a stop a hundred meters from its sister ship and the alien vessel that was attached to it.

"We've suffered minor damage, Captain, but the regenerative armor kept most of it out," said Commander Banks, peering down at her console. "It's nothing the repair drones can't take care of, and the armor is already regenerating."

Sterling nodded then stepped to Banks' side. "What about communications? Can you raise them?"

"I'm not getting any response on standard comms channels, and I can't connect to anyone on the Imperium through a neural link, either," said Commander Banks. She then tore her eyes away from her console to look up at Sterling. "If Captain McQueen is still alive, I have no way to know."

"Let me try, I know her better than you do," said Sterling, returning to his console. His emotions were ramped up from the adrenalin of battle, which made his comment sound more snappish than he'd wished-for. While it hadn't been his intention to offend his second-in-command, the dirty look that Banks shot him in return suggested he had done so.

Turning back to the viewscreen, Sterling tried to visualize Captain Lana McQueen standing at her console. Then he tapped his neural interface and reached out to her. His mind was immediately assaulted with a jumble of white noise, like an old-fashioned detuned analog radio. He closed his eyes and tried to sift through the clutter, looking for order amongst the chaos.

"Lana... this is Lucas, can you hear me?" Sterling said, reaching out across the Void through his neural interface. There was no reply, but the confusion of noise was beginning to subside. "Lana, are you there?"

"Lucas, is that you?" came the voice of Captain

McQueen. It filled Sterling's mind and drowned out the noise.

"We responded to your distress call," said Sterling. "Two of the Skirmishers are atoms. What's your status?"

"We've been overrun by a Sa'Nerran boarding party," Captain McQueen replied. The mental and physical stress she was experiencing was even more evident through their intimate neural link. "They were playing possum, pretending to be dead in space. I ran into one of their torpedoes that they'd dropped like mines, and it took out main power. Half my crew is dead or turned, and the Sa'Nerra have the rest locked down on deck five.

"Is your position secure?" asked Sterling. He was, admittedly, partly concerned for the wellbeing of his fellow Captain. However, he also needed to know if they were already too late to assist. If that were the case, it would require an intervention on his part of a very different kind, though he didn't want to go there just yet.

"I've sealed the doors to the bridge, but there are only three of us left up here," replied McQueen. "I could sure use your help, Lucas, especially if you have the hulk on-board."

Sterling smiled. "If you mean Commander Banks, then yes, she's here," he replied. He then considered his options, of which there were only two. Attempt to secure the Imperium from enemy hands, or blow it and the Sa'Nerran Skirmisher into atoms where they were. He tapped his finger on the console, pondering the two options, before declaring his decision across the neural link. "Sit tight, Lana, and hold them off. I'm coming to get you." Sterling was about to sever his neural link when Captain McQueen's voice again filled his mind.

"You know as well as I do that Griffin would tell you to blast the Imperium and everyone on it to hell," said McQueen. "We're a prime candidate for an Omega Directive. Don't pretend you haven't considered it."

"We're not there yet, Lana," Sterling replied. "But if it comes to that, I will do it." This wasn't just talk – he meant it. However, saving the Imperium was still the rational choice. There were only twelve full-blown Omega officers in the fleet. Losing McQueen and the Imperium would set back Griffin's plans, prolong the war and ultimately mean that more people died. Yet while his reasoning was sound, there was more to Sterling's decision than simple logic. Lana McQueen was one of their own. "Now stand and fight until we get there," Sterling added, this time intentionally sharpening his tone. He then tapped his neural interface to sever the connection and opened his eyes. It was then that he realized his bridge crew were all anxiously waiting on his orders.

"Ensign, warm up the shuttle, we're going to board the Imperium and take it back," announced Sterling.

Lieutenant Shade immediately tapped her neural interface, and in his mind, Sterling heard her issue orders for her alpha commando squad to form up in the shuttle bay. Commander Banks then stepped beside him, her inhumanly strong arms folded across her chest.

"Griffin will have your ass for this little stunt, you do realize that, don't you?" Commander Banks said.

"Only if it goes wrong," replied Sterling. "So, let's make sure it doesn't, okay?"

Banks nodded then slapped Sterling on the shoulder, almost knocking him off his command platform. "Let's call this impromptu rescue the Sterling Directive then," she said, smiling. "Besides, if you get court-martialed or killed, then I get your command."

Sterling laughed, though considering that an Omega officer's humor was generally darker than a black hole, he knew that she wasn't entirely joking either.

"If I survive, try not to be too disappointed," replied Sterling. He then stepped off the command platform and headed for the door, with his second-in-command close by his side.

STERLING LEANED across Ensign Keller and entered his captain's command override code into the console of their combat shuttle. There was an anxious wait while the computer transmitted the codes to the Fleet Marauder Imperium, during which time Sterling impatiently tapped his finger on the console.

"Command override accepted. Opening shuttle bay doors," the computer replied, cheerfully.

Sterling removed his hand from the console and placed it onto the shoulder of his helmsman. "Take us in, Ensign. And let's ignore Fleet regulations regarding maximum approach speeds for docking maneuvers, shall we?"

"In that case, you'd better sit back down, Captain," replied Keller, though his expression was still deadly serious.

Sterling slid his hand off the young man's shoulder and planted himself back down into his seat, opposite Commander Banks. He fastened his harness, drew his plasma pistol then glanced toward the rear of the shuttle. Lieutenant Shade was seated next to Banks, along with four of her commandos, each in full combat armor and armed with a plasma rifle. Shade, like Banks and Sterling, preferred her regular Fleet uniform, with the added protection of a combat vest.

"Combat landing in ten," Ensign Keller called back to the waiting assault squad.

Sterling knew that he'd told the ensign to land quickly, but the speed with which the compact combat shuttle was hurtling toward the docking bay was unsettling. He found himself gripping the side of his chair, as if he were on a rollercoaster that was about to head over a sheer drop. Then he realized that the docking bay doors were already closing.

"Ensign, the doors!" Sterling called out, noting to his dismay that his helmsman had not adjusted course.

"Don't worry, Captain, we'll make it," said Keller. There was a confidence in the ensign's voice that made Sterling feel a little more at ease, but a quick glance across to Commander Banks told him that his first-officer was not persuaded.

Sterling looked back through the cockpit glass and gritted his teeth as the shuttle punched through the narrowing gap leading into the shuttle bay. The deck shuddered and the screech of metal grinding against metal filled the cabin, but in the blink of an eye they were through. The shuttle thudded onto the deck and skidded forward, then Keller yanked back on the mag-lock lever and the vessel stopped like a fish caught in a net.

Lieutenant Shade was on her feet even before Sterling had released his harness. The weapons officer hammered the hatch release and the rear ramp of the shuttle slammed to the deck, like the door of an ancient tomb falling open.

"Squad move out!" Shade yelled, following her commandos out into the hangar, where they took up positions in two fire teams of two.

"Ensign, keep the shuttle's weapons trained on those double doors," Sterling said to Keller, pointing directly ahead through the cockpit glass. "If anyone comes out, blast them. You got that?"

"Anyone, sir?" said Keller, sounding hesitant.

"Anyone, Ensign. We can't afford to take any chances," Sterling confirmed.

"Aye, Captain," said Keller. Sterling still thought he detected some reticence in the young officer's voice, but he knew that Keller would do as he was ordered. He always did.

Sterling then ran down the rear ramp of the shuttle with Banks close behind, but his feet had barely hit the deck of the Imperium before plasma blasts started flying inside the hangar. Sterling used the shuttle for cover and peeked out, spotting four Sa'Nerran warriors. He leaned around the side of the shuttle and fired, hitting one of the aliens in the shoulder. However, Shade's commandos had taken the rest down before he'd had the chance to fire a second shot.

"The Sa'Nerra are holding most of the crew on this deck. Send your squad up the port-side auxiliary stairwells to deck one," Sterling called out, directing the instruction to Lieutenant Shade. "Securing the bridge is our top priority."

"Aye, Captain," his weapons officer called back before issuing the orders to her commandos. "And remember, the Omega Directive is in effect," Sterling added, his tone grave. "Anyone on this ship who has been turned by the Sa'Nerran neural weapon is no different to the enemy. That means *anyone*, understand?"

"Understood, Captain," said Shade, not showing a flicker of emotion. She then moved ahead to join her squad, while Sterling and Banks followed a short distance behind, weapons held ready.

"You do realize that if the situation were reversed, Captain McQueen would probably just let the Invictus fend for itself against the Sa'Nerra?" said Banks, while sweeping her pistol to cover their rear.

"She wouldn't do that," said Sterling, moving into cover while one of the commandos set to work trying to force open a door. Then he noticed Banks looking at him, eyebrow raised. "Okay, she *might* do that," Sterling admitted, cracking under the pressure of his first officer's fierce stare. "But I'm not doing this out of some sense of honor. If we can't stop the Sa'Nerra from taking the Imperium then Griffin will just order us to destroy it, anyway. I want to give Lana a fighting chance to survive first. I'd like to think she'd do the same for us."

The door that the commando had been working on slid open and plasma blasts immediately flew through the opening. The commando took a hit and was pulled into cover, while the rest of Shade's squad returned fire.

"Still sounds a bit sentimental to me," said Banks, over the fizz and thrum of plasma weapons fire. "I thought you were supposed to be a 'cold-hearted bastard'?"

Sterling was about to answer when a service hatch to his side swung open and a hand grabbed around his neck. Sterling grasped the hand, but the grip was almost inhumanly strong. Banks shot across the corridor, risking being hit by the plasma blasts that were still flying wildly past them and seized the attacker's hand. Her own phenomenal strength managed to prize the fingers away from Sterling's neck, then she pulled the body through the hatch and threw it to the deck. Sterling scrambled back into cover, one hand rubbing his bruised neck while the other aimed his plasma pistol at his attacker. However, it wasn't a Sa'Nerran warrior, but a member of the Imperium's crew. Sterling saw the spidery pattern of corruption around the officer's neural implant, before looking into the woman's distant, vacant eyes. The officer had clearly been turned. Without hesitation, Sterling adjusted the aim of his pistol and fired, blasting the crew member's head clean from its body.

"I am a cold-hearted bastard," said Sterling, again meeting Banks' eyes. "If I have to, I'll blow this ship and its crew to hell and not shed a tear about it. But the Imperium isn't lost yet."

Sterling heard Lieutenant Shade call out "clear" then order her squad to advance. The injured commando had treated his wound and advanced with the rest of the squad. "Come on, before there's no-one left to save," Sterling said.

Sterling and Banks ran up the bare metal stairwells that

supplemented the lift systems that connected the five decks of the compact warship. He could hear bootsteps echoing along the corridors behind them then waited until he saw the shadows of the approaching Sa'Nerran warriors and opened fire. Three aliens fell without even getting a chance to see who shot them.

"Lucas, are you on board?"

It was the voice of Captain Lana McQueen, speaking through their neural link. "I'm here, what's your status?" Sterling replied in his mind.

"Can you get a squad to deck three, auxiliary systems control?" said McQueen. "If you can cycle the secondary power systems, all of the interior doors should unlock. Then whatever is left of my crew can mop up these alien bastards." Sterling clicked his fingers loudly three times. Lieutenant Shade heard the signal and ordered her squad to hold position. "We're approaching deck three now," said Sterling through the neural link. "I'll send a squad, and meet you on the bridge."

Lieutenant Shade arrived at Sterling's side, looking at him expectantly. "Lieutenant, take your squad to the secondary power systems control room on this deck. If we cycle secondary power, all the doors will unlock, and we can get the Imperium's crew back into the fight."

"Aye, Captain," replied Shade, waving over her corporal. "I take it you're heading to the bridge?" she added. Sterling nodded as the corporal arrived and crouched at Shade's side. "Then I should come with you, sir. My commandos can handle the job here. My job is to protect you."

Sterling glanced to Banks, who returned an acquiescent little shrug. "Okay, Lieutenant, you're with us," he replied. Shade relayed her orders to the corporal, who then ran back to the rest of the commando squad. "We'll continue to use the auxiliary stairwells," Sterling continued. "But we should move fast. If the Sa'Nerra manage to secure the bridge then we may have no choice but to fall back and destroy the ship."

Lieutenant Shade moved out ahead, boots clattering up the bare metal staircase to deck two. The sound of plasma blasts and anguished screaming filtered along the corridors as they pushed on.

"Our best chance to access deck one is through the crawlspace hatch that leads into the rest room behind the bridge," said Banks, stalking ahead alongside Sterling. "We can then assault the bridge through the port egress."

Sterling turned up his nose. "The restroom?"

"Don't worry, I don't think we'll catch any Sa'Nerran warriors using the head," replied Banks. Then she frowned. "Do those things even pee?"

Sterling had no idea what the answer to Banks' bizarre and pointless question was, and he didn't care. However, he also didn't get an opportunity to answer before the door leading into the ship's infirmary slid open. A Sa'Nerran warrior was standing behind it. The alien's egg-shaped, yellow eyes met Sterling's, though if the warrior was as surprised to see him as Sterling was to see it, he couldn't tell. Shade reacted first, grabbing the alien by its leathery throat and driving it back inside the infirmary. Sterling and Banks followed, spotting two more of the warriors inside, standing beside medical bays, which were occupied with members of the Imperium's crew. Sterling could see Sa'Nerran neural control devices attached to their heads.

Sterling opened fire, hitting one of the aliens before he was tackled from the side by another. Moments later, his plasma pistol was wrenched from his grasp and he soaked up a hard punch to the ribs. Sterling pushed on through the pain and drove his elbow into the alien's solid gut. The warrior staggered back then drew a serrated, semi-circular blade from a stow on its armor. This was the traditional weapon of the belligerent alien species. It was a cruel implement, designed to inflict maximum pain and suffering on whomever it was used on. However, Sterling had faced warriors armed with this crude but lethal weapon before and come out on top. This would be no different, he vowed.

Sterling watched the alien's movements, waiting for it to attack first, as he knew it would. The serrated blade flashed through the air, but Sterling dodged back then caught the alien's wrist as it tried to turn the weapon back toward him. He snapped a kick to the Sa'Nerran's knee – a weak point in their otherwise tough, leathery frames – and the alien buckled, letting out a long, waspish hiss as it did so. Sterling stripped the blade from the warrior's hand then drove his elbow down onto the pressure point at the back of the alien's neck. He heard the crunch and snap of bone, and the warrior dropped to the deck, dead.

Lungs burning, Sterling glanced up to check on the others. With one hand, Commander Banks had another of the aliens pressed up against the wall of the infirmary by its thick neck. She held her pistol in her other hand and was firing across to the other side of the room. Sterling followed the line of the plasma blasts and saw that she was aiming at the side door to the infirmary, where more of the alien warriors were trying to force their way inside. Lieutenant Shade had progressed deeper into the infirmary. Four dead warriors already lay on the deck behind her, the smell of their burned alien flesh permeating the air like a budget crematorium.

"Seal the main entrance," Sterling called over to Banks, while grabbing his pistol off the deck and running toward the side door.

Using her inhuman strength, Banks snapped the powerful, muscular neck of the Sa'Nerran she was holding up against the wall then let it slump to the deck. Sterling fired through the side door, killing one of the warriors that was trying to enter. He then glanced behind to see Banks push one of the heavy medical bays in front of the main door and flip it onto its side to block the entrance. Plasma blasts flew toward him and he took a hit to his chest. Sterling was knocked down, but recovered quickly and moved into cover. The smell of charred material now mixed with that of the alien's smoldering flesh. It was a stench that Sterling had never gotten used to, despite the frequency with which his senses had been assaulted by the foul smell. Four more warriors rushed inside the infirmary, using the lull in suppressing fire to press their assault. The head of the first warrior was blasted clean off by Lieutenant Shade before it had progressed more than a few paces inside. However, the remaining warriors came on, serrated blades in hand.

Sterling sprang up and shot one of the warriors through the gut at point blank range, the weapon burning a hole straight through its body. His pistol was then again smashed from his hand and a Sa'Nerran blade sliced through the air, carving a deep furrow into his armor. Sterling felt the sharp sting of pain and knew that the blade had penetrated, but there was no time to check how badly. He landed a swinging haymaker to the alien's face, which felt like hitting a sack of cement, then drove the blade into the warriors' chest. However, the Sa'Nerran armor stopped the weapon from penetrating the alien's thick skin, and moments later the warrior's leathery fingers were around his throat. The warrior then dropped its own blade and pulled a neural control device from its belt.

Sterling's eyes widened as the unique weapon was pressed toward his neural implant, but then another hand reached out and grabbed the warrior's arm; a human hand. Sterling glanced back and saw Commander Banks, blood trickling from a cut to her temple. Her eyes were wild, bloodlust having taken hold of the usually calm and controlled officer. When angered, Mercedes Banks was the most dangerous person Sterling had ever known, and he included himself in that equation. Banks twisted the Sa'Nerran's wrist, and Sterling heard the thick alien bone snap. The warrior hissed and rasped as she drove it back and away from Sterling. The serrated blade that he had thrust into its armor remained lodged in place. Banks grabbed the handle of the alien weapon and pulled her arm back, face still twisted with rage. Then with a force unlike anything Sterling had ever witnessed, Commander Banks thrust the weapon back into the Sa'Nerran's chest. Except this time the armor did not resist the blade. This time the weapon, along with Bank's forearm right up to the elbow was driven through the alien armor, through its flesh and clean out the other side. Removing her hand, Banks tossed the carcass aside and stood over it, chest heaving and teeth bared.

"Thanks," said Sterling, standing in front of Banks, though she didn't appear to see him. It was like she herself had been turned. Sterling tapped his neural interface and spoke again, though this time in his mind. "Mercedes, come back to me," he said, and this time there was recognition in the Commander's eyes. She looked at him and her face transformed so that she no longer appeared wild and feral.

"I hate these alien bastards," she said, wiping her hand on her pants to remove the alien's blood and guts from it.

"I can tell," said Sterling, picking up his plasma pistol for a second time. "Keep channeling that anger and strength," he added, meeting his first officer's eyes. "We aren't finished yet."

Above all else, Sterling valued and respected strength, which is why he valued Mercedes Banks for more than just her obvious fighting abilities. Weakness angered him, especially weak people who wore the UG Fleet uniform. Humanity was at war with an enemy that despised them, and that was now turning human against human through their devious neural weapon. There was no room for weakness. There was no space for moralizing. That was the point of the Omega Taskforce – to do what the rest of the Fleet could not, or would not. It was their *raison d'être*. And it was something Sterling believed in, despite him not agreeing with Admiral Griffin's macabre methods of recruitment.

Lieutenant Shade then moved past them both, closed the side door and used a cutting beam on her plasma rifle to melt the seams and seal the entrance.

"We can reach deck one through the crawlspace hatch in the infirmary," Shade said, turning back to Sterling.

Sterling nodded then remembered about the crew of the Imperium that were lying on the medical beds, with Sa'Nerran neural devices attached to their implants. He walked over to them, closely followed by Banks and Shade. There were six crew members in total, and each was showing the spidery tell-tale signs of neural corruption around their implant. In the short time since the neural weapon had been developed, Fleet scientists had discovered little about how it worked, and nothing about how to correct the mutilation once a person had been affected. The brain damage was permanent, which meant that the six crew members lying in front of him were ticking time-bombs and could turn on him and his crew at any moment.

"We can't help these people," said Sterling, while lowering the power setting on his plasma pistol. He shot each of the six crew members in the head, with barely a second's pause between each shot. Each crew member spasmed then lay still, a flat-line tone emanating from their bed's medical sensors. "But there are still crew on this ship who we can save," Sterling added.

Shade moved over to the crawlspace hatch and

removed the panel. She then checked and tossed down her rifle, which Sterling could see was already depleted, and took a pistol from one of the crew Sterling had just killed. Neither Shade nor Banks showed a flicker of emotion at what Sterling had done. They were all Omega officers. This wasn't the first time they'd had to kill members of the Fleet, and each of them knew it wouldn't be the last.

CAPTAIN STERLING HAULED himself out of the compact crawlspace and into the deck one rest rooms. He immediately caught a strong whiff of the chemical cleaning agent that was used to sanitize the restrooms on Fleet ships. The scent was as distinctive as the pungent smell of burning Sa'Nerran flesh and – at least to Sterling's nose – no less unpleasant.

"Lana had better appreciate this," he muttered, dusting down his hands then wiping them on his pants. "This is the twenty-fourth century equivalent of crawling through the sewers."

Lieutenant Shade moved up to the restroom door and pressed her ear to it. "I can't hear anything outside," she said, speaking through a neural link to Sterling and Banks.

"That doesn't mean there isn't one of those alien bastards lurking outside," replied Sterling, while turning up the power setting on his plasma pistol to maximum. The energy cell in the weapon was already almost depleted, and he estimated he'd get three or four shots at most before he was out. However, thanks to the armor the Sa'Nerran warriors all wore, Sterling also knew that maximum power was the only way to guarantee a one-shot kill. "We should expect heavy contact, so be ready," Sterling added.

Shade nodded then also adjusted the power setting on her weapon to maximum. "It's a straight line from here to the port egress onto the bridge," the weapons officer said, indicating the line of attack with the flat of her hand. "But we may need to blast or cut our way through the bridge door."

"I'll try to reach Captain McQueen and let her know we're coming," said Sterling. "The last thing we need is friendly fire." He then tapped his neural interface and reached out to Captain McQueen. Lana's voice immediately filled his head.

"Lucas, if that's you, now would be a good time to get in here!" said Captain McQueen. Neural communication omitted any extraneous noises, such as the sound of weapons fire or the cry of the alien warriors, so Sterling couldn't gauge the severity of the situation on the bridge. However, the sound of Lana's frantic cry, framed and isolated inside his mind, was chilling enough for him to know she was in deep trouble.

"We're out of time," said Sterling, moving up beside Shade. "We need to get in there now. Nothing fancy, just a straight up power play." Turning to Banks, Sterling added, "You're up, Commander."

Commander Banks moved to the door and tightened her grip around the handle. She then braced her back against the wall and jammed her leg up on one of the sinks before hauling back with all her extraordinary strength. The metal door creaked and groaned then unwillingly slid open, unable to withstand Banks' raw muscle. Shade moved through first, with Sterling close behind, both swiftly and proficiently checking the corners then moving into cover. The corridor was clear and Sterling was able to advance to the port egress unchallenged. The sound of urgent voices and weapons fire bled through the thick metal door that led onto the bridge. Sterling felt his pulse quicken and body flood with adrenalin. However, it wasn't fear that prompted this reaction, but anticipation. Like the naval warship captains in the age of sail, Sterling relished getting into close-quarters action.

"On three," said Sterling, aiming his pistol at the door before beginning the countdown. "Three, two, one..."

A fierce torrent of plasma blasts then surged toward the door. The energy cell in Sterling's pistol was quickly depleted, but with Banks and Shade also concentrating their fire, the door soon gave way. Smoke from the melted remains of the material provided cover for their assault, and as usual it was Lieutenant Shade who advanced first, followed by Commander Banks. With his pistol useless, Sterling drew a Sa'Nerran blade from his belt – he'd kept the alien weapon just in case – and followed his crewmates, keeping his head low. The smoke stung his eyes and burned his lungs, but he pushed on, ignoring the pain and discomfort. Banks and Shade were already locked in combat with Sa'Nerran warriors on the bridge, making full use of the element of surprise. Confident that his crew could handle the alien invaders, Sterling focused his attention to the command platform. Captain McQueen would have been the primary target for the Sa'Nerran assault force. A Fleet captain under Sa'Nerran control would be a powerful weapon. He had to prevent McQueen from being turned and captured.

The smoke dissipated enough for Sterling to get a clear view of the captain's console. Lana McQueen was locked in a struggle with two warriors, one of which was trying to force a neural control device onto her head. Sterling ran toward her but was struck to the body by a plasma blast and bowled over. The fall winded him, but he pushed himself up just in time to see the warrior charging at him, weapon raised. The barrel of the alien rifle flashed but the blast flew wide, giving Sterling an opening to attack. Throwing the serrated Sa'Nerran blade like a shuriken star, the alien weapon impaled itself into the warrior's eye socket. The alien crumpled to the deck and let out a harsh, waspish cry, pressing its leathery hands to the wound. The alien then yanked the blade clear and Sterling felt a spray of hot Sa'Nerran blood lash his face. Glancing across to the command platform, Sterling saw that the other aliens had almost succeeded in fixing the neural device to Captain's McQueen head. He scrambled toward her, but the wounded warrior grabbed his ankle and yanked him back. Sterling roared with frustration and twisted his body to face the alien. One of its yellow eyes was now just a bloody mess, but the other was fixed onto him, wide and unblinking. Unlike human eyes, which expressed more about a person's state-of-mind than even words did,

Sa'Nerran eyes were blank and soulless. The look on its leathery face gave no indication as to whether the creature was angry or afraid, or even if it felt pain at all. However, Sterling didn't care what the warrior felt, if it felt anything. He only cared that it had invaded a Fleet ship and attacked its crew, and that meant it had to die.

Grabbing the alien by its neck, Sterling drove his fingers through the warrior's gaping wound and into its eye socket. The creature's rasps and hisses grew to a near deafening level as blood gushed from the wound and poured down Sterling's arm. Using the alien's eye socket for leverage, he then hammered the warrior's head against the command platform, focusing on the weak point of the alien's otherwise robust anatomy until it lay dead. The smell of Sa'Nerran blood invaded his nostrils, so thick that he could practically taste it. Wasting no time, Sterling grabbed the alien's pistol and spun around to face the captain's console. He aimed the alien weapon at the warriors that were still wrestling with Captain McQueen and fired, killing one instantly. The second reacted swiftly and swung the body of McQueen in front of itself, using the ship's captain as a shield. Sterling cursed then checked on Banks and Shade. His weapons officer was fighting an alien warrior hand-to-hand, hammering kicks and punches into the Sa'Nerran's body as if it were a training bag. Across the other side of the bridge, Banks had her hands wrapped around a warrior's throat, crushing the life out of the alien. Her teeth were gritted and bared. Sterling tapped his neural interface and called out to his first officer.

"Mercedes, get to Captain McQueen!" he yelled out to

her through his mind, but Banks didn't respond. "Commander!" he tried again, but it was clear that Banks had given herself over to bloodlust, and that he wouldn't be able to reach her until the fire in her belly died down. If McQueen was going to survive then it was down to him, and Sterling knew that if he couldn't save her then he'd be the one who had to kill her.

Sterling pushed himself up and tried to get a clear shot at the Sa'Nerran warrior, but the creature cleverly shifted its position, keeping McQueen in the line of fire. His eyes flicked up to the neural control device. It had yet to be secured over McQueen's implant, but Sterling knew that his fellow captain could not resist the alien's superior strength for long. If she were turned, then he'd only have to fight her too. Cursing again he adjusted his aim, pointing the Sa'Nerran plasma pistol at Captain McQueen's head. McQueen's eyes met his own, but he saw no fear behind them. McQueen knew what Sterling had to do. This was one of the reasons why he had been chosen as an Omega Captain. When faced with an impossible situation, where doing the unconscionable was the only option, Sterling would not falter. If McQueen were in his position, she'd do the same. Sterling slipped his finger onto the trigger and squeezed.

The plasma blast flashed through the air and burned a hole into the viewscreen behind the command platform. Perhaps anticipating his actions, the Sa'Nerran had pulled McQueen aside at the last moment. Sterling adjusted his aim, but before he could fire again, Commander Banks had rushed over to the command platform and tackled the alien. The mutilated body of the warrior Banks had been strangling lay slumped up against the far wall, its neck crumpled to half its former thickness. Sterling ran to the command platform just as Lieutenant Shade landed the final two blows in a ferocious flurry of martial art strikes that left her opponent broken and bloodied. Only the warrior that had attacked McQueen now remained. Reaching the command platform, Sterling saw Banks grab the Sa'Nerran's wrist and snap it like a twig. Eyes still wild, she then lifted the two-hundred-and-fifty-pound alien warrior up as if it were a sack of cotton wool. Sterling dropped down beside Captain McQueen and tore the neural device off her head. McQueen's interface showed no evidence of corruption, but Sterling barely got a look at it before his fellow captain was back on her feet. She stood in front of the warrior that Banks was now holding up like a prized Christmas turkey and glowered at it. Without a word, McQueen pulled the warrior's semi-circular blade from its belt. Then with a single swift swing of the crude weapon, she slashed opened the alien's throat. Banks continued to hold the warrior as blood gushed from the wound and spilled onto the deck.

Suddenly the other doors leading onto the bridge unlocked and slid open. Sterling dropped into cover, aiming his weapon at the nearest opening, anticipating another wave of warriors to rush in, but no-one came.

"Tactical report, Lieutenant," said Sterling, switching his aim from one door to the next, still expecting an attack. Lieutenant Shade dropped into cover and tapped her neural interface. For a few long seconds the bridge was as silent as the dead of night.

"Our commandos have secured the secondary power systems control room," Shade said, her face showing the intense concentration required to conduct verbal and neural conversations simultaneously. "The Imperium's crew is now moving through the ship and taking down what remains of the Sa'Nerran invasion force. Deck one is secure. We're safe up here."

Sterling nodded then turned to Captain McQueen as Shade continued to liaise with her commandos and co-ordinate with the Imperium's forces. Banks finally released her grip on the bleeding Sa'Nerran warrior and allowed its body to thump into the deck like a butchered carcass. The smell of alien blood surrounded them, though Sterling at least preferred this to the odor of burning Sa'Nerran flesh.

"You took your damn time," said McQueen, folding her arms and shifting her weight onto her back foot.

"Space is pretty big," replied Sterling with matching sternness. "You could have at least gotten into trouble a bit closer to us."

McQueen then smiled and unfurled her arms. "You just can't stay away from me, admit it," she continued, dropping the pretense of being angry at him. "My knight in shining armor, riding to my rescue."

Sterling laughed, though Commander Banks looked distinctly uncomfortable, like she was a third wheel on a date.

"Ignore her, it's just her way of saying 'thanks for saving my ass'," Sterling said to Banks, which succeeded in breaking the tension. He knew McQueen well enough to understand that she struggled with genuine displays of emotion, preferring to make light of situations instead. And if he was honest, he was the same. "What the hell happened here, anyway, Lana?" he continued, turning to more serious matters to save all their blushes. "How did three Skirmishers get the jump on you?"

Captain McQueen shrugged while mopping blood from her face and neck with the sleeve of her tunic. "We had an Omega Directive to neutralize Artemis Colony. When we got here, these Skirmishers were hiding in the asteroids. The alien trash jumped us before we'd even had time to scratch our asses."

Sterling frowned. "Artemis Colony has been abandoned for years. It seems like a damned strange target for an Omega Directive."

"That's what I thought too," replied McQueen, pushing the Sa'Nerran she'd killed off her command platform with the side of her boot. "But intelligence from our recon probes in the Void showed there to be Sa'Nerran prisoner transports in the system. It looked like they were trying to use captured and turned Fleet crew and colonists to start up the mining operation again."

"That's brazen, especially so close to Fleet space," said Commander Banks. The fire had left her eyes now, though her muscles were still taut, as if she were about to spring into action again at any moment.

"The Sa'Nerra are nothing if not audacious," replied McQueen. "Anyways, it seems that our arrival spooked them. There's nothing here now, except the crippled Skirmisher that's still docked to us."

Sterling rubbed the back of his neck, trying to massage away the tension. However, it wasn't the stress of the battle that was causing his muscles to spasm. Something about McQueen's experience at Artemis Colony didn't add up.

"This all still seems damned odd to me," said Sterling, folding his arms. "But I guess we'll never know. It's not like we can interrogate Sa'Nerran survivors and get any intel out of them. Not unless you speak 'alien hiss', that is."

McQueen shrugged again. "That won't stop my weapons officer from trying." She then turned to Commander Banks, eyeing her up like a prized bull at a market. "Are you sure you don't want to transfer to the Imperium, Commander? You're one hell of a useful lady in a fight."

"Thanks for the offer, sir, but the Invictus is my ship," said Commander Banks, politely, but firmly. She then straightened her tunic, which was ripped and looked more red than blue thanks to the copious amount of Sa'Nerran blood it had absorbed. "Besides, my next post after the Invictus will be as captain of my own Omega Taskforce ship," she added, though without any hint of irony.

McQueen nodded and smiled. "I'll put a word in with Admiral Griffin. We could do with more Omega Taskforce ships on the front lines." McQueen then touched her neural implant, which Sterling was glad to see still appeared to be perfectly normal. McQueen was silent for a few moments, while receiving a message from one of her crew. "The Imperium is secure, thanks to your help,"

McQueen then said, lowering her hand back to her side. "My crew are boarding the Sa'Nerran ship now. Hopefully, we'll be able to take a few prisoners for Griffin to use in her next round of Omega Directive tests."

Sterling nodded, remembering how the hard-nosed Admiral had used captured warriors during his own Omega Directive test on the Fleet Dreadnaught Hammer. "The Omega Directive test has to be real," Admiral Griffin had explained to him, over a glass of Calvados – the flag officer's favourite tipple. "It's the only way we can discover officers with the grit that we need."

"Well, if you're all good here then we need to get moving," said Sterling, reminding himself that they had their own Omega Directive mission to carry out. "We've been ordered to Vega Two."

"Vega Two?" replied McQueen, scowling. "That's another little backwater nothing place, like Artemis."

"It will certainly be a nothing place once we're through with it," replied Sterling, thinking about the unenviable task that lay before him. "I can leave you a few extra repair drones, if you like?" he added, recalling that the Imperium's engines had taken damage.

"Thank you, Captain, that would be appreciated," replied McQueen, sincerely. Then she looked around the bridge, which was pockmarked and scorched with plasma blasts and splattered with human and Sa'Nerran blood. "I think I'm going to need them," she added.

Sterling felt Ensign Keller reach out to him, and he touched his neural implant to allow the connection.

"Captain, the hangar bay is now secure," the Ensign

reported. "The Imperium's crew are in control. But…" Keller hesitated, though because of their intimate neural link, Sterling could feel his discomfort and even guilt.

"What is it, Ensign?" Sterling pressed.

"While defending the hangar with the shuttle, I'm afraid I killed two Imperium crew members who hadn't been turned. They were caught up in the fighting, and I couldn't have known…"

"You did what you had to, Ensign Keller," Sterling cut in, his own voice strong and unwavering. "Your actions helped save the ship, and that's all there is to it. Do you understand?"

Keller was silent for a couple of seconds. Then when the young man's voice again filled Sterling's mind, the hesitation and doubt was gone.

"Yes, Captain. I understand," Keller said.

"Stand by, we'll be back with you in a few minutes," Sterling added before tapping his neural interface to sever the connection. He then addressed Captain McQueen, speaking out loud. "Hopefully, the next time we meet it will be under better circumstances, Captain," Sterling said, offering McQueen his hand.

"I very much doubt it," McQueen replied, still smiling. She then took Sterling's hand and shook it. "Till next time, Captain."

"Till next time," Sterling replied. He relaxed his grip, but as McQueen let go, she slowly stroked her thumb across the back of his hand. Sterling nonchalantly acted as if it hadn't happened, but a quick glance across to

Commander Banks told him that his eagle-eyed first-officer had observed the subtle gesture of affection.

Sterling and Banks then regrouped with Lieutenant Shade, stepping over dead alien warriors to reach the door they'd blasted through only minutes earlier. However, he'd barely taken a step off the bridge when Captain McQueen called out to him.

"And Captain Sterling, thanks for saving our collective ass," McQueen called out, breaking character and offering her gratitude sincerely and openly. "We both know that Griffin would have had you blow us out of space if I'd been turned and captured. I won't forget it."

"No problem, Captain," replied Sterling, feeling both buoyed and discomposed by his fellow captain's candid admission. "You'd do the same for us," he added.

McQueen shrugged. "Don't count on it, Captain," she said, a wicked smile curling her lips. Then she turned to her captain's console and set to work on the task of getting her ship back in order.

Sterling huffed a laugh then headed out of the door. However, he hadn't gone far, before he felt Commander Banks' eyes drilling into him. He stopped and turned to her.

"Go on, say it," said Sterling, folding his arms. "I can tell that you're dying to."

Banks also folded her arms, mirroring Sterling's defensive stance. "I told you she wouldn't have done the same for us," she said, huffily.

THE VIVID, blue-green planet that was home to Colony Vega Two shone out of the viewscreen like a jewel in the Void, but Captain Sterling's eyes were focused down on his console. They'd exited the aperture expecting to find a squadron of Sa'Nerran warships waiting for them. However, their scanners were suspiciously clear.

"Are you sure there's nothing out there?" said Sterling, directing the question to Commander Banks.

His first-officer shrugged and shook her head. "If there is then they've managed to hide from our scanners somehow," she replied. "It could be that they're on the surface, powered down, but if they are then it won't be easy to find them."

Sterling sighed then started tapping his finger on his console like an impatient schoolmaster. Based on the information Admiral Griffin had sent him, the colonists on Vega Two had been turned and set to work manufacturing weapons components for the Sa'Nerra. That being the case, he would have expected at least one enemy ship in orbit around the planet. If nothing more, this ship would act as an early warning system to call for reinforcements through the aperture relays should a Fleet vessel come snooping, as they had just done.

"Take us closer, Ensign," said Sterling, still tapping his finger on the side of his console. "But stay alert, and keep your eyes out for anywhere that a Sa'Nerran ship might hide. The magnetic poles of a moon, dense asteroid fields, any area of high EM chop, that sort of thing."

"Aye, Captain," replied the ensign, increasing power to the main engines to propel them closer to the world.

The door to the bridge then swung open and Lieutenant Commander Clinton Crow walked in. As always, the ship's chief engineer had his multi-tool attached to his belt and a modular computer wrapped around his left forearm. The display was malleable, so that when not in use it simply flowed like the material of his tunic, but when active would stiffen and become glassy.

"Repairs are complete, captain," said Crow standing beside the command platform and fiddling with the multi-tool on his belt.

"You could have told me that over neural comms, Lieutenant Commander," replied Sterling. "What brings you all the way up here?"

Sterling wasn't annoyed to see his chief engineer, not in the same way that the sudden arrival of his morbid medical officer would disturb him. He was at least thankful that it was his engineer rather than his doctor that was paying him a house call. Sterling had already spent enough time with Graves of late, due to the need to have the wounds he sustained on the Imperium tended to and healed. However, Crow rarely came to the bridge, unless ordered to do so, which meant the engineer's arrival was unexpected.

"I just wanted to get a better view of Vega Two," replied the engineer. "The viewscreen in engineering doesn't quite have the resolution of this one on the bridge."

Sterling shot Banks a knowing look. Clinton Crow's specialty may have been starships and engines, but his real passion was exploration and discovery. It was the only reason he'd joined Fleet in the first place, though even if Crow hadn't willingly chosen to serve in the UG Fleet, his valuable talents and skillset meant that he would have been drafted anyway. Most people who were forced into Fleet service resented it, even if they buried this resentment deep down. Crow on the other hand would have welcomed it.

"Vega Two is an interesting world," Crow went on, still fiddling with his multi-tool. "It has some unique metals and mineral compositions that could have exciting applications in starship hull materials and more."

"Fascinating..." said Banks, drolly.

Sterling tapped his neural interface and spoke to his first officer over a private link. "Be nice, this is the guy who keeps us flying," he said, glancing across to her.

"I know, but he's sooooo dull," replied Banks. Her words were so loud and clear in Sterling's head that he subconsciously turned to Crow to make sure he hadn't overheard, before remembering that he was speaking neurally.

"If you don't mind, Captain, I'd like to accompany any landing party," Crow went on. Sterling noticed that the engineer's multi tool was now in Crow's hand and that he was using it to adjust the captain's console. The brightness and fidelity of the digitized display suddenly increased.

"This is an Omega Directive, not a scientific mission, Lieutenant Commander," Sterling replied. His tone was intentionally stern. The notion that they'd arrived at Vega Two just so Crow could go rock hunting angered him. It wasn't the first time his engineer had put his own considerations above those of the mission.

"Of course, Captain, I just meant if there's time after the mission is over," Crow replied, seemingly undeterred.

"I'm detecting a five percent variance in regenerative armor integrity on the port quarter," Commander Banks then announced out loud. Sterling raised an eyebrow and looked over his at first officer. She was staring down at her console with a look of intense concentration that Sterling could tell at once was faked.

"Really?" said Crow, returning the multi-tool to the clip on his belt. "A five per cent variance? That can't be right."

Banks shrugged. "Perhaps you'd better check it out, rather than waste time up here. We're about to fly to a hostile planet."

Lieutenant Commander Crow quickly scurried to the exit before stopping and turning back to Sterling. "Permission to leave the bridge, sir," he said, straightening to attention.

"Granted," replied Sterling. His engineer didn't need his explicit permission to enter or leave the bridge, but he granted it anyway just to expedite Crow's exit. The chief engineer then practically ran through the door, which swooshed shut behind him.

"I'm not detecting any variance in armor integrity," said Lieutenant Shade, who was frowning down at her weapons console.

"That's odd," said Banks, who was clearly trying to suppress a smile. "I could have sworn it was there a moment ago."

Lieutenant Shade still looked confused and even a little embarrassed, though Sterling knew why. If anyone should have picked up a problem with their armor, it was Shade. The fact she'd missed the non-existent variance was clearly bothering her.

"Relax, Lieutenant, the armor is fine," said Sterling. "It's probably just a sensor glitch." Then he turned to Banks. "You should probably get that checked out, Commander," he added, with a subtle eyebrow raise.

"I'll get right on it, sir," said Banks, still trying to suppress a smile.

"Coming into orbit above Colony Vega Two now, captain," said Ensign Keller, pulling Sterling's focus back to the viewscreen.

"Still no sign of any Sa'Nerran vessels, sir," said Shade. "And I'm not picking up anything moving around on the surface of the colony, either, other than native animals."

Sterling switched his own console to the planetary scans of the colony and saw that Shade was right. There appeared to be no-one moving around on the surface, though there were clear energy signatures that suggested the buildings and factories still had power and were operating as normal.

"The lights are still on down there, so either the Sa'Nerra have already cleaned the colony out and abandoned it, or everyone is indoors," said Sterling. He found that his finger was again tapping out its usual, regular pattern on the side of his console.

"Are you thinking it's a trap?" said Banks.

"After what happened to McQueen, it's a strong possibility," replied Sterling. Though like his fellow captain's situation at Artemis, there was something about their mission that didn't add up, and it was gnawing at him, like an itch that couldn't be scratched. "But how would the Sa'Nerra know we were coming?" he added.

"We could just bombard the whole site from orbit, sir," offered Lieutenant Shade. "I can program a spread of plasma fire that would level the entire area in a couple of minutes."

Sterling pondered his weapons officer's extreme yet practical solution, but there was still doubt in his mind.

"If the colonists aren't down in those buildings anymore, we'd have no way to confirm the success of our mission," Sterling eventually answered. "No matter whether they're hiding out somewhere else on the planet, or the Sa'Nerra have already taken them away, we need to know."

Commander Banks nodded. "Even if we blitz Vega Two from orbit, we could be leaving the Sa'Nerra potentially hundreds of brainwashed human slaves to transport to another one of their factories."

Ensign Keller then spoke up. "I can leave a scanner buoy in orbit and land the Invictus near the colony," the helmsman said. "That way if the Sa'Nerra do show up in the system, we'll know straight away and have time to recover the landing party."

Sterling weighed up the options. He didn't like the idea of taking the Invictus down to the surface of a hostile world, but Keller's idea was an effective safeguard. Destroying the colony and moving on was the easy option, but Sterling was never one to take the easy route.

"Okay, Ensign, launch the buoy," he said, straightening up and pressing his hands behind his back. Then he turned to Shade. "Take us to battle stations, Lieutenant, and prepare your commandos for a surface recon."

"Aye, Captain," replied Shade, smartly.

"I still think this is a trap," said Banks, though she was again speaking to Sterling privately through their neural link.

"So, do I," Sterling answered, also in his mind. "But if it is then I want to know how the Sa'Nerra knew we were coming. Those alien bastards are ruthless, but so far, they've at least been predicable. If they've changed their tactics, we need to understand how and why."

A scanner buoy shot out ahead of the ship then took up position in orbit. Sterling saw the data feed appear on his console. The signal was strong.

"Buoy deployed, Captain," said Ensign Keller.

Sterling peered out at the planet, which now filled the

entire viewscreen. He took one last look at the scan data from the Vega Two system, probing the readings for any hint of enemy activity, but there was none. He then exhaled slowly, gripped the sides of his console and leaned forward.

"Take us down, Ensign, smartly."

Vega Two was a cold, desolate world that seemed to be comprised of nothing but dull, yellow-brown rocks and thick, straw-like grasses. Sterling stepped off the cargo ramp of the Invictus and peered up into the steel grey sky, feeling a light misty rain wash over his face. Ahead of him was the main colony block, which contained the living quarters, shops, bars and other amenities that serviced the inhabitants. Doors banged in the bitter wind and rainwater dripped from broken or clogged gutters, creating sludgy bogs in the dirt surrounding most of the pre-fab buildings.

"What a dump," Commander Banks observed, pulling her jacket tighter around her body. Sterling smiled. His second-in-command may have possessed inhuman strength, but when it came to braving the elements, she was a bit of a wimp. "We'll be doing this place a favor by razing it to the ground," Banks added, unkindly.

Sterling looked around the dreary complex and had to agree with his first officer's assessment. Prior to the Earth-

Sa'Nerra war, Vega Two had been supported by UG Fleet under the Outer Colonies Expansion Program. This rewarded pioneers like those who ventured to Vega Two with supplies and high-rates of compensation, in return for harvesting unique and valuable resources from the planets they settled on. As such, the colonies became prosperous and were generally well appointed. Providing you had an adventurous spirit and didn't mind living dozens of light years from Earth, it was a good life. Then the Sa'Nerran invasion happened and the Void was established. Almost overnight, Vega Two and the hundreds of colonies like it became cut off from the Fleet and from Earth. They had to fend for themselves or die. Most died.

Sterling was then snapped back into the moment by Lieutenant Shade. She was jogging back from her position ahead of the ship, where four commando fire teams had already taken up position behind the rocks, covering the seemingly abandoned town.

"Scanners aren't picking up any movement inside these buildings, beyond the odd local rodent, anyway," said Shade. The rain was dripping from her nose and chin, but she seemed unfazed by it, as if the water were merely an illusion. "And the heat signatures are not organic. Just generators, lights and space heaters most likely."

Sterling shook his head. Like Banks, he had taken an immediate dislike to Vega Two before even setting foot onto its muddy surface, but the unexplained absence of the colonists made him hate it even more.

"According to Griffin, this place should be crawling with Sa'Nerra and turned colonists, churning out torpedoes, power cells and who knows what else," said Sterling. "So, where the hell is everyone?"

Shade became distracted and touched her fingers to her neural implant, turning back to look at her commandos as she did so. One of the unit was looking back in her direction.

"There's a cluster of individual heat signatures about ten meters below the surface," said Shade, still with her hand to her implant. "It looks like it's directly below the large building at the end of this main street, sir," she continued, turning back to Sterling.

Sterling peered along the unmetalled road that ran through the center of the ramshackle town to the building Shade had indicated. "It looks like some sort of town hall. Or maybe a bank?"

Commander Banks lifted her wrist and activated the computer that was wrapped around her forearm. The screen solidified into a rectangular sheet as she did so. "I'd say bank vault is on the money, so to speak," said Banks, scanning the building with the device. "Maybe some of the colonists are hiding down there? Though it can't be all of them. Twenty at most."

Sterling nodded. "There's only one way to find out," he said, though at the back of his mind he was still wondering where the other three-hundred-plus colonists were. "Lieutenant, move your squad up to the building and create a secure perimeter," he then said to his weapons officer.

Shade replied with a brisk acknowledgement then ran back to her commandos, heavy boots splattering the backs of her combat pants with yellow-brown mud as she went. Sterling then tapped his own neural interface and connected to Lieutenant Commander Crow, who had temporary command on the bridge.

"Lieutenant Commander Crow, we're advancing to the building at the end of the street," he said in his mind. "Commander Banks will send you the exact location. Keep our defense turrets active. If you see so much as a possum approach that structure while we're inside, I want you to vaporize it, understood?"

"Aye, Captain," replied Crow, though Sterling knew instinctively that there was a "but" coming. "But if possible, sir, I'd rather not kill the local critters. One of the large rodent species on this planet is an excellent bioreactor. I would like to study it and…"

"Lieutenant Commander, I don't care if you see Rudolf the Red Nosed Reindeer walking down the street," Sterling cut in, again annoyed by his engineer's skewed priorities. "If anything looks like its stalking us, you blast it, is that understood?"

"Yes, Captain, fully understood," replied Crow, sounding very much like a scolded child.

Sterling tapped his neural interface then shook his head. "Is being weird a requisite qualification for being an Omega officer?" he asked Banks.

"Don't look at me, I'm not weird," replied Banks, while examining one of the planet's yellow-brown rocks in her hand. She then crushed it like it was an egg and brushed the dust from her palms.

"You were saying?" said Sterling.

Banks scowled at him. "Freakish strength doesn't make me a freak," she hit back. "Doing fifty push-ups every morning, even when there's a general alert sounding, however..."

This time it was Sterling that frowned. "I wish I'd never told you about that," he said, setting off down the road in pursuit of the commandos. One of the plasma turrets on the port bow of the Invictus steadily tracked them as they moved.

"The building is clear, sir," came the voice of Lieutenant Shade though a neural link. "There's a vault in the basement level. The door is sealed."

"Continue to secure the perimeter, Lieutenant, we're on our way," replied Sterling. He tapped to close the link then glanced over at Banks. "How are you at tearing open bank vault doors?" he asked.

"Depends on the size of the vault," replied Banks, casually. She then drew her plasma pistol and dialed the power level up to maximum. "There are other ways to break into a bank, though."

Sterling stepped off the road and underneath the welcome shelter of the bank's veranda, closely watched by two of Shade's commandos. The rain had started to come down harder during the time they had been walking through the main street of the settlement and he was glad to be under cover again. Smoothing the water off his close-cropped number three-cut hair, Sterling then opened the door and stepped inside.

"This place looks like time forgot it centuries ago," said

Banks, stepping in beside Sterling and shaking the water off her jacket.

"The people here had to rebuild almost from scratch once the United Governments abandoned them," said Sterling, looking around the wooden interior of the bank. "Between the Sa'Nerra and the Void pirates that prey on these non-affiliated colony worlds, they've had to fight to survive almost every day of their lives."

Banks cocked her head and shot a sideways glance at Sterling. "You admire them?"

"They're strong," said Sterling, as they made their way toward the staircase leading down to the vault room. "Life out here is hard, so these colonists are survivors. We could use more like them in the Fleet."

Banks gave a noncommittal shrug. "Maybe. But what we really need is more people like us."

Sterling descended the stairs toward the vault, the heels of his boots making a satisfying clack against the polished hardwood floor. This was a material that was rarely used or even seen in the twenty-fourth century, outside of colonies like Vega Two. However, despite the pleasing, hollow note his bootsteps produced, Sterling preferred the clean, clinicality of a starship's interior to the dark, irregular look of the wooden structure.

"The vault is sealed up tight, but there are definitely people inside," said Lieutenant Shade, straightening almost to attention as Sterling approached. "It's an old locking system, though. We've already almost cracked it."

Sterling saw that one of the commandos was kneeling in front of the vault door. He considered that he should spend some time to get to know these soldiers by name, especially considering the small crew complement of the Invictus. However, the fact he expected some or all of them to die in the near future always held him back. In the year he'd spent as captain of the Invictus, he'd already lost fifty-two commandoes, either due to injury or death. In many ways, it was simply easier to see them as faceless soldiers.

"The tech in here must be ancient if he's having to use a cable," said Banks. She was running her hand along the surface of the steel door, apparently gauging whether she thought she could force it open.

Sterling frowned then spotted the wire snaking from the computer attached to the commando's wrist into the vault's locking mechanism. Like the rest of Vega Two, it was a relic from a time before he was even born. Suddenly there came a series of heavy thuds and the commando backed away, jerking the cable free then aiming his rifle at the door. The three other commandos in the vault room also jolted into action, covering the steel slab with their plasma rifles. Shade, however, remained cool and simply walked up to the door and placed her hand on the release lever.

"With your permission, Captain," said Shade, poised and ready to open the door.

Sterling backed up behind the commandos, but slightly off to the side of the door and held his own weapon ready. "Go ahead, Lieutenant."

Shade pulled the lever then hauled back on the steel slab. There was a hiss of air as the door began to swing outward, but it had barely opened by a crack before it slammed shut again.

"Damn it, they're pulling it closed again from the inside," said Shade, trying but failing to overwhelm whoever was holding the door shut on the other side. She then waved one of the commandos over and together they tried again, but still they could barely open the vault door by more than a crack.

"This is Captain Lucas Sterling of the Fleet Marauder Invictus," Sterling called out, edging closer to the door and trying to peek through the narrow opening. "You can come out. The Sa'Nerra have gone."

Everyone stayed silent, waiting for a response, which came a few seconds later.

"It's a trick!" a voice called out. "We've seen how the Sa'Nerra twist people's minds. We're not coming out, so piss off!"

Sterling's brow scrunched into a frown and he raised an eyebrow at Banks. "I'm already bored of this," he said, waving her over.

Commander Banks holstered her plasma pistol then moved up to the vault door. "Everyone, get back," she said, flexing her arms and shoulders as if limbering up for fight. Banks then tested a few handholds on the door, like a rock-climber scouting a route up a mountain, before she finally indicated she was ready. Sterling, Shade and the commandos took several steps back, while keeping their weapons trained on the edge of the door. Banks then sucked in a deep breath, dug her heels into the wooden floor and took up the strain.

"On three..." said Banks.

Sterling started the silent countdown in his head then watched as Commander Banks heaved back on the door. The massive slab of metal creaked opened and this time the colonists were unable to slam it shut again. Sterling could see the heels of Banks' boots practically chiseling grooves into the wooden floor as she stepped back, pulling the door, and five colonists, along with her.

"Hold it right there," yelled one of the commandos. "On your knees. Show me your hands!"

The colonists immediately dropped to the floor and thrust their hands toward the ceiling. Sterling peered through the now open vault door and saw six more inside.

"You, inside the vault. Step outside. Slowly!" Lieutenant Shade ordered, moving into the center of the door with her pistol aimed at the hiding colonists.

"Check their implants," commanded Sterling, grabbing the colonist closest to him and tilting the man's head back so he could scrutinize the neural implant. However, there was no visible corruption. The implant appeared normal.

"We haven't been turned, if that's what you're worried about," the colonist snapped, yanking his head out of Sterling's grasp. "We just thought you were pirates. They often claim to be members of Fleet, like you did."

Sterling hauled the man to his feet and pressed his pistol underneath the colonist's chin. So far, the man's story seemed to check out, but he wasn't taking any chances, and he also wasn't taking any crap. "Where are all the other colonists from Vega Two?" Sterling demanded, as the commandos lined up the other eleven people who were hiding in the vault against the wall.

"The Sa'Nerra took them," the colonist replied, displaying the sort of grit Sterling expected from someone who had been raised in the Void. "We were forced to work or those alien bastards would kill us. The ships came every week to pick up the weapons and supplies we made. Then a few days ago, a Sa'Nerran transport arrived and took everyone off world."

"So, how come you escaped capture?" asked Banks, stepping to Sterling's side and glowering at the colonist. Sterling liked that his first-officer was as naturally cynical as he was. The colonist recoiled from Banks, as if the Commander was on fire. Sterling smiled; clearly his first officer's frightening display of strength had made an impression.

"We hid, obviously," the colonist replied, managing to muster the courage to give attitude back to Banks. "Then we got down here. One of the others works in the bank," the man added, nodding in the direction of the colonists lined up against the wall as he said this. "He got us all inside the vault, with some supplies. But we had no way of knowing when the Sa'Nerra had gone. We had a couple more days of supplies, so we just planned to wait as long as we could."

Sterling looked at Commander Banks and her skeptical eyes met his. She clearly wasn't buying the colonist's story, and while on the surface it seemed to check out, Sterling felt a nugget of doubt burrowing away at the back of his mind.

"There's nothing on the surface but mud," replied Sterling, nodding to Shade. His weapons officer then rounded up the colonists and began to march them back up the stairs to the main hall of the bank.

"What are you going to do with us?" said the colonist, nervously watching his companions get herded up the staircase.

"We're going to get our medical officer to check you all out, that's all," said Sterling, tying to make it sound like this was for their own benefit. However, in truth, he wanted to be doubly sure the colonists were who they said they were. And he also wanted to check that there was no corruption beneath the surface of their implants that would make them mind-controlled ticking time bombs. The mention of pirates had also raised his suspicions that this gang of twelve people hiding in a bank vault weren't native to Vega Two.

"Then what are you going to do?" replied the man. "Will you take us back to United Governments space? Or to Earth?"

Sterling waved the man on with the barrel of his pistol then followed a couple of meters behind, with Banks still at his side. "We're a ship of war, not a taxi service," said Sterling. "If you want to get back to Earth, you'll have to make your own way there."

They reached the top of the stairs and Sterling entered the main hall of the bank. The other eleven colonists were again lined up against the wall, being watched vigilantly by three of the commandos.

"Did you come here alone?" asked the colonist as

Sterling ushered him into the center of the room. "Is your ship in orbit or on the surface? I didn't see a shuttle landing."

Sterling's eyes narrowed. "Do you see much, holed up behind a three-foot-thick steel door ten meters below ground?"

Commander Banks became alert and slowly stepped to the side of the colonist, her eyes fixed on the man.

"Oh, one of us scouted outside when we heard the thrusters firing," said the colonist, offering Sterling a smile. "We thought it might have been the Sa'Nerra leaving."

Sterling kept his eyes locked on the man. "You just asked me if my ship is in orbit," he said, tightening his grip on his pistol. "You'd already know it wasn't if you watched us land."

"I meant other than that one," the colonist replied, still smiling. "You know, I just wondered how many of you are here." The man's voice wasn't showing any signs of stress, nor had the colonist's expression altered, beyond adopting a smile. This only made Sterling more suspicious. Then he noticed a name tag on the colonist's shirt. It was just visible beneath the man's animal-skin jacket, though he could only make out the surname, which read "Gillian".

"You'll see soon enough, once you're on-board," said Sterling, changing tack and returning the man's warm, insincere smile. "First, let's get you all medically checked out. I'll need your name for the record."

The man's plastic-looking smile remained on his face as he answered. "Kyle. My name is Kyle," he said.

"Do you have a surname, Kyle?" asked Sterling, maintaining his own smile.

The colonist again vacillated. "Jones," he eventually answered, after another pregnant pause. "My name is Kyle Jones."

Sterling nodded and smiled. The man had fallen into his trap. Then without warning he grabbed a clump of the colonist's hair and yanked the man's head back, thrusting the barrel of his plasma pistol underneath his chin once again.

"Why don't you tell me who you really are, 'Kyle Jones,'" Sterling said, practically spitting the words into the colonist's face. "And I want to know what the hell happened to the other colonists. The truth this time!" he snarled, pressing the barrel of the pistol so hard against the man's skin that he drew blood.

"You can't win," the colonist replied, his voice suddenly coarse and aggressive. "They'll never stop hunting you."

"Who?" replied Sterling, pushing the man to his knees and this time holding the pistol to the colonist's forehead. Banks moved behind the man and pressed down on the colonist's shoulders to make sure he couldn't run. "Who the hell are you talking about?" Sterling barked, growing increasingly impatient.

"The Sa'Nerra, of course!" the colonist spat back. "You're vermin to them. You have infested their space, and they will not stop until you are eradicated."

Sterling cursed and threw the man down to the ground. "You're siding with the Sa'Nerra?" he asked, his eyes briefly flicking up to Banks, who looked as stunned as he felt.

"It's better this way," the colonist replied. "Just give in to them! They'll win anyway, there's no sense in fighting."

Banks stepped on the colonist's hand and applied pressure with the heel of her boot. "Answer the question," she yelled. "Are you working with the aliens? Have you been feeding them intelligence?" However, despite practically crushing the man's fingers, the colonist showed no pain. He simply peered up into Banks' eyes, almost willing her to apply more pressure.

"He's been turned," said Sterling, suddenly understanding what was happening.

"How can that be? His implant is normal," Banks hit back, lifting her boot off the man's hand. Three of the colonist's fingers were broken, yet still the man acted as if he was unhurt. "And he's cognizant. The others we've see who are turned are like zombies," Banks added, glowering down at the man as he lifted his mangled hand off the floor and smiled at her.

Sterling shook his head. "I don't understand it either," he said. Then he leant in closer, grabbing the colonist's jaw and forcing the man to look at him. "But I'm going to have Commander Graves dissect you like a lab rat until I find out why," he continued. Though again the colonist displayed no fear whatsoever.

"You won't have time for that," the man replied, the plastic smile returning to his face. "We told them you were coming. And now they are here."

The man then slapped the breast pocket of his jacket, and every light in the building went dead.

STERLING HEARD a grunt of pain and a scuffle of boots against the solid wood floor, but with the lights suddenly going out, he was temporarily blinded.

"Mercedes, talk to me..." Sterling called out, taking cautious steps back while trying to compel his eyes to adjust, but he could no longer see the colonist or his first officer.

"Damn it, I've lost him!" Banks replied. "He hit me and ran, I don't know where."

Sterling followed the sound of Banks' voice, but he could barely make her out in the gloom.

"Everyone, stay sharp, this is a trap," Sterling called out, continuing to back away from the colonist's last known location with his weapon raised.

Sterling then felt a hard thump to the gut and he was driven back across the polished hardwood floor of the bank. The attack caught him completely unawares and stole the breath from his lungs, so that he was unable to call out for help. Before he knew it, his attacker had driven him hard into the wall, bruising his back and shoulders. Then he felt hands sliding around his throat and begin to tighten their grip, squeezing his windpipe so that he couldn't breathe. His training kicked in and Sterling thrust his arm up through the colonist's hands to break the hold. Twisting his body, he then drove his elbow into the man's sternum as hard as he could. The colonist staggered away, but considering the force with which Sterling had struck him, the man should have been on his knees, gasping for breath. Instead, the turned colonist barely showed a flicker of discomfort.

"Open fire!" Sterling heard Lieutenant Shade call out, but the fizz of plasma weapons was conspicuous by its absence. His vision was adjusting, but he could still barely see Shade or Banks in the gloom. However, the scuffles of boots, shouts and dull thuds of flesh striking flesh told him that fighting had broken out.

"You can't beat them," the turned colonist said, continuing to stalk Sterling. The man was now a shadowy outline in front of him, growing clearer by the second. "They're stronger than you. They're smarter than you. There's more of them than you. It's only a matter of time before humanity falls. Give in to the Sa'Nerra and they will make you understand. It's better this way."

Keeping one eye on the colonist, Sterling peered around the room, looking for anything he could use as an improvised weapon. A bar from one of the bank teller windows was rusted and loose. He grabbed it and yanked it clear with one swift, powerful motion. The metal bar felt cool and reassuringly weighty in his hand.

"You seem to know a lot about the Sa'Nerra," said Sterling, circling around the colonist. He wanted to extract as much information from the man as possible, before extracting as much pain from him as the turned traitor could stand.

"I'm one of the lucky ones," the colonist replied. "The Sa'Nerran neural education granted me the gift of understanding. The Sa'Nerra now speak to me." Then then man tapped his neural implant so hard that Sterling thought he would poke a hole through his skull. "They speak to me in here."

"And what do the Sa'Nerra tell you?" Sterling asked, dodging back to avoid an attempt by the man to grab his arm.

"They tell me that humanity will be exterminated," the colonist replied, "but that I will be spared. That I will live under their rule, once Earth and all of the worlds that humankind infests are cleansed of those that refuse to bow to their will."

Sterling had seen and heard enough. All the colonist had done was confirm what he, Admiral Griffin and the other Omega officers already suspected. That peace with the Sa'Nerra was not an option. Neither was surrender. And because of this, victory had to be achieved at any cost. Because even if the cost was high, it was still better than annihilation or servitude.

"You can tell your new masters that humanity doesn't take kindly to threats," Sterling hit back, feinting and drawing the colonist into an attack. The colonist rushed forward and Sterling slammed the metal bar into the man's throat, crushing his windpipe. Yet, incredibly, still the man did not go down. Undeterred, Sterling reversed his grip on the bar then drove it inside the colonist's mouth and down his throat, scraping and cracking teeth as he pushed harder. The man croaked and flailed his arms, but looked more confused than in pain. "And you can tell them that Captain Lucas Sterling will never bow to their will," he added before smashing the man's face into the hardwood floor and driving the bar deep into the colonist's gullet. Sterling watched the man flounder on the wooden floor like a stranded salmon. He could have ended the man's suffering, but he had no desire to do so. The Sa'Nerra would show humanity no mercy. He would return the compliment. It didn't matter that the man was human – he was turned. He was no different to the Sa'Nerra, and Sterling would treat him the same as his enemy.

The colonist's thrashes finally died down and Sterling looked up to see Commander Banks and Lieutenant Shade coming toward him. Two commandos flanked Shade, but Sterling could see that the rest of the squad was dead on the floor, alongside the bodies of the other turned colonists.

"It was an EMP, sir, powerful enough to fry the circuits in our plasma weapons," said Lieutenant Shade, holding an object out to Sterling. "They planned this."

Sterling took the object and saw that it was a remote activator. He cursed and threw the activator down. "At least in the past, we knew who we were facing," Sterling said, as the floor and walls of the bank vault began to shake.

"This is different. This makes the Sa'Nerra even more dangerous." The floor then began to shake even harder, as if the area was being subjected to a low intensity earthquake.

"The turned colonist said that they're already here," Shade added, looking around the room. Dust and loose mortar were crumbling from the ceiling. "The man must mean the Sa'Nerra."

"If that EMP was powerful enough to knock out our weapons, it could have affected the Invictus too," said Commander Banks, ramping up the sense of urgency even higher. "The ship is hardened against any such strikes, but it might still scramble the systems long enough for the Sa'Nerra to attack."

"We need to get off the ground," said Sterling, running to the window and peering outside. The two commandos who had been standing watch on the veranda were now sprawled out on the ground. Sterling could see blood-stained holes to their foreheads. "There are more turned colonists outside," Sterling continued, moving away from the window. "They're using conventional firearms. The commandos outside are dead."

The glass in the windows then smashed and Sterling ducked, shielding his head from the razor-sharp shards that were tumbling onto him.

"Get down!" Sterling called out to the others, while shaking the glass from his head and neck. Then he saw that the two remaining commandos were dead, shot in the head and neck by whoever was lurking outside.

"I'll try to find us another way out of here," said Banks, rushing to the row of teller counters and leaping over them.

"And I'll scout the place for some weapons," added Lieutenant Shade. "Commander Banks may be strong enough to snap these colonist's necks, but the rest of us aren't."

Sterling nodded then closed and barred the door from the inside. The floor was shaking harder still and there was a rumble in the air like distant thunder. He chanced another look through a window and saw a ship descending though the atmosphere. Sa'Nerran vessels were easy to discern from their Fleet adversaries. They were crude and ugly, like their crews, but also tough and battle-hardened. The ship that was approaching was equivalent in size and combat potency to a Fleet Light Cruiser. And it could pulverize the Invictus in a matter of seconds, unless they could get their ship off the ground. However, Sterling suspected that if the Sa'Nerran ship was landing it was because the warriors had other plans for him and his crew.

"Captain, over here," Commander Banks called out, waving him over. Sterling ran across the polished hardwood floor, ducking low beneath the window line in case anyone outside tried to take a potshot at him. "There's an exit through here. We can then move through the side streets and alleys back to the ship."

Sterling tapped his neural implant, watching as Lieutenant Shade approached, holding two ancient-looking sidearms and a longer weapon that was an elegant combination of wood and metal.

"Lieutenant Commander Crow, do you read me?" said Sterling over his neural link, but there was no reply. "Crow, come in," he repeated, but still there was no answer.

Sterling cursed then spoke out loud to Banks and Shade. "I can't raise the ship over a neural link."

"Perhaps the EMP knocked out our implants too?" suggested Shade.

Sterling shook his head. "The implants are organic, an EMP wouldn't impact them."

"The neural comms relays on the ship's hull aren't through," Banks chipped in. "If they were affected by the pulse, it would scramble the link. And without those relays, our signals will struggle to penetrate the hull of the Invictus."

Sterling took one of the conventional sidearms from Lieutenant Shade and handed it to Banks, before taking the second for himself. "I assume you're comfortable with whatever that thing is?" he said, nodding at the rifle-sized weapon that remained with Shade.

"It's a shotgun, sir," replied Shade. "And there's no weapon that I'm not comfortable with," she added, coolly. It wasn't a boast, and didn't come across as one. Shade never overstated her capabilities, or gave understated responses. She said exactly what she meant, whether you liked it or not. "I've already loaded your weapons, and they're ready to fire."

Sterling tried the handle of the side door, but it wouldn't open. Stepping back, he nodded to Commander Banks, who grabbed the handle and pushed the door open, snapping the lock like it was made of a brittle clay. Shade moved out first, running into cover behind a commercial waste bin. Sterling and Banks followed, moving across to the opposite side of the narrow back alley.

"The ship is a few hundred meters in that direction," said Shade, pointing with the flat of her hand. Then she adjusted the aim of her fingers. "Based on the shots from outside the bank, I'd say our snipers are either on the roof or an upper floor of a building to the west side of the street.

"We won't be able to take them down with these," said Sterling, examining the ancient weapon that Shade had found. It felt heavier than a plasma pistol, but the ergonomics were similar. "We should work our way around, and stay off the main street."

The rumble of thunder continued to rise and Sterling glanced into the murky grey sky to see the Sa'Nerran light cruiser creeping ever lower and closer. Its landing struts were already kicked out, which simply confirmed Sterling's earlier suspicions.

"They're here to capture the Invictus and its crew," said Sterling, feeling his grip on the handle of the pistol tighten. There wasn't a chance in hell he was letting the Sa'Nerra take his ship. "We need to move fast."

Lieutenant Shade took the lead as the group weaved through the back alleys and side-streets. The rain had stopped, but the mud underfoot still hampered their progress, and made stealth almost impossible. Sterling rounded a corner in pursuit of Shade, getting a clear glimpse of the Invictus for the first time, then caught movement in his peripheral vision. He slid to stop and aimed his weapon.

"Shade, get down!" Sterling yelled, firing up toward the roofline of the building to their side. He hit a turned colonist in the leg and the man tumbled off the roof and landed face-first in the yellow-brown mud. Then more colonists appeared on the roof and bullets hammered into the wall and clattered off metal shutters all around them. Shade took a hit to her combat vest, but it only seemed to make her angry. Aiming the ancient shotgun skyward, she unloaded the weapon, filling the air with a boom that made their plasma weapons sounds like toys. Two more colonists fell from the rooftop, but the final attacker took cover behind a metal chimney vent that ran down the side of the building into the ground beside them.

"Damn it, we need to clear him off there before we can move onto the ship," said Sterling, shuffling around in order to get a better angle, but the man remained hidden.

Banks shoved the handgun into the holster for her plasma pistol, which fitted the weapon surprisingly well, then grasped the metal chimney.

"Get ready," Banks said, looking at Lieutenant Shade as she said this. Then she sucked in a lungful of the cold, damp air and heaved on the chimney stack. The groans and creaks of twisted and broken metal filled the air as the chimney was torn away from the wall. Mortar and brick fell from the roofline, closely followed by the colonist, who had apparently been resting back against the chimney to catch his breath. The man bounced off the metal tower and landed hard, snapping his knee in the process. Yet, despite the brutal fall and injury, the man didn't cry out in pain. Shade raised her shotgun, ready to fire, but before she could squeeze the trigger, Banks had slammed the metal chimney stack down across the felled colonist, crushing its body into the mud.

"I thought you said get ready?" said Shade, frowning at Banks.

"Get ready in case I missed," replied Banks, breathing heavily as a result of her stupefying feat of strength. Then the Invictus' first officer pointed down to the flattened colonist. "But as you can see, I didn't miss."

Sterling moved ahead this time, slapping his first officer on the shoulder as he darted past. "Come on, before that ship changes its mind and decides to just blast us into atoms instead."

No sooner had Sterling said this than plasma blasts erupted from the Sa'Nerran Light Cruiser. Sterling skidded to a stop, hands pressed to his head, watching the energy shards strike the hull of his ship. Energy crackled across the surface, and black scars appeared. Sterling was helpless to intervene as another volley struck the ship, this time to its port quarter. The regenerative armor again soaked up the impact, but the attack whittled down the ship's protective coating to the bone. Another strike would cripple the ship, but Sterling was powerless to intervene. Teeth gritted and blood pumping furiously in his veins, Sterling looked on, waiting for the Sa'Nerran warship to deal the death blow. Then another flash of plasma lit up the sky, but this time it wasn't from the Sa'Nerran Light Cruiser. The alien ship was struck hard on the command section, and began to veer wildly off course. Another roar of thunder surrounded them, this time near-deafening in its intensity. Sterling peered into the sky and saw another vessel puncturing through the clouds. He wasn't a man to give himself over to overt displays of emotion, but even

Sterling couldn't help but shake his fist and let out a primal roar of exaltation.

"It's the Imperium!" cried Commander Banks, sliding to a stop at Sterling's side.

Their sister ship unleased another full volley from its forward plasma rail guns, striking the Sa'Nerran light cruiser cleanly across its back. The ship exploded violently in mid-air, like a nuclear airburst. Sterling's eyes widened as hunks of the ship flew out in all directions. Banks threw her arm around him and pulled them both into cover as debris peppered the buildings all around them, smashing walls like they were made of sand. Fragments of brick and splinters of wood began tumbling down on top of them. Sterling and Banks held onto each other, cowering under what little cover they had. Then when the falling debris had subsided, Sterling discovered that he was smiling.

"What's so amusing?" said Banks, shaking dust from her hair. Then her eyes widened and she cottoned on to the reason Sterling was looking so smug. She folded her arms, which were stained with blood, yellow-brown mud and dust. "Go on then, say it," she said. "I'm know you're dying to."

"I told you that Captain McQueen would do the same for us..." Sterling said, unable to shake the smile from his lips.

CAPTAIN STERLING WATCHED the Fleet Marauder Imperium kick out its landing struts and drop into the mud beside the Invictus. The two lean and mean Fleet warships cut an impressive sight against the stormy backdrop of Vega Two, especially with the burning wreckage from the downed Sa'Nerran ship adding to the sense of atmosphere.

"Captain, this is Lieutenant Commander Crow, can you read me?" came the voice of Sterling's chief engineer in his mind.

Crow sounded oddly calm and even a little bored considering the engineer had almost been blown up only minutes earlier. All of the Omega officers were a little closed off and aloof in their own ways, so in itself this fact shouldn't have surprised him. However, that his crew had gelled as a unit at all was remarkable, and testament to Admiral Griffin's ability to pair the right people into a team.

"I'm here Lieutenant Commander, what's the damage?" replied Sterling over the neural link. He wanted to get straight to business, before Crow selfishly decided to raise the subject of rock hunting again.

"We've sustained moderate damage, Captain," the engineer replied. "My quick and decisive actions in diverting power to our regenerative armor matrix ensured the ship is fully-repairable. However, I'm afraid we'll need to return to a major repair dock."

Sterling balled his hand into a fist then pressed it against his leg to stop himself shaking it angrily into the dark sky. "Are you sure you can't just fix her up out here?" he hit back. He wanted to avoid the need to return to one of the larger repair stations in UG Fleet space if he could help it.

"Even with my superior engineering abilities, I estimate that we'll be operating at no more than seventy percent," Crow replied, as haughtily as ever. "Should we, as is likely I suspect, end up in a battle with another Sa'Nerran vessel, our chances of survival would be greatly reduced."

Sterling cursed under his breath then hovered his hand beside his neural implant. "Understood, Lieutenant Commander, continue what repairs you can and I'll return shortly." He then tapped his neural interface a little harder than intended and shook his head.

"Bad news?" asked Commander Banks, who Sterling now realized had been watching him.

"We'll need to return to Fleet space for repairs," said Sterling, unable to hide his disappointment and frustration.

"Griffin is going to eat you for breakfast," said Banks, her smile as inappropriate as her comment.

"Thanks, Mercedes, it's good to know that you're always on hand to cheer me up," Sterling hit back.

"Relax," said Banks, slapping Sterling on the shoulder and knocking him two paces forward. "That old battle-axe loves you more than she loves her own son."

"She hates her son," Sterling replied, raising his eyebrows. "She calls him a moron and a disgrace to the Griffin name."

"There you go then!" said Banks.

Sterling frowned, unsure of whether Banks was still teasing him or if she genuinely thought her comment was complimentary. However, the appearance of Captain Lana McQueen in his peripheral vision diverted his attention. His fellow Omega Captain was trudging toward them, practically ankle-deep in the mud.

"What took you so long?" said Sterling, folding his arms and attempting to mimic the pose McQueen had adopted after he'd stormed onto her bridge.

"Space is pretty big," replied McQueen, with a wicked grin. "Besides, I can't stand the fact that I owed you one, so I thought I'd settle the score."

Sterling nodded his head to McQueen, respectfully. "Well, thank you Captain. You got here literally in the nick of time."

McQueen returned the nod. "You could have picked a nicer planet to need rescuing on, though," she said, gesturing the mud coating her boots and the bottoms of her pants.

"How the hell did you know to come after us, anyway?" Sterling asked with a curious scowl. "Just a few seconds longer, and the Invictus would be the one burning to cinders on this rotten world, instead of that Sa'Nerran hunk of crap." Sterling cast his eyes over the flaming orange inferno, which was all that remained of the Sa'Nerran warship McQueen had pulverized.

The smug look on McQueen's face suggested that she was glad Sterling had asked. "Well, here's the thing," she began, sounding like a TV detective that was about to launch into a startlingly-brilliant monologue revealing who had committed the crime and why. "When we were sweeping up the rest of the Sa'Nerra on my ship, we found that some had a yellowy-brown mud dried to their boots. You mentioned Vega Two, which is the yellowy-brownest ball of mud I know."

Sterling's scowl deepened. "That's pretty tenuous. There are a hundred muddy planets where that warrior could have been."

McQueen then raised her finger in a classic "ah ha!" gesture, again like a cheesy TV detective. "If you hadn't mentioned Vega Two, I wouldn't have thought anything of it either," she continued. "But we managed to get enough information out of their navigation computer to learn the recent comings and goings in the Vega Two system. And one of the goings was a Sa'Nerran Light Cruisier."

Sterling shrugged. He was already getting bored. "So? Still seems like a leap to me. Not that I'm complaining."

"It sure sounds like you're complaining, Captain," McQueen snapped back. "Anyway, long story short, the cruiser navigated above the pole then disappeared. That's when I knew you were heading into a trap."

Sterling shrugged again, but he was smiling too. "Pretty smart. I guess," he said, making a concerted effort not to sound too impressed. McQueen just shook her head at him.

"The bigger question is how the hell that Sa'Nerran cruiser knew we were coming," said Commander Banks, cutting to the chase. "And also why the 'turned' colonists on this rock all sound like brainwashed cultists."

This time it was McQueen who scowled. "What do you mean? The turned colonists here could actually talk?"

"That's an understatement, I could barely shut one of them up," Sterling replied, thinking back to the verbose colonist that he'd eventually silenced by shoving a metal bar down the man's throat. "It seems that the Sa'Nerra have enhanced their neural control weapon. To what extent, I don't know. But there's a chance some of the other turned colonists aren't entirely dead yet, which means we can take a couple back for analysis."

McQueen scrunched up her nose then shook her head. "Damn, that opens a can of worms," she said, anxiously looking around herself in case a colonist might have been sneaking up on her. "I'll have my team scout the area for any survivors."

Sterling nodded then turned to Lieutenant Shade, who had been standing to the side, silently observing and awaiting orders.

"Lieutenant, check to see if any of the colonists in the bank are still breathing," Sterling said. Then he noticed that only two commandos were flanking his weapons officer and frowned. "Did we lose all the rest?"

Shade nodded. "Yes, sir. I'll need to take on new men

when we return to Fleet space," she replied, speaking as though she were talking about collecting a few extra bags of groceries from the store.

"Very well," said Sterling with matching aloofness. "I'll contact Admiral Griffin and let her know what happened. We should make ready to leave in thirty. We don't know how many other alien ships are lurking around here."

"Aye, Captain," Shade replied, then she moved off through the rain with the two commandos in tow.

"I like her," said Captain McQueen, hooking at thumb toward the departing weapons officer.

"No, you can't have her either," said Sterling, a little more defensively than he'd intended. McQueen was always trying to thieve his top officers. Then he had a thought. "Though, if you need a medical officer..."

Captain McQueen snorted a laugh. "Graves?" she said, derisively. "I heard the guy is so good he could surgically re-attach an eyelash, but he's also one creepy S.O.B. So, no thanks."

Sterling shrugged. "Worth a shot."

Captain McQueen then tapped her neural implant and was silent for a moment while conversing with one or other members of her crew. Sterling waited for her to finish her neural conversation, then McQueen tapped her implant and blew out a sigh.

"We dropped a sensor buoy in orbit before we came down here," McQueen said, speaking out loud again. "Four phase three Sa'Nerran Destroyers are heading this way. Time to leave I think."

Sterling cursed. He could have done with more time on

Vega Two to piece together what had happened. However, he knew they were in no shape for another fight. Resigning himself to the inevitable need to withdraw, sterling tapped his neural implant and ordered Ensign Keller to prepare to take off. Then he again turned to McQueen.

"Where are you headed from here?" Sterling asked his counterpart.

"We've been ordered to return to F-Sector COP," McQueen replied. "Admiral Griffin apparently wants to speak to me, so I assume that's where you'll be heading too."

Sterling glanced at Banks, who appeared unimpressed by McQueen's news. Neither of them liked the Combat Outposts, or COPs as they were known. They were the highest-ranking outposts in each sector, and were usually teeming with Fleet personnel. Most of these officers and crew, and even the civilian inhabitants, looked at the unique uniforms of the clandestine "Void Recon Unit" with more than a little suspicion. The Omega Taskforce was top secret, so naturally half the fleet had heard rumors about it. Many of these rumors revolved around the idea that the VRU was simply a cover for this super-secret elite unit. For once, the rumor mill had churned out the truth.

"I'll confirm our destination before we leave and let you know," said Sterling. Then he shot McQueen a wicked smile that she herself would have been proud of. "You can perhaps be my escort back to Fleet space, if you like?"

"Like hell," McQueen snorted. "But if you want a race back to F-COP, you're on."

Sterling snorted right back. "I'm surprised you think I'd

entertain such a petty endeavor," he replied, with a haughtiness worthy of Lieutenant Commander Crow. It was a bare-faced lie, of course – Sterling fully intended to beat Captain McQueen back to F-COP.

"Suit yourself, loser," said McQueen. Then she shot them both a lazy salute. "I'll see you slowpokes back at the COP."

Sterling waited for McQueen to trudge off back toward the Imperium then surreptitiously went to tap his neural interface. His intention was to order Ensign Keller to ramp up their engines and prepare for a high-power burn to the aperture. However, he noticed that Commander Banks was already in communication with someone. Curious as to who she was speaking to, Sterling waited until she tapped her interface to sever the link, then meet his eyes.

"Who were you just speaking to?" Sterling asked.

"Ensign Keller, of course," replied Banks, smiling. "You want to beat McQueen back to F-COP, right?"

THE FLEET MARAUDER INVICTUS surged through the aperture and all the sights, sounds and senses of the universe exploded back into existence. Any trip through an aperture was disorientating, but the multiple surges in close succession that Ensign Keller had performed in their race to F-Sector COP had left Sterling's head feeling like jelly. The deck plating was also still shuddering from the frankly unsafe velocity that Ensign Keller had exited the aperture at. However, even after Keller had throttled back and the rattle through the ship had subsided, Sterling discovered that his legs were still quivering like a frightened puppy.

"Did we make it?" said Commander Banks, practically falling over the top of her console. "Did we beat them?" There was a flash of light on the viewscreen, like a million camera bulbs all going off at the same time. Then the Fleet Marauder Imperium emerged from the aperture and immediately initiated a hard deceleration burn.

Commander Banks whooped uncouthly then thumped her fist onto her console, creating a dent in the far-right corner.

"You did it, Keller!" Banks hollered. "You beat them, and with a ship that's well below one-hundred percent, too!"

Ensign Keller spun his chair around to face the command platform, a smile beaming from ear to ear. Sterling threw up a casual salute in his helmsman's direction.

"Good job, Ensign!" said Sterling with an enthusiasm almost matching that of Banks. "Captain McQueen will be sore about this one for months." Sterling then glanced over to the weapons console to also congratulate Lieutenant Shade. However, Shade was simply standing at her post, hands pressed to the small of her back, looking like she was attending a funeral. "Come on, Lieutenant, how about a little holler? We won!"

Lieutenant Shade sighed then reluctantly raised her fist in a half-assed gesture of solidarity.

"Well done, sir," Shade said, though it sounded more like she was telling a waiter how she liked her steaks cooked.

The communications system then chimed an incoming message on Banks' console. However, Sterling already knew who was on the other end of the line.

"Shall I put her through?" said Commander Banks, with a smug look on her face.

"By all means," said Sterling, extending a hand toward the viewscreen. Captain McQueen appeared before them; hands pressed to her hips with a face like a winter storm.

"Luck..." McQueen snapped. Even the act of prizing her lips apart far enough to utter this single word was clearly a struggle. "Either that or you cheated."

Sterling smoothed down the front of his tunic and stood tall. "Don't be a sore loser, Captain. The best ship won, that's all there is to it."

"My ass the best ship..." McQueen replied, pouting.

Sterling and McQueen were then both interrupted by an aggressive-sounding alert that blared out from the weapons consoles of both Marauders.

"Sir, the Fleet Gatekeeper Odin has locked it weapons onto the Invictus and the Imperium," said Shade.

Considering that the Odin could obliterate a small moon, this news should have been deeply perturbing to the lieutenant. However, as usual, Shade was displaying all the emotion of a dry rock.

"Don't worry, Lieutenant, the Odin is just making a statement," Sterling replied. It was obvious that Shade wasn't in the slightest bit worried, but Sterling's statement was more for the benefit of the rest of the bridge crew, Ensign Keller in particular. "We busted through the aperture at well over regulation surge velocity. It's just the Odin's way of reminding us that they're watching."

Then Commander Banks' console chimed another incoming communication. Sterling checked his own console and saw that the message was being broadcast on the alert channel. Someone other than the Odin was now vying for their attention, and as Sterling assimilated the data on his screen, he quickly realized who it was.

"Captain, the Fleet Dreadnaught Hammer is

approaching, and they're hailing us," said Commander Banks. "In fact, they're practically on top of us, already."

Banks then tapped her console and the Hammer appeared on the viewscreen. The giant ship was looming over them, blocking the light from the sun and casting the diminutive Marauder-class vessels into darkness.

"Put him through," said Sterling, reluctantly. The viewscreen then switched to the image of Captain Oscar Blake, the Hammer's commanding officer, and Sterling's former boss.

"Captain Sterling, are you lost?" said Captain Blake, with a scolding tone that immediately got Sterling's hackles up. "You seem to believe this aperture is part of some sort of galactic racing circuit."

Sterling had to force himself not to roll his eyes at the man. He and Blake had never truly seen eye-to-eye, despite there being a grudging respect between them.

"I'm just eager to get back to base and receive new orders," Sterling replied, cheerfully. "New orders from the Fleet Admiral, that is."

Sterling had thrown the Admiral's name into the mix to remind Blake that the red-haired captain of the Fleet's flagship was no longer his superior.

Blake's eyes narrowed. "I know who you report to, Captain," he said, clearly having taken the hint, and some offence in the process. "But this sector is under my protection. So, while you're here, I suggest you abide by standard regulations." Then Blake straightened up and lifted his chin, peering at Sterling down his nose. "I realize that your unique little taskforce isn't used to standard regulations. However, while you're at F-COP, I should remind you that you're no different to any other ship."

Sterling smiled back at Blake. In some ways, he'd missed sparring with his old Captain, but not enough to want to continue his conversation with the man.

"Of course, Captain, thank you for the friendly advice," he replied, sarcastically.

Sterling had never been entirely sure quite how much Captain Blake knew about the Omega Directive. However, his fellow captain's subtle use of the word "taskforce" and the jibes about not following standard regulations reminded him that Blake knew more than most. His former captain had been in on Admiral Griffin's Omega Directive test while Sterling was a commander on the Hammer. It was possible he was an Omega captain himself, Sterling mused. It made sense for Griffin to have senior officers loyal to her strategically placed within the regular Fleet too.

Blake then ended the transmission without another word and McQueen reappeared on the viewscreen.

"That was rather rude," said McQueen, her arms now folded across her chest.

"It's Blake, what do you expect?" replied Sterling with a shrug. "How about we meet up on F-COP once we're docked and I have our repairs underway?" Commander Banks' console then chimed another message. This time it came through on their secure Omega Taskforce channel. "Hold that thought, Captain..." Sterling said to McQueen on the viewscreen before turning to Banks.

"Admiral Griffin wants to see you and Captain

McQueen in her office in thirty," announced Commander Banks, with a knowing gleam in her eyes.

Sterling tutted and shook his head. "It'll take us longer than thirty minutes just to dock the damn ship," he complained.

"No rest for the wicked, eh, Captain?" said McQueen.

Sterling then noticed that the Imperium had already gotten underway again and was on-course F-COP, at the fastest possible regulation-permitted speed. Sterling cursed under his breath, realizing this meant she'd get docking clearance first, which would only delay his arrival further.

"I'll apologize to the Fleet Admiral on your behalf for your tardiness," McQueen added with her usual wicked smile. "Catch you later, slow poke," and she abruptly cut the transmission.

Captain Sterling had only been waiting outside Fleet Admiral Griffin's office on F-COP for a couple of minutes, but already his unique uniform was attracting anxious stares. Despite the nature of Sterling's command being a secret, rumors still circuited as to the true purpose of the mysterious officers and crew that bore the silver stripe on their tunics.

In order to conceal the Omega Taskforce from the government and from public view, Admiral Griffin had established it under the cover name, "Void Recon Unit." The mandate of the Void Recon Unit was to conduct manned reconnaissance patrols deep inside the Sa'Nerran half of the Void, in order to report intelligence regarding enemy movements. This itself had raised some eyebrows, since automated recon probes had served that function well enough for decades. However, Griffin's high rank and pugnacious attitude had allowed her to push it through. No elected official in the UG War Council was willing to block a program that Griffin argued could save millions of lives. The enhanced need for deep space recon was also the only way Griffin could explain the frequency with which the Invictus and Imperium would enter the no-man's land between Fleet and Sa'Nerran space.

Over the last year, however, more and more people, both in the government and the Fleet, had grown suspicious of the Void Recon Unit. Rumors abounded of their true role, all of which were inaccurate, and some of which were even wild. Sterling particularly enjoyed the theory that the Invictus and Imperium had established an aperture into a parallel universe where the Sa'Nerra did not exist, in order to prepare for a mass human exodus. However, in recent weeks, stories of the Void Recon Unit's more extreme remit had begun to circulate, and there were even whispers of its true name. As such, the distinctive silver stripe that Sterling wore on his uniform had become more than merely a symbol of suspicion. It had become a symbol of fear.

On the fringe of the Void, or even at the smaller outposts in the outer sectors, it was easy for Sterling and his crew to remain out of the public eye. However, there was no such possibility on F-COP. A far cry from the small combat outposts of Earth's own domestic conflicts in the time before space travel, Fleet COPs were more like giant forward operating bases built in space. They were constructed to protect the only aperture route that linked the Void to the solar system, but they were also thriving military communities in their own right. The COP in Sector-F bore the unimaginative yet logical and accurate name, Fleet F-COP. It was home to more than a quarter of a million Fleet personnel and their families, plus a host of private businesses and united governments staff. F-COP was the largest space-based installation close to the Void. It was also the only base in the sector that was large enough to support a Dreadnaught-class ship, such as the Hammer. That alone accounted for the Hammer's presence in the sector. The mighty warship was now the only remaining Dreadnaught in the fleet, after the capture of its sister ship, the Vanguard, which had not been seen for over a year. As such, the Hammer was rarely risked on the front line. Its role now was to act a deterrent to the Sa'Nerran armada attempting a more coordinated incursion into Fleet space. Together with the firepower of the Gatekeeper Odin and F-COP itself, the key aperture in Sector F, quadrant two was well-guarded. However, if the Hammer was to fall, the Gatekeeper alone would not be able to stop the Sa'Nerra from flooding into Fleet space and making a run for Earth.

The sound of Admiral Griffin's voice suddenly invaded Sterling's mind, blotting out any thoughts of gatekeepers, conspiracy theories and his old ship, the Hammer.

"You can come in now, Captain Sterling," said the voice of Admiral Griffin. The sound of her strident, commanding tones felt like thorns being raked across his brain. "Now that you've finally decided to turn up, that is..." she added, with extra prickliness.

Sterling sighed, realizing that Lana McQueen must already be inside, and that she'd likely made a point about Sterling's disrespectful tardiness. He walked up to the door, which dutifully opened for him, and stepped into Fleet

Admiral Griffin's office. The Admiral was seated at her imposing desk with Captain McQueen sitting opposite, grinning in Sterling's direction. The room was stately in a twenty-fourth century kind of way. There may have been no wooded panels or animal-head trophies on the walls, but the silver-grey room still had an imposing character about it. It was also both larger and more well-equipped than the entire bridge of his own ship.

"Apologies for the delay in arriving, Admiral," Sterling began, marching toward the desk. His muscles felt suddenly tense and he realized he was walking more stiffly than usual, as if he was a rookie on parade. Despite his atypically informal relationship with Griffin, she still had an unopposable power over him, like gravity. "My ship was damaged during the last mission and so we had to take it a little slower on the docking approach."

Griffin cocked her head a little to the side. "Is that so, Captain?" she said, in a way that told Sterling in no uncertain terms that she hadn't bought his story. "Because based on your arrival through the aperture at double the regulation surge speed, I find that surprising."

Sterling winced but stayed silent, hoping the Admiral had more important things to do than chew his ear off for the next few minutes. Mercifully, he was correct. "Just sit down, Captain, we have a lot to talk about," the Admiral continued, while turning her attention to one of the computer consoles built into her desk.

Sterling wasted no time in planting himself in the seat beside Captain McQueen, who was smiling innocently at him. He slyly tapped his neural interface, disguising the gesture by scratching his temple, then spoke to Captain McQueen through the link. "Nobody likes a sore loser..." he said, also shooting her an innocent smile.

"Call me old-fashioned, Captain Sterling, but I prefer the ancient art of verbal communication," Griffin said, still focused on her consoles. "So, leave your little neural chit-chat until later." Sterling abruptly severed the link to McQueen, though his fellow captain looked as shocked as he did that the wily admiral had managed to detect their neural connection.

"I have a neural scanner, before you ask," said Griffin, raising her eyes to meet Sterling's. "I don't like people talking behind my back, either out loud or in their heads."

"I thought those things were illegal?" replied Sterling. He'd heard of the neural scanning technology, but it had been outlawed at the start of the war because of privacy and security concerns.

"They are," replied Griffin, coolly. She left her statement hanging in the air for a moment then changed the subject. "I've read your reports," Griffin continued, still focused on Sterling. "And as admirable and heartwarming as it is to see you two rushing to one another's aid, do not forget that you are under my command," she went on. Despite the Admiral speaking out loud, Sterling again felt like thorns were being dragged across his brain. "I shouldn't have to remind either of you that you are to follow my orders, not whatever whim takes you in the moment. While the outcome was favorable, your actions could have cost us two advanced war vessels and two Omega crews."

Sterling straightened up and sat to attention. "Yes,

Admiral, I understand," he replied, accepting the dressing down. However, all told, Sterling thought he had gotten off lightly. Griffin was usually much more painstaking in her dissections.

"The same applies to you, Captain McQueen," the Admiral added. Griffin's intense eyes, framed by dark circles and crow's feet, peered at McQueen with no less ferocity.

"I understand, Admiral," McQueen replied, also straightening to attention.

"That being said, your foolish heroics gained us some valuable intel," Admiral Griffin said, seemingly satisfied that her captains had fallen in line. She then tapped her console and a holo image of a neural control device appeared to the side of her enormous desk. Next to it was a medical scan of a human head, which was highlighting brain activity specifically in connection to the neural implant. "This neural weapon is one that Captain McQueen's crew recovered from the Skirmisher that ambushed the Imperium near Artemis Colony," the Admiral went on. The image of the device began to rotate and was overlaid with technical data while Griffin spoke. "As you can see, it is identical to all the others we have encountered." Griffin then tapped her console and a second neural weapon and scan of a human head appeared alongside the other images. "This is a device that was recovered from Vega Two," the Admiral continued. "Although the appearance is the same, this weapon is new and far more sophisticated than the existing models." Griffin then pointed to the medical scan of the second head. "This image shows the initial medical data obtained by Commander Graves from one of the surviving colonists on Vega Two." The second image showed an identical looking scan, but even to Sterling's inexpert eye, he could see the huge difference in brain activity. "Compared to the brain activity of 'turned' prisoners we have experimented on in the past, the difference is clear, as you can see," Griffin concluded.

Captain McQueen pushed herself out of her chair and stood in front of the two medical scans, scrutinizing them with the intensity of a chess grand master.

"The number and density of neural interfaces in this recent subject is orders of magnitude above what I've seen before," McQueen said, pointing to the second brain scan. Sterling remembered that prior to being recruited by Griffin for the Omega Taskforce, McQueen had been the chief medical officer on board the Fleet Heavy Battlecruiser Nimrod. "There's a distinct focus on manipulating electrical signals in the frontal, temporal and parietal lobes," McQueen went on, talking excitedly, "but this new corruption extends to nearly all the eighty-six million neurons in the human brain."

Griffin nodded then cleared the images so that McQueen could no longer be distracted by them. "We're dealing with a level of brain manipulation that we previously thought was impossible," the Admiral continued. "Memory, behavior, personality, even beliefs can all be modified, and the person affected wouldn't even realize."

McQueen cursed under her breath then sat back down.

"With this device the Sa'Nerra could turn an entire ship's crew against their own people," she said, crossing her legs and flapping her foot up and down like a paddle. "We could see mass mutinies across the fleet."

Sterling rubbed the back of his neck, which still felt stiff and sore. He may not have understood anything about neurons and lobes, but he knew what the implications of the new Sa'Nerran weapon were, and they weren't good.

"It's worse than that," Sterling said, looking at McQueen first before meeting Griffin's eyes. "If these turned crew are made to genuinely believe in the Sa'Nerran cause, like those on Vega Two did, it means we could effectively have enemy agents already moving throughout the fleet. It means we can no longer be sure who to trust."

"Correct, Captain," replied Griffin. For the briefest moment Sterling thought that the Admiral sounded impressed with him. "Which is why we have to keep this knowledge under tight control. If word got out then Fleet would be at each other's throats within days. Trust in the chain of command would rapidly erode."

McQueen cursed again, this time more bitterly. "Give me the turned colonist," she said to Griffin, suddenly growing more agitated. "Let me dig around in his brain and see if there's a way to undo this damage. We have to find a way to counteract this weapon. We can't allow the Sa'Nerra to twist our own people against the Fleet."

"The subject that Commander Graves experimented on is already dead," said Griffin, with a dismissive waft of her hand, "but that doesn't matter. There are plenty of convicts scratching their assess in outpost brigs to provide more test subjects. I've already begun experiments on the worst of them. Murderers, rapists, deserters and the like."

Admiral Griffin's admission of human experimentation would have shocked most other people, but Sterling considered the use of prisoners to be a perfectly sensible option. And from McQueen's response, it appeared she did too.

"Request permission to transfer to the advanced research division," McQueen said, leaning forward and almost sliding off her chair. "I can figure this thing out, Admiral. Just give me a chance."

Griffin shook her head and waved McQueen off again. "I need you doing what I recruited you to do, Captain," she said, not even entertaining McQueen's request for a millisecond. "There are thousands of doctors and scientists in the advanced research division as it is. But I only have two Omega Captains." Then Admiral Griffin removed two devices from her desk drawer and slid them across the surface toward Sterling and McQueen. Sterling recognized the objects as encrypted communications chips. "Install these once you get back to your ships. It's a new scrambled private channel for Omega Directive use only." Sterling picked up one of the chips and pocketed it. "Based on the ambushes at Artemis and Vega Two, we have to assume someone inside the Fleet is already feeding intelligence back to the Sa'Nerra," she went on. "I'll deal with implementing tighter communications within the regular Fleet, but I need to be doubly sure our exchanges remain private."

"So, what's our next move, Admiral?" said Sterling. He knew Griffin well enough to understand that everything she'd said up to this point was just a preamble.

"In light of this information, the Omega Taskforce has never been more necessary," Admiral Griffin replied, suddenly sitting more upright, as if she were giving an address to conference delegates. "However, this new neural weapon is not our only problem. Recon probes from within the Sa'Nerran half of the Void recently picked up what appears to be a massive ship-building project."

Griffin entered another command on her console and a group of blurry, long-range recon images appeared on the wall to their side. Sterling examined the images, but nothing about them appeared to stand out.

"Why are they building a ship in the Void?" asked Captain McQueen. "Surely it would be safer to build inside their own territory?"

"We believe their resources are already stretched, and that this location in the Void is a rich source of materials," replied Admiral Griffin.

Sterling was only half paying attention to McQueen's question. He was still studying the images, looking for the reason Griffin considered them so important. However, the answer eluded him.

"It just looks like a regular ship, on a regular shipyard," Sterling said, sounding almost disappointed. He was expecting some bigger news. "The design of the vessel is similar to a Sa'Nerran Heavy Battlecruiser. Perhaps it's a new phase four design?"

"Look again, Captain," said Griffin.

The Admiral also sounded disappointed, but her disappointment was directed at Sterling, rather than the seemingly anticlimactic news. Like a child seeking the approval of his mother, Sterling was duly spurred on to impress. He looked at the images again, then noticed the scale bar in the bottom corner. At first, he thought he'd misread it and so stood up to get a closer look. However, the scale appeared to be correct.

"This can't be right," said Sterling, turning back to the Admiral. "If this is accurate then that ship would be over ten kilometers long. That's way more than double the size of the Hammer."

"The scale is correct, Captain," said Griffin, flatly.

Sterling shook his head, marveling at how such an enormous vessel could be built. Then he noticed something else in the background of the recon images.

"Are they building this new ship inside a planetary ring system?" He shot Griffin a perplexed frown.

"We believe so," the Admiral replied. "But where and how they are building it is not what concerns me," she added, darkly. "The Sa'Nerra have always focused on fighting in greater numbers, not in the might of individual battleships," Griffin went on. "This is a major tactical shift. We need to know what the purpose of this vessel is."

McQueen then also stood up and scowled at the images. However, she appeared unimpressed, and even a little annoyed. "So, send a regular Fleet ship to scout it out. Recon is hardly work suited to our talents."

Griffin sat back and folded her arms, suddenly appearing even more hacked off than usual. "I can't. The

United Governments have ordered that all regular Fleet actions in the Void must cease."

"Why the hell would they do that?" said Sterling, throwing his hands up. "If we don't engage them in the Void, we're inviting them to invade our borders."

Griffin let out a sort of half-sigh, half grunt, then opened a large desk drawer and pulled out a bottle of Calvados. "The UG knows we're losing and wants to push for a diplomatic solution," Griffin replied, speaking the words, "diplomatic solution" in a mocking tone. "They believe that continued incursions into the Void are provocative, and that to establish a dialogue, we need to take the first step in de-escalation."

Sterling snorted. "A dialogue? We haven't worked out what a single one of their hisses means in over fifty years! We need to crush the Sa'Nerra, not chat with them around the campfire."

"Do you think I don't know that, Captain?" snapped Griffin, wearily. She then slid three tulip-shaped glasses onto the table and filled each of them from the bottle. "That's why it's up to us. You are the 'Void Recon Unit', after all. As of right now, I've managed to convince the war council that the Invictus and Imperium still be allowed to gather intelligence, but that may not last for long. We have to act fast."

Sterling slid back into his chair and accepted the glass that Griffin offered him. "I'll get under way as soon as my repairs are complete," he said.

"No, Captain McQueen will take the Imperium," said Griffin, handing a glass to McQueen, who frowned.

However, Sterling wasn't sure if she was frowning at the order, or at the drink. "I want to take the opportunity to refit the Invictus while you're in repair dock," Griffin continued, sitting back in her chair and relaxing for the first time since Sterling had entered the room. "I had intended to introduce additional Omega Taskforce ships in the coming months, but this new order blocks me from adding to the ranks of the Void Recon Unit." She paused to take a drink from her glass, and Sterling used the opportunity to do the same. The taste had become familiar to him, like a well-worn sweater. Then Griffin turned to Captain McQueen. "The Imperium leaves at twelve hundred hours," Griffin added, "so, I suggest you get some rest."

Captain McQueen nodded then downed the contents of her tulip-shaped glass before standing up. "I'll brief my officers," she said. Then she turned to Sterling. "Do you have any time to grab some food? The wardroom here is pretty good."

Sterling shrugged and also downed the rest of his calvados. "It appears that I'm not going anywhere soon," he said. Then he turned to Griffin. "With your permission, of course, Admiral?"

Griffin just frowned back at him. "You don't need my permission to eat dinner, Captain," she said, crabbily. "But if you mean are you dismissed, then yes, you can go."

Seizing the opportunity to leave early, Sterling stood up and headed to the door with Captain McQueen. It slid open and they stepped out into the corridor, immediately attracting interested stares from passersby. The door slid shut behind them, and Sterling felt like a weight had literally been lifted from his shoulders.

"I'd happily take on squad of Sa'Nerran warriors by myself than deal with Griffin's erratic moods," he said, as they set off toward the wardroom.

"We're lucky to have her," replied McQueen. "If the United Governments have their way, we'll all be hissing like Sa'Nerrans in a few months' time."

Sterling laughed, though it was a half-hearted, despairing sound. The only thing funny about McQueen's quip was that it was probably true.

"Come on, I need a proper drink," said Sterling, quickening his pace to the wardroom.

STERLING OPENED the compact wardrobe in his quarters on the Invictus and grabbed a clean tunic off its hanger. The one he'd worn the previous night was still in a bundle on the floor, creased and crumpled. He was in the process of pulling the tunic on when the door chime sounded.

"Computer, who is at the door?" said Sterling. The door then slid open and he tutted loudly. "Damn it, computer, I said 'who is at the door', not 'open the door'."

"Apologies, Captain," said the computer, cheerfully. "My analysis of your question suggested that once I explained who was at the door, your next response would be to ask me to open it. Therefore, I thought that it would be more expedient to simply open the door straight away."

"What have I told you about thinking, computer?" Sterling said, while fastening the buttons on his tunic.

"You have mentioned nothing specific about me thinking, Captain," the computer chirped back. "Though you did say I talked too much."

"Well, you do too much of both," Sterling hit back. He then swung over to the door and saw Commander Mercedes Banks standing outside. He froze up, as if he'd seen the ghost of his mother and father in the corridor.

"So, you're still alive then?" Banks said, hands on hips.

"Mercedes..." said Sterling, anxiously glancing over his shoulder. "What are you doing here?"

"Your neural link is off," replied Banks, now sounding a little peeved. "I always call you in the morning, remember, and today you didn't answer."

Captain Lana McQueen then appeared beside Sterling. She was also buttoning up her tunic. Commander Banks straightened up, though Sterling could see this was more out of surprise than in response to the presence of another superior officer.

"Captain McQueen, I didn't..." Banks began, but then she quicky started falling over her words. "I mean, I didn't know you two. I didn't know..."

Captain McQueen reached out and slapped Banks on the shoulder. "Don't worry, Commander, no need to feel awkward," she said, returning to fastening her buttons.

"Well, I don't feel awkward," replied Banks, though Sterling thought that she couldn't have looked any more awkward if she'd tried. He caught a glimpse of himself in the mirror beside his door and realized he looked like a man who'd just been caught cheating on his wife. Then he felt ridiculous for thinking this; there was no reason for him to feel guilty.

"That's great then," said McQueen. She then turned to Sterling, straightened his tunic and smoothed the fabric down with the palm of her hand. "I'll have to skip breakfast. The Imperium ships out in an hour on this damned recon mission," she said, adopting a more formal, 'captainly' pose.

"Hopefully you won't need us to save your ass this time," replied Sterling, casting a glance across to Banks, who still looked like she'd seen her parents snogging in a nightclub.

Captain McQueen just snorted in response then stepped out into the corridor. "Enjoy your downtime, while the Imperium does all the hard work," she said before turning and strolling away down the corridor without another glance back.

Sterling waited until McQueen was out of earshot then turned his attention to his first officer, who had her hands pressed to her hips again. The shock of seeing Captain McQueen in his quarters appeared to have worn off, and any embarrassment she had shown had been replaced by irritation.

"You could have warned me," said Banks.

Sterling frowned. "The last time I checked, Fleet regulations don't require me to report my personal relationships to my subordinates." Banks shot him a look that could have turned milk sour. "Look, it's no big deal, and frankly it's also none of your business," Sterling added, taking a forceful tone with Banks. He felt like he was being judged, and he didn't like it.

Commander Banks straightened up again, though this time it was in order to stand to attention. "My apologies, Captain," she said, pressing her hands to the small of her back. The apology seemed sincere, which for some reason made Sterling feel worse. "I only came to ask if you wanted to join me for breakfast, but since you're busy, I'll see you at the refit update briefing in an hour."

Sterling threw his arms out wide. "I'm not busy, but I am hungry." Then he folded his arms around his chest. "Unless you and I now have a problem, Commander?"

"No sir, no problem," replied Banks, crisply.

Sterling studied Banks' expression for a moment, but she was unflinching. If they had been paying poker, he would have had no clue as to the strength of her hand. "Okay then," said Sterling, inviting Banks to take the lead out along the corridor. "How about we head into the outpost and find out what meal packs they're serving on F-COP this morning?"

"You're just after that elusive number twenty-seven meal tray, admit it..." said Banks, stepping out in front.

"Guilty as charged," replied Sterling, smiling.

The journey to get breakfast on F-COP took considerably longer than the short hop to the Invictus' wardroom. Sterling and Banks filled the time with their typical mixture of work-related chat, news and gossip from around the Fleet. As usual, their conversation was frequently interrupted by the need for both Sterling and Banks to acknowledge greetings from the crew. However, once they had traversed the docking tunnel into F-COP, the dynamic shifted quickly. Instead of respectful nods and smiling faces, they were met with suspicious glances and deliberate attempts by other Fleet crew members to avoid them. It was the space-station equivalent of crossing the street to dodge having to meet someone.

"Considering the way people look at us, you'd think we were Sa'Nerran warriors wandering the station," said Banks, jumping onto one of the trams that extended throughout the vast command outpost.

"It's gotten worse, especially in the last few weeks," said Sterling, grabbing the handrail beside Banks. He then noticed four Fleet crew jump off the tram coincidently straight after they had gotten onboard. The remaining passengers were trying hard not to look in their direction, or were subtly edging themselves away from the two officers with silver stripes on their uniforms. "At least now we have an inkling about why," he continued, lowering his voice.

Banks leant in, bringing her lips so close to Sterling's ear that he thought she was going to bite it. "Why are you whispering..." she said, the breath of her voice barely brushing his face.

Sterling then felt stupid and tapped his neural implant. "Sometimes I forget about this method of talking," Sterling said, reaching out to Banks in his mind.

"Do you think the Sa'Nerra turned someone who knows about the Omega Taskforce?" Banks replied, picking up the thread of the conversation again.

Sterling had already briefed Banks on the pertinent points from the meeting with Admiral Griffin the night before. This had been before Captain McQueen had convinced him to do shots, which had been the main reason they'd ended up in bed together.

"Honestly, I don't know," Sterling admitted. "Besides

the Omega officers and crew, Admiral Griffin herself, and perhaps Captain Blake from the Hammer, I don't know who else knows."

Banks nodded then caught the eye of a Crewman who was looking at her furtively. The Crewman's head spun away so sharply that Sterling thought he heard the vertebrae in the man's neck snapping. The tram then slowed to a stop and the computer announced their destination.

"Command level fourteen, section alpha, zone one," the computer announced. The synthesized voice was dreary and monosyllabic compared to the Invictus' irksome computer. However, Sterling much preferred his quirky gen-fourteen AI to the drab regulation-standard computers the rest of the Fleet relied upon.

"This is our stop," said Sterling, loudly enough that others in the tram carriage could hear. He was then sure he could detect audible gasps, as if some of the other occupants had been holding their breaths since the moment he and Banks had boarded.

Banks hopped off onto the platform and Sterling followed, still feeling the eyes of the other passengers drilling into his back. Sterling then looked around the wide, open spaces of F-COP's command level fourteen and suddenly felt exposed. It was like he had walked on stage in the middle of a play then forgotten his lines.

"I've gotten used to the Invictus and it's narrow spaces and compact decks," said Sterling, again noticing that other Fleet crew were giving them a wide berth. "I'd almost forgotten how huge these COPs are."

"Why do I feel like this is a zoo and we're the animals?" replied Banks, glowering at the many people who were surreptitiously sneaking looks at them. "I think I prefer the Void to Fleet space these days."

Sterling led the way through the crowds, separating them like Moses parting the Red Sea. When the entrance to the wardroom finally came into view, he was glad to get out of the public eye. However, as soon as he'd set foot inside the wardroom, Sterling realized that they were not about to escape scrutiny there, either.

"Damn, they could fit the entire crew of a Dreadnaught in this place," said Sterling, heading further inside the wardroom. Sterling noted that the wall, floors and ceilings were all constructed from the usual, staid-looking silver-gray composite materials Fleet employed in all its ships and bases. However, he had to admit it was certainly grander than most wardrooms he'd seen.

Banks headed up to one of the serving counters, which was generously staffed, unlike the mostly automated serving hatches Sterling was used to, and perused the menu options.

"One number nine and a fourteen, please," Banks said to the crewman behind the counter. Like pretty much everyone else they'd seen, the man appeared anxious in the presence of the fabled "Void Recon Unit". The crewman nodded then slid the trays Banks had ordered into the processor.

"I'll take a twenty-seven, if you have it," Sterling said. He noticed Banks rolling her eyes at him. "What, we haven't had twenty-seven on the Invictus for over three months," said Sterling shrugging. "I love that grilled ham and cheese."

The crewman behind the counter then let out an apologetic cough. "I'm sorry, sir, I thought the commander ordered for both of you," the crewman said. "Regulations state only one meal tray per person, sir." The man then added, looking like he wanted the deck to open up and swallow him.

"She eats for two," said Sterling, undeterred by the crewman's push-back. He knew the regulations, but he also wanted his grilled ham and cheese.

"Oh, congratulations, Commander," the crewmen said, managing a weak smile.

Sterling almost laughed, but held his composure. Banks shot him a dirty sideways glance then addressed the crewman. "I'm not pregnant, I just have a fast metabolism," she said, causing the crewman's face to fall faster than a headman's axe. "A nine and a twenty-seven will do fine, crewman," Banks then added. The crewman hastily departed and switched up the order, while Banks continued to glower at Sterling.

"You'll eat half of my tray anyway, so I don't know what you're looking at me like that for," said Sterling.

The crewman then returned with all three meal-trays. A nine, a fourteen, and Sterling's favorite number twenty-seven.

"I'd already put the nine and fourteen in the processor, so you may as well have them both," the crewman said, offering Banks a weak smile.

"Thank you, crewman," Banks said brightly, grabbing both trays.

The crewman nodded then beat a hasty retreat. Sterling collected his tray and followed Banks to a nearby table.

"I guess this silver stripe has some perks after all," said Sterling sliding the tray onto the table then sitting down.

"It was my charming personality, rather than our threatening mystique that got me a second breakfast," said Banks, tucking into a pile of maple syrup pancakes.

Sterling snorted a laugh then set to work on the grilled ham and cheese. It was every bit as good as he remembered. Coffee was then brought to their table by another nervous-looking crewman, and several minutes elapsed, during which time Sterling and Banks chatted as they always did. And as usual, Banks put away more food than seemed humanly possible for one person to eat. When they were finished, Sterling threw his paper napkin down onto the tray, feeling suitably sated.

"We should probably head off to the refit briefing," said Sterling, pushing his chair back. "I've given the crew leave while the upgrades are being taken care of, but hopefully we won't be here all that long."

Banks reached over the table, grabbed the crust of the grilled ham and cheese that Sterling always left uneaten and began nibbling on it. "So long as I keep getting two breakfasts, I don't mind staying here a few days longer."

Sterling looked around the wardroom, noticing that most of the other officers finally seemed to have forgotten about them in the time they'd been sitting. Then he noticed that one of the officers on a table behind him was staring in his direction. He almost looked away, paying it no mind, but then recognized the man and cursed.

"What is it?" said Commander Banks, becoming suddenly alert as a chair screeched back from the table to Sterling's rear.

"Just someone I hoped never to see again," said Sterling. He was then aware of bootsteps approaching from behind him and a second later he could practically feel the man breathing down his neck.

"Captain Sterling, fancy seeing you here," said the man.

"Captain Wessel, what a coincidence," replied Sterling, shifting in his seat to face the man. "I didn't think you ever ventured to the outer sectors. You were always more of a near-Earth guy."

Sterling could see Banks out of the corner of his eye. She'd picked up the tension between the two captains straight away, and appeared both vigilant and deeply curious.

"Well, the war is pushing us all out closer to the Void, these days," Captain Wessel said, sliding into the empty seat to Sterling's side. "You don't mind if I sit down, do you?"

"Whether I did or I didn't, it appears that you already have done," Sterling hit back, straight faced.

Wessel shot him an oily smile then began tapping his fingers on the table. "So, what has the mysterious 'Void Recon Unit' been up to recently?" Wessel continued. He hadn't looked at or even acknowledged Banks' presence.

"Well, Vernon, I think you'll find that the clue is in the name," said Sterling, switching to the man's given name. He knew Wessel had no love for it.

Wessel laughed, though it was more artificial than the gravity that was keeping them all in their seats. "With the new orders from the UG War Council forbidding incursions into the Void, I guess your little taskforce has its days numbered."

Sterling smiled back at his fellow captain, but maintained a poker face that Commander Banks would have been proud of. The use by Wessel of the word "taskforce" had not gone unnoticed to him. And Sterling didn't believe for one second it was accidental either.

"Maybe you should read your orders and intel reports more carefully, Vernon," said Sterling, with more hostility. He detested Wessel and was no longer interested in being polite. The man had already barged in on them uninvited and now he was deliberately trying to tweak his nipples. "The Void Recon Unit still has special dispensation to operate in the Void. By order of Fleet Admiral Griffin, who I think you know."

Wessel's oily smile faded slightly at the mention of Griffin and his finger finally stopped tapping on the table. "For now, you do," Wessel admitted, reluctantly, "but things are changing fast, Captain. For you more than others." Sterling could tell that Wessel wanted to say more, but he appeared to fight the urge and instead stood up. "I'm sure we'll meet again soon, Captain Sterling," the officer then said.

"I can hardly wait," replied Sterling, impersonating Wessel's oily, insincere smile.

"Until then," Captain Wessel said. Then the man turned and walked away, still without acknowledging or even glancing in Banks' direction.

"What the hell was all that about?" said Banks, glowering at the back of Captain Wessel's head as the snide officer exited the wardroom.

Sterling ran a hand over his close-cut hair and shook his head. "Honestly, I'm not sure," he said, still trying to process the motive for Wessel's unwanted visit. "Vernon Wessel and I were at the academy together. He's a suck-up and an asshole."

Banks smiled. "I take it you two never really got along then?"

"You could say that," replied Sterling, though he wasn't smiling. The memories of his academy days with Wessel were not his fondest ones. "Wessel was always trying to be the big man, name dropping his father and other senior Fleet personnel and making promises he had no intention of keeping. I either called out his bull or ignored him. Both seemed to infuriate him equally."

Banks leaned forward and flashed her eyes at Sterling. "Tell me you popped him in the mouth at least once?"

"Those are the only memories of him I cherish," said Sterling, watching Banks steal a fruit cookie from his tray. "Wessel is a grifter who only made captain because his father is an admiral."

Banks nodded. "He didn't seem to like it when you brought up Admiral Griffin. Do they know each other?"

"Let's just say that Fleet Admiral Griffin and Admiral Wessel don't see eye-to-eye, either," replied Sterling. "Admiral Wessel commands the Earth Defense Fleet, and his pissant son is the captain of a Heavy Destroyer in the Perimeter Defense Taskforce. My left toe has seen more action than the two of them put together."

"The perimeter taskforce operates on the edge of the solar system," said Banks, mopping up some jam with a crust of bread. "Captain Wessel is a long way from home out here." Then she paused, jam-soaked crust held midway to her mouth. "Do you think his mention of our unit as a 'taskforce' was just a slip of the tongue?"

Sterling stroked his top lip with his thumb and cast his eyes in the direction of the exit, as if Wessel was still standing there, watching him.

"No, I don't think it was a slip-up at all," Sterling answered, feeling his stomach knot slightly. "But whatever the reason is that he's here, I have a feeling that it's bad news for us."

Sterling stood at the viewing gallery window and gazed out at his ship, the Fleet Marauder Invictus. The Heavy Cruiser that was in a dock two pylons along dwarfed the Marauder-class Destroyer in terms of size, but the Invictus still managed to look more aggressive. It was like a scorpion compared to a pit bull terrier.

"Repairs and upgrades are all done, Captain," came a voice from behind him. Startled, Sterling jerked around to see Lieutenant Commander Crow, smiling amiably at him.

"How long have you been there?" snapped Sterling, wondering how the engineer had managed to sneak up on him unawares.

"Only for a few seconds, Captain," replied Crow. The engineer was apparently unaware he'd startled his captain. "I was admiring the Invictus too."

Sterling nodded then saw that Crow was holding a personal digital assistant in his right hand. "So, what upgrades have F-COP's engineers, in their infinite wisdom, decided to bestow on my ship?" he said, nodding toward the PDA.

"Nothing much, I'm afraid, sir," replied Crow, the disappointment evident in his voice. "It was mainly routine updates to processing cores and software, plus some enhanced power relays and rail gun components."

"So, no 'death rays' then?" said Sterling, smiling.

Sterling's question caused Crow to frown down at his PDA. A holographic screen then extended in front of the engineer, projected from the small device, which itself was no larger than a deck of playing cards.

"I don't see any death rays, sir," Crow said, scrolling through the work orders. "They must have missed that. I'll speak to the project manager right away."

"Relax, Lieutenant Commander, I was joking," said Sterling, stopping Crow from scurrying away.

"Oh," replied Crow, looking more perplexed than he did embarrassed. Humor was a concept the engineer struggled with. "Very funny, sir," Crow then added, faking a smile and a polite laugh.

Sterling turned back to the window and looked out at the Invictus again. F-COP had already begun to feel stifling and claustrophobic to him, despite its vast size. And now he was looking out at his ship, tethered to the station like a captive animal, he had a growing urge to get on board and get underway. With the upgrades complete, there was no longer any reason to stay, so in that moment, Sterling decided to unhook the chain and leave. Tapping his neural interface, he reached out to Commander Banks to notify his first-officer of his decision.

"Mercedes, let the crew know that we get underway at oh-eight-hundred tomorrow," Sterling said to Banks in his mind. "That way they can have one final hurrah in the bars on F-COP tonight."

"Aye, Captain," said Banks. However, his first officer hadn't replied inside his head – the voice was real and had come from behind him. Sterling again jerked around and saw the commander standing to the side of Crow, hands on her hips. "Are you planning a final hurrah too?"

"Damn it, will you all stop sneaking up on me?" complained Sterling. "And no, I'm not planning a final hurrah, or even a first one, for that matter."

Banks frowned. "Someone is cranky this evening," she said, snatching the PDA from Crow's hand and scanning the work orders.

"Sorry, it's just that I've had enough of F-COP," replied Sterling, staring over at the Invictus again. "I'm sick of people looking at us like we're escaped murderers. This place is all talk and noise and no action."

"Well, at least one of us got some action," Banks replied, with a not-so-subtle raising of her eyebrows.

Commander Crow's eyebrows also climbed toward his hairline and he suddenly looked deeply uncomfortable. However, the engineer simply remained where he was, standing as still as possible, perhaps in the hope that neither Banks nor Sterling would remember he was there.

"There's still time to arrange some transfer orders," Sterling hit back, glowering at his first officer. The jibe about his casual liaison with Captain McQueen was so thinly veiled that Banks may as well not have bothered trying to hide it.

"Apologies, Captain," said Commander Banks, appearing to actually mean it.

Sterling decided to let it slide. Joking at inappropriate moments was not an uncommon trait of Omega officers, and it was a flaw that Mercedes Banks, in particular, struggled with. However, nobody was perfect, Sterling considered, least of all himself, so if he couldn't forgive the flaws in others, it would simply make him a hypocrite.

"The rest of the crew have been enjoying the break from the confines of the Invictus," Banks continued, scanning through the entries on Crow's PDA. "All except one person, anyway."

Sterling huffed a laugh. "Let me guess. Lieutenant Shade?"

Banks smiled and nodded. "She doesn't really like Fleet, to put it mildly. She hasn't left the ship since we docked."

"I don't give a damn what she does in her spare time, so long as she keeps killing Sa'Nerrans with the same proficiency she's shown so far," said Sterling. He spoke the words with the sort of icy detachment that Shade herself would have been proud of.

Commander Banks then held the PDA back out to Crow, who took it without saying a word before resuming his statuesque pose.

"These upgrades hardly seem worth hanging around here for," Banks said. "Other than the moderate boost to our plasma rail gun efficiency, the upgrades won't count for a lot in the field."

"Any extra advantage is worth it, Commander," replied Sterling, again staring out at the Invictus. He found the sight of the vessel soothing and was absorbed by its sharp lines and smooth panels.

"Captain Sterling."

Sterling jerked around again, this time seeing Fleet Admiral Natasha Griffin standing behind him. Banks appeared her usual, unflustered self, but the proximity of the Fleet Admiral had made Crow look like a schoolboy waiting outside the principal's office.

"Are you okay, Captain?" Griffin asked. "You look like you've just seen a ghost."

"I'm fine, Admiral," said Sterling, checking to make sure that Banks wasn't about to make an inappropriate quip. Mercifully, this time she remained silent. "I'm just itching to get back into action, that's all," Sterling added.

Admiral Griffin nodded, clearly satisfied with Sterling's answer. "Well, you'll get your chance soon enough, Captain," she said. She then turned to Lieutenant Commander Crow, who returned a slightly manic-looking smile. Unfortunately, Sterling's chief engineer was not one to smile often and the unfamiliar expression made him look like a simpleton. "Take a walk, Lieutenant Commander," said Griffin, glaring at the engineer like he'd just barged in on her in the rest room. Crow's uncomfortable smile fell away and the officer scurried off, again without a word.

Commander Banks also made to leave, but Griffin raised a finger to stop her. "You can stay, Commander

Banks," the Admiral said. Banks halted and stepped back, standing to attention. However, Sterling could read his first-officer like a book. Banks' expression conveyed her clear surprise that the Admiral had not told her to get lost as well.

"What's wrong Admiral?" said Sterling. "I haven't seen that look on your face since the Dreadnaught Vanguard went missing."

Griffin checked around her then tapped a device on her wrist. The doors to the observation lounge closed and Sterling immediately felt light-headed, as if he was experiencing vertigo, but then the sensation quickly passed. Banks was gently slapping the side of her head, like she was trying to shake out water that had become lodged in her ear during a shower.

"That was just a neural and EM inhibitor field," said Griffin, answering the unspoken question. "I want to be sure we're not overheard."

Sterling frowned. "Aren't they illegal?" he asked, still curious as to where Griffin was getting her secret gadgets from.

"Yes, captain, they are," Griffin replied in a way that told Sterling this was the only answer he would get.

Sterling then noticed that Banks was frowning at the Admiral. He could see the hyper-defined muscles in her arms had tensed up.

"Has something happened to the Imperium, Admiral?" Commander Banks then said. Sterling couldn't deny that his first-officer's question was far more relevant than the one he'd asked.

"I've lost contact with Captain McQueen," confirmed Admiral Griffin, stoically. "She was due to report back over twenty-four hours ago. Encrypted aperture relays were in-place to transmit her reports, but so far nothing."

"The relays could have been destroyed, or perhaps just malfunctioned?" suggested Sterling.

Griffin shook her head. "They're operational, Captain. The Invictus and the Imperium may be the only two Omega Taskforce warships in active service, but I have additional resources in and around the Void too," she said, mysteriously. Sterling would usually take the opportunity to push Griffin a little harder to reveal more details. However, there was too much urgency on this occasion, and all he wanted to do was learn more about the Imperium and the fate of McQueen.

"I'll cancel leave immediately. We can be underway in an hour," said Sterling, nodding to Banks. His first-officer then moved far enough away from the admiral to escape her jamming field. Banks then tapped her neural implant to relay the order to the crew.

"I would usually say good hunting, Captain, but on this occasion, I urge caution," said Admiral Griffin. This surprised Sterling more than Griffin's request for Banks to remain present during the snap briefing. The Admiral was never one to urge caution. "Whatever the Sa'Nerra are building, I have no doubt that its purpose it to bring Fleet to its knees. The United Governments' senators are gaining traction with the admiralty to pursue a negotiated peace. They are wary of committing battleships to the front-line for fear of them being captured. Once word of the new neural weapon reaches the UG senators, it will only strengthen their resolve to pursue negotiations."

Sterling shook his head, feeling his muscles tense up and adrenalin surge through his veins. "The Sa'Nerra aren't interested in peace or talking," he spat, scarcely able to believe what was happening. "If we go on the back foot now, the Sa'Nerra will surge out of the Void and crush us like bugs."

"That's why I need you to find out what they're building, Captain," said Griffin, seeming to draw from Sterling's energy and thirst for combat. "Get the evidence I need to show the council the Sa'Nerra are gearing up for an invasion."

Commander Banks tapped her neural interface to close the link to the ship's crew then hurried back to Sterling's side. Sterling could even observe the precise moment his first-officer had entered the neural jamming field from the sudden, pained look in her eyes. Sterling then turned to see the Invictus powering up through the window of the observation deck.

"And what about the Imperium, sir?" Banks asked the Admiral. Sterling could see that she was as eager to get back into space as he was. Her energy was infectious. "Should we attempt to find them?"

"If you can recover the Imperium without risk to the Invictus then do so," replied the Admiral. Then her eyes sharpened and her lined faced became harder than diamond. "Otherwise, destroy it with all hands on-board. That is an Omega Directive." Griffin then fixed her steely eyes onto Sterling. "Are we clear, Captain Sterling? I will tolerate no noble rescues this time."

Sterling nodded. "Perfectly clear, Admiral," he replied, smartly. He didn't like it, but he also couldn't deny it was the right thing to do. The Imperium was small, but it was also a powerhouse. Should it fall into Sa'Nerran hands, it could surge through the apertures, potentially avoiding the watchful cannons of the gatekeepers, and wreak havoc before it was finally taken down.

"Then you have your orders, Captain," said Admiral Griffin. She tapped the device attached to her wrist, causing the same brief sensation of vertigo to return, before turning on her heels and marching out of the observation lounge.

Captain Lucas Sterling tapped his finger on the side of his console and anxiously peered out through the viewscreen at the flashing beacons surrounding the aperture. He knew that this aperture was, structurally speaking, no different to any of the dozens of other apertures he regularly surged through. However, there was something unique about it. It was the last aperture that humanity had ever constructed. It was the aperture that had surged the human race into Sa'Nerran space. And it was the aperture that, indirectly, caused the fifty-year war that Fleet was now losing. Every other aperture beyond the interplanetary gateway that hung in space in front of the Invictus was engineered by the warmongering alien race. It was like a border crossing of sorts, except there were no guards or papers, and also no guarantees of what might lie on the other side.

"Approaching the aperture threshold now, Captain," Ensign Keller announced. "Co-ordinates for star system

Void quebec two, zulu two, dash two-eight-six, Lima, locked in and holding," the helmsman continued. Keller had read off the string of numbers and letters like he was reading from a phone book.

"Snappy name," said Commander Banks, smiling.

"Let's hope the system is a boring as it sounds," replied Sterling, though he suspected this was wishful thinking.

"We're in position to surge, Captain," said Ensign Keller, glancing over his shoulder to look at Sterling.

"We have one contact on the scanner," said Banks from her station beside the captain's console. "It's a light freighter of some kind. Probably a Void Pirate."

"Are they heading our way?" asked Sterling, still tapping his finger on the side of his console. Hundreds of thousands of people still lived inside the Void, on the planets and frontier outposts left behind after the start of the war. Cut off from Earth and the Fleet, they'd formed their own community of sorts. However, it was a mostly lawless society, where it was literally every man and woman for themselves. If you were lucky enough to own a ship – or be able to salvage one of the many wrecks from the war - piracy was a good way to make a living. It was also a good way to get yourself killed, especially if you were bold enough to take on a Fleet warship.

Banks was quiet for a moment while she studied the readings, then shook her head. "No, they're heading away, on course to the entry aperture," she said, lifting her eyes from the console to look at Sterling. "Looks like they're not desperate or stupid enough to pick a fight with us today."

Sterling nodded. "Note their last position and

trajectory and log the vessel in case we run into it on the way back," he said. "It may just be waiting until we head home again. A battle-damaged ship makes for easier pickings."

"Aye, Captain," said Banks, returning to work at her console.

Sterling then blew out his cheeks and turned to Lieutenant Shade. "Take us to battle stations, Lieutenant," he said, meeting the weapons officers' eyes, which were as cool and emotionless as always. Shade acknowledged the order then the bridge darkened and red strip lights at floor level cast a crimson hue over her face. Sterling then faced the viewscreen and stood tall. He didn't enjoy making speeches, and didn't believe himself to be very good at them. However, considering where they were about to go, he wanted the crew to be clear on their orders, and on the dangers that lay ahead.

"We're about to surge deep into the Sa'Nerran half of the Void, further than we've ever gone before," said Sterling, causing all eyes to fall on him. "The aliens are building a new ship of war. A new weapon designed to crush the Fleet and humanity. We won't allow that to happen." Suddenly, Sterling's thoughts were filled with Captain McQueen and her crew, and what the Omega Directive would require him to do should it turn out the Imperium had been turned. "The Imperium is also out there somewhere," Sterling continued, rallying his thoughts. "If we can, we'll bring them home with us. If not, we'll take them down." Sterling then sucked in a lungful of the ship's cool, recycled air and let it out slowly, meeting the eyes of each of his bridge crew in turn. All of them peered back at him, displaying the courage and steadfastness he'd come to expect. "The Omega Directive is in effect," Sterling announced. The words were chilling even coming out of his own mouth. "Let's hope it's not needed." He then turned to Ensign Keller, whose gaze was fixed on his captain, awaiting the final order. "Take us in, Ensign," Sterling said.

Keller called out a crisp acknowledgment then eased the Invictus forward. Sterling braced himself, knowing that it would be a long surge. He had ordered Keller to plot a surge vector that would take them far beyond Captain McQueen's surge exit point. His reasoning had been that if the Imperium had been captured, the Sa'Nerra would be expecting a rescue party to enter the system, and be lying in wait. Pushing their surge boundary was not without risk, however. The further beyond the safe surge limit of the vessel, the more unpredictable the end coordinates became. It was like trying to throw a baseball too hard and too fast and losing control. The distance achieved might still be greater than a more measured throw, but where the ball ended up was anyone's guess.

The Invictus slipped beyond the flashing beacons that marked the perimeter of the gateway. Then Sterling felt the universe collapse into the peaceful nothingness that existed in the space between apertures. His thoughts drifted and he found himself on the bridge of the Fleet Dreadnaught Hammer, aiming his plasma pistol at Ariel Gunn.

"Ariel, get out of the way..." Sterling heard himself saying, though this time he sounded angry, not desperate.

Then his weapon fizzed and the head of his former colleague and friend was blasted clean off. It was like his nightmare all over again, except somehow it felt more real, like he was inside his own memory.

No, I won't let you torment me! Sterling thought, pushing the headless image of Ariel Gunn to the far depths of his mind. *It was your choice. Your mistake. I did what I had to do. And if I had a do-over, I'd make the same damn choice again!*

The bridge of the Invictus then rushed back in around him and Sterling fell forward, just managing to catch the corners of his console. The soft red glow from the battle stations lights flooded into his eyes and he felt suddenly queasy. Then an alert blared out, assaulting his ears like a foghorn. He peered up at the viewscreen and saw that they'd emerged from the aperture inside the ring system of a planet.

"Divert power to regenerative armor!" Sterling called out as rocks and clumps of ice hammered into their hull. Sterling's eyes then widened as a lump of frozen rock and ice the size of a light freighter approached them. He turned to Lieutenant Shade, though he could already tell she was alert to the danger. "Lieutenant, point defense guns to maximum," he ordered. Shade acknowledged the command then moments later a swarm of weapons fire erupted from the Invictus, creating a volatile shield around the ship. "Shoot anything big enough to cause us a problem. Your discretion," he added, staring anxiously out at the giant boulder ahead of them.

"Aye, Captain," replied Shade, still as cool as ice tea.

The forward plasma railguns erupted into action, pulverizing the frozen boulder with a single volley. However, Sterling could see on the viewscreen and on his console that thousands more rocks just like it or bigger were swirling all around them.

"Ensign Keller, I need you to find us a big-ass rock and land us on it," Sterling called out to his helmsman. "Any port in a storm, you understand?"

"Aye, sir," replied Keller, his fingers working the helm controls like a virtuoso pianist.

The Invictus turned hard, and Sterling again found himself grasping the console to steady himself. A clump of rock the size of a shopping mall came into view dead ahead. It looked like a misshapen avocado that had been cut in half and the stone removed. Sterling then realized where his helmsman was taking them.

"Are you heading where I think you're heading, Ensign?" asked Sterling, shooting an anxious glance across to Commander Banks. However, she appeared to be as much intrigued by Keller's apparent destination as she was perturbed by it.

"Any port in a storm, Captain," Keller replied, adjusting the pitch and roll of the ship to align with the neat-looking hole in the center of the massive rock.

Sterling tapped his neural interface and opened his mind to everyone on the ship. "All hands, brace for impact," Sterling announced, his mental voice conveying urgency, but also calm.

Meanwhile, Keller had successfully managed to align the rotation of the Invictus with that of the ring fragment.

That maneuver alone would have been worthy of celebration, but the ensign had more to do yet. Keller fired the thrusters to arrest their still rapid approach. Sterling felt his heart leap into his mouth as a hard thump resounded through the deck, throwing him off balance again. Another alert blared out and Sterling saw the hull stress indicator flash up on his panel. Then the alarm wail ceased and the dozen red lights on his board all slowly blinked away.

"We're down, Captain," shouted Keller, more than a little breathlessly. "Sorry for the rough landing, sir."

Sterling almost laughed. "I'll take a rough landing over been smashed like an egg, Ensign. Well done," replied Sterling. Then he looked out through the viewscreen at the dense mass of rock and ice that comprised the ring system and blew out a sigh. "Now, any idea where the hell we are?"

Commander Banks had already been working on that problem and answered immediately.

"We're inside the ring system of the fifth planet," Banks said, throwing up a rudimentary star chart onto the viewscreen. "Based on the very limited scan data we have so far, the Sa'Nerran shipyard is on the far side of this planet." Banks was then silent for a moment while she worked her console before she shook her head and cursed under her breath. "From what I can tell, the shipyard has been constructed inside the gap between the planet's a-ring and the outermost ring. There appears to be a high concentration of shepherd moons in that region, but until we get closer, that's all we know."

Sterling nodded. "Launch a probe to survey the ring

system, so we know where the hell we're going and what we're dealing with," he said. "I want an analysis in one hour. For now, we sit tight and wait for any damage to our armor to regenerate."

The crew all acknowledged the order and set to work. Sterling rested forward on his console, again tapping the side of the smooth metal panel with his finger. Then he glanced at Banks and activated his neural interface.

"Well, that was almost the shortest mission in Fleet history," Sterling called out to his first-officer in his mind.

Sterling's tone had been playful and Banks responded with a smile. Others might have considered Sterling's comment to be an unusually dark and inappropriate response to their near-death experience. However, both he and Banks had learned to find perverse amusement in any wild twist of fate whenever it benefited them. And this had been a happy accident.

"We couldn't have picked a better surge exit point if we'd tried," Banks replied, also appearing to recognize their stroke of fortune. "This ring system provides perfect camouflage, which is probably why they built the shipyard here in the first place. If we hadn't surged inside it, we might never have found the installation at all. Even better, all this swirling rock and ice will have blinded the Sa'Nerra to our arrival."

Sterling nodded and again peered out at the mass of rock and ice that was spinning around them. "The only problem is that we also don't know how many of those alien bastards are camped out in this system too," he replied.

Banks' console chimed an alert and she checked the

new information that was flooding in from the probe they'd launched. Sterling was still connected to Banks through their neural link, and he could feel the anxiety grip her, like a vice gently squeezing her brain.

"Whatever they're building out here is the least of our concerns right now," said Banks over their link.

Sterling checked the new data on his own console and the meaning of Banks' statement became crystal clear. Hanging in space in front of the aperture that led back into the Fleet-half of the Void was not just a squadron of Sa'Nerran warships, but an entire strike group. It was comprised of a squadron of six Skirmishers and four of the latest phase-three Destroyers, led by a single Heavy Destroyer. It was not an uncommon formation of Sa'Nerran ships, but there was one aspect about the strike force that made it uniquely dangerous. The lead vessel was one that Sterling had come across before, as had dozens of other Fleet ships. It was a bruised and battle-scarred beast that was credited with the destruction of forty-six Fleet warships; more than any other ship on either side of the war. Officially, its designation was Sa'Nerran Heavy Destroyer M4-U1. To every front-line crew member in the fleet, it was simply known as MAUL.

Ensign Kieran Keller eased the Invictus toward the Sa'Nerran shipyard, navigating through the maze of rock and ice inside the ring system of the fifth planet. Fortunately, the Sa'Nerran strike group had remained ignorant of the Invictus and its stealthy progress toward the secret installation. The group of warships had remained at the mouth of the aperture, waiting for an unsuspecting Fleet vessel or taskforce to surge through it. However, the strike group, and its formidable lead warship, was a problem for another time, Sterling had told himself. Their priority was to learn more about the new Sa'Nerran vessel that was under construction inside the ring system of the Saturn-sized planet.

"Steady as she goes, Ensign," said Sterling, as another chunk of rock bounced off their hull. The alien shipyard should have already been visible on the viewscreen, but the sheer mass of material in front of them was blinding their view of it.

"Aye, Captain," replied Keller, whose hands and fingers had been a near-constant flurry of action for the last thirty minutes. "I'm almost through to the gap, sir," Keller continued. "The stellar material is particularly dense around the edge of the ring."

Sterling tapped his finger impatiently on the side of his console, occasionally glancing across to Commander Banks. Creeping around in the shadows was not his style, and he could see from the tension in his first officer's shoulders and the uneasy look in her eyes that she felt the same way.

"Coming into position now, sir," said Ensign Keller.

Sterling looked out through the viewscreen and saw the mass of rock finally begin to clear. "Hold position just on the fringe of the ring, Ensign," said Sterling. He then turned to Lieutenant Shade. "Hold fire on the point defense guns, unless absolutely necessary, Lieutenant. I don't want to tip off the Sa'Nerra to our presence. If we can take the hit then take the hit."

"Aye Captain," Shade replied, in chorus with a series of thumps to the hull from flying rocks and ice.

Ensign Keller finished maneuvering the Invictus into position at the edge of the ring and Sterling finally got his first clear look at the shipyard. It was so close that he didn't even need to magnify the image on the viewscreen.

"Now that is a big ship," said Commander Banks, flicking her eyes from the readings flooding her console to the viewscreen and back again. "That monster is more than eleven thousand meters long. What the hell do they need a ship that big for? It would be as maneuverable as an asteroid."

Sterling studied the vessel on the viewscreen, occasionally glancing down to the more intricate readouts on his console. More than half of the ship appeared to be given over to a large tubular section running through the center line. He tapped his neural interface and opened a link to Lieutenant Commander Crow, allowing the rest of the bridge crew to monitor the conversation.

"Lieutenant Commander Crow, what do you make of that ship, and the center section in particular?" Sterling asked.

Crow's voice then filled his mind. "I'm unable to get a detailed scan from this range, sir, but from what I can tell, it looks like an aperture tunneling array."

Sterling frowned. "So, you're saying this isn't a warship at all?" he asked, quickly beginning to grow frustrated. "It's just some kind of giant aperture construction tool?"

Sterling waited eagerly for engineer's response, which was not immediately forthcoming. He could feel his pulse quicken. If he'd come out all this way and risked his crew only to take snapshots of what was essentially a giant road building machine, he was going to be majorly pissed off.

"I am not entirely clear on the function of the array as yet, Captain," Crow eventually replied.

"That's not good enough, Lieutenant Commander," Sterling said, gripping the side of his console.

"I shall expedite my analysis, sir," Crow replied, a little gloomily. "Besides the tunneling array, the vessel is heavily armed and armored," Crow continued, trying to offer something of worth. "However, they are mostly defensive armaments. The vessel alone appears to have very limited offensive capabilities."

Sterling sighed and shook his head. "Keep scanning, Lieutenant Commander, and let me know as soon as you figure out what this thing is," he said. Sterling then tapped his interface to sever the link.

"It normally takes an entire fleet of construction ships to assemble a new aperture route, and they're all easy pickings in a warzone," said Banks, speaking out loud. "Perhaps the Sa'Nerra are looking for a quick way to create their own route to Earth, avoiding the gatekeepers and Fleet forces that defend the lane to the solar system?"

Sterling considered this for a moment then realized that Commander Banks' suggestion made sense. If the Sa'Nerra could open an aperture directly into the solar system they could bypass the first, second, third and fourth fleets in a single leap. This would leave them only the Earth Defense Fleet and Perimeter Defense Taskforce standing in their way. The plan wasn't without problems, however, not least of which was creating an aperture to Earth in the first place.

"It's a strong suggestion, Commander, but I still sense that we're missing something," said Sterling, tapping his finger on his console again. "The gatekeepers and COPs in the solar system would need taking down quickly in order to make that work. I don't see how the Sa'Nerra could surge enough ships in quickly enough to have the firepower to pull it off."

"This is odd," said Banks, frowning down at her

console. "One of the moons inside the ring gap seems to have a hole cored straight through its center."

Banks then threw up an enlarged image of the moon on the viewscreen. It wasn't a large moon, measuring a little over two hundred kilometers across at its widest point, and was pockmarked with craters so that it looked like a giant potato. Then Sterling saw that Banks was right. Cut directly through the moon's center was a perfectly spherical hole that measured five kilometers in diameter.

Sterling's finger-tapping had now grown to a level where the tip of his nail was throbbing from the repeated knocks against the hard metal of his console. He was about to activate his neural interface and ask Lieutenant Commander Crow for his opinion when the entire shipyard began to move.

"Standing by to withdraw, Captain," said Ensign Keller, the rising intonation in his voice betraying his anxiety.

"Hold position, Ensign," ordered Sterling, firmly. "Let's just see what it does."

The shipyard and its titanic contents moved with all the grace of an oil tanker. However, contrary to Sterling's expectations, it was not nearly as lumbering and slow as its size suggested it should be.

"That's about as fast as a Dreadnaught turns," commented Commander Banks, also apparently having noted the vessel's surprising agility. "It must be packing an enormous number of thrusters and maneuvering engines in order to move like that."

Sterling continued to watch as the giant ship's

cylindrical aperture was aimed at the shepherd moon that orbited inside the ring system. Commander Banks' console then chimed an alert and his first-officer's brow furrowed with concern.

"I'm reading a massive power spike, Captain," said Banks, studying the readings intently. "But the energy signature is like nothing I've ever seen before."

Sterling turned his attention back to the viewscreen, noting that the front section of the modular shipyard had peeled away from the bow of the ship. The door to the bridge then opened and Lieutenant Commander Crow stepped inside. The inquisitive engineer looked excited, which Sterling knew probably meant bad news.

"I believe I now know what the aperture array in the ship is for," said Crow. The engineer then hurried over to one of the auxiliary consoles on the bridge and accessed his engineering systems. However, before Crow could continue, a distorted ripple of dark energy erupted from the end of the Sa'Nerran vessel's aperture array. It was barely visible against the darkness of space, but set against the backdrop of the ring system, it was like a powerful heat haze or mirage effect. The ripple extended out into space, expanding at it did so until it hit the shepherd moon. Sterling watched in astonishment as the moon then slowly disintegrated. It was as if a titanic space creature was taking bites from it like an apple. Then in a matter of seconds the moon was gone, leaving no trace of it behind, not even a single speck of moon dust. With the shepherd moon gone, the ripple of energy emanating from the giant vessel's aperture array shut down.

"As I was about to say, Captain," Crow said, breaking the sudden, awed silence that had fallen over the bridge. "The aperture array is not designed to build tunnels through space. "It itself is the weapon."

"I can see that, Lieutenant Commander," replied Sterling, still struggling to believe what he'd just witnessed. "The question is, what kind of weapon is it? And how the hell did it just destroy a moon?"

"I would need days to study this data more in order to answer that question, Captain," Crow replied. The engineer then shuffled on the spot and rubbed the back of his hands, anxiously. Sterling could tell he was working up the courage to ask one of his unreasonable requests. "However, in order to truly understand the workings of this incredible machine, I would need direct access to it."

Sterling cast a sideways glance to Crow. "You want to go on-board the alien shipyard?" he asked, not sure if he'd understood Crow correctly.

"It may be our only opportunity, sir," replied Crow, only indirectly answering Sterling's question.

The familiar sound of Banks' console chiming an alert then turned Sterling's attention to his first-officer's station.

"You're not going to believe this, but I've just located the Imperium," said Banks, a twinge of excitement in her voice. "It appears to be docked to the shipyard."

Banks tapped a sequence of commands into her console then a moment later an image of the Fleet Marauder Imperium appeared on the viewscreen. It was tucked inside a hexagonal docking port at the far extremities of the shipyard. Sterling then noted that there were similar docking ports of varying sizes all across the enormous structure. However, while the dock had fully-enclosed the Imperium it was not pressured and the fleet vessel was still exposed to space.

"Are there any Sa'Nerran ships in the adjacent docking pods?" Sterling asked, glancing across to Banks.

"No sir," Banks replied, smartly. There are dozens of Sa'Nerran vessels docked in other parts of the station, but in that area it's just the Imperium."

Sterling sighed then peered out at the viewscreen again. After the Sa'Nerran shipyard had reorientated itself to destroy the shepherd moon, part of it had brushed up against the inner ring in which the Invictus was hiding. He then heard Banks' voice in his mind.

"Are you thinking what I think you're thinking?" Banks asked. However, she didn't sound concerned. If anything, she sounded hopeful that Sterling had the same thing in mind as she did.

"It's like Crow just said. We may never get another chance to see this thing up close," Sterling replied in his mind, though he was still staring at the Imperium on the viewscreen. "And if we can get more data and take the Imperium back home with us, then all the better."

Sterling closed the link to Banks then turned to Lieutenant Commander Crow, who was still looking at him expectantly.

"Lieutenant Commander, how long would you need inside that shipyard in order to extract some meaningful data?" Sterling asked.

The question appeared to shock Crow and for several

seconds the engineer's mouth just hung open. The ever-inquisitive officer had evidently been expecting his captain to deny the request.

"Sometime today, please, Lieutenant Commander..." Sterling pressed, trying to snap Crow out of his daze.

"At a rudimentary level, their computers speak the same language as ours." Crow spoke with fervent excitement. "It's all just ones and zeroes when you boil it down to the fundamentals," he continued. "If I can get access to a computer interface, I can brute force my way in and download the encrypted data. Then the supercomputer clusters at F-COP might be able to decrypt some of the information and get access to the raw data. We'd obviously have no understanding of the written content, but images, schematics, raw numbers... this we can understand."

"How quickly could we decode the information?" asked Commander Banks.

The engineer shrugged. "It could take weeks or even months to make any sense of it," Crow replied. "But it could give us the edge we need to defeat this new weapon, before it's used in anger against us."

Banks let out a long low whistle and glanced over at the shipyard on the viewscreen. "Something tells me that once Fleet sees what we've just seen, they'll find a way to speed that process up," said Banks. However, she was as much talking to herself as to Crow.

Sterling nodded. He'd already made up his mind what to do next. He stopped tapping his finger against the side of his console and turned to Ensign Keller.

"Ensign, can you get us close enough to that shipyard to attach a docking tunnel onto the Imperium?" Sterling said to his helmsman.

Keller looked like Sterling had just asked him to fly the ship blindfolded. "A docking tunnel, sir?" the helmsman replied, eyes wide.

"Yes or no, Ensign, can you do it?" Sterling pressed, maintaining the firmness in his voice.

Keller turned back to his helm controls, his fingers again moving like a blur for several seconds. Then he turned back to his captain and simply said, "Yes."

STERLING FELT a solid thump resonate through the deck, letting him know that their docking tunnel had latched on to the Imperium. With his usual skill and deftness, Ensign Keller had managed to navigate the Invictus to within docking range of their sister ship without being detected. This feat was aided by the fact that part of the enormous alien shipyard was still nestled just inside the shelter of the planetary ring system. However, Sterling was acutely aware that there was no guarantee the flying shipyard would remain in its current position for long. The safe thing to do would have been to withdraw and take what information they had back to Admiral Griffin. However, playing it safe wasn't Lucas Sterling's style.

Despite this, Sterling would have been the first to admit that their plan to enter the shipyard bordered on gung-ho bravado. He may have been willing to take risks, but he wasn't reckless. However, on this occasion the reward was worth the inevitable cost in lives. Fleet was losing the war and it was clear to Sterling that the titanic ship was being built in secret for one purpose alone - to hammer the final nail into humanity's coffin. If he could find out more about the vessel and its powerful aperture-based weapon then he had to try. And if he could liberate the Imperium from the clutches of the Sa'Nerra in the process, so much the better. Even if that were possible, Sterling held out little hope that Captain McQueen or her crew had been spared the mind-altering effects of the Sa'Nerran neural weapon.

The docking seal turned green and Captain Sterling entered his command override codes to force the Imperium's hatch to unlock. Sterling tapped his finger against the control pad as he waited, glancing across to Commander Banks, who was at his side as always, plasma rifle in hand. Behind Banks was Lieutenant Shade and five of her commandos, some of whom had only just joined the Invictus crew while they had been docked at F-COP. He met each of the commandos' eyes in turn, failing to recognize any of them. This was despite knowing for certain that at least one of the commandos had fought at his side before.

Perhaps it's better this way, Sterling told himself. There was no point in forming a connection when in all likelihood there would be a different group of commandos at his side for the next mission. So long as they did their jobs, it didn't matter what their names were. Suddenly, the image of Ariel Gunn sprang into his thoughts, causing his muscles to tense up. Sterling pushed the memory of killing his friend into the deeper recesses of his mind, as he had trained himself to do, and the tight feeling in his gut subsided.

Sterling then looked beyond the squad of commandos and saw Lieutenant Commander Clinton Crow at the rear of the formation. Like the rest of them, he was wearing standard Fleet combat armor. However, while a plasma pistol rested in a holster on Crow's hip, the engineer's real weapons were inside the metal case he carried at his side.

"We get in and out as fast as possible," said Sterling, finger resting on the button to release the two docking hatches at either side of the tunnel. Then he looked to Lieutenant Commander Crow specifically. "As soon as you have what you need, you signal us," he said. Crow nodded, but Sterling hadn't finished. "No dallying, no poking around in other systems, no diversions because you found something fascinating to investigate. Do you understand me, Lieutenant Commander?" Sterling knew of Crow's love of exploration and discovery, and wanted to pre-empt any possibility of the engineer faffing around and indulging himself while all their lives hung in the balance.

"I understand completely, Captain," said Crow. Sterling held the engineer's eyes for a moment to make sure there wasn't a "but" coming. However, for once Crow had seemed to get the message.

Turning away from his engineer, Sterling then signaled Shade to get ready to move. His weapon's officer acknowledged the command then focused ahead, waiting for the hatch to open. She looked like an Olympic relay runner, waiting impatiently on her marks for the baton to be passed.

Sterling hit the button and the hatch released. Air hissed

through the gaps and moments later the door had retracted into its housing. Shade was the first to move through, leading her troop of commandos into the docking tunnel. Sterling and Banks entered next with Crow picking up the rear.

"Ensign Keller, we're moving inside the Imperium now," Sterling said through a neural link to his helmsman. "Make sure you keep the engine running…"

"Aye, Captain," Keller replied without delay. "Waypoint markers are locked in and I'll be ready to move as soon as you return," the ensign continued.

Sterling could sense the young officer's restlessness in his mental voice. Like all pilots, Keller wasn't comfortable with just sitting still and waiting around.

Shade and the commandos pushed on through the hatch at the far end of the tunnel and boarded the Imperium. Sterling heard the weapons officer call out "clear" in his mind. They'd all created an open neural link to one another shortly after they'd assembled at the docking hatch. Like a group of people all talking over each other in a bar, the overlapping voices could sometimes feel overwhelming. However, Sterling and the others had learned to filter out the noise and concentrate on a specific person. And right now, it was Lieutenant Shade that Sterling was intently focused on.

"The ship appears to be in low-power mode, Captain," said Shade, coming through strongly in Sterling's mind, as if she were standing right beside him. "I've yet to come across any crew."

Sterling stepped through the docking hatch, following

the route they'd planned to cut through the Imperium and onto the shipyard as quickly as possible.

"Standby, we've found something," said Shade. Her voice in Sterling's head fell silent for a moment, during which time he felt his pulse climb, like mercury rising in a thermometer. "There are crew still in their bunks on this level," Shade finally added. "They appear to be unconscious. There is no visible corruption to their neural implants, but there are devices attached to the bunks. It doesn't look like Fleet tech."

Sterling quickened his pace, briefly glancing behind to make sure Crow was still with them. "Keep them covered, I'm on my way," he said to Shade, hurrying through the narrow corridors of the ship on instinct, since he knew the layout of the Marauder-class like the back of his hand.

Sterling and Banks arrived at the door to the crew bunk and the commandos stepped back to allow them both through. Sterling frowned at the two enlisted crew members, lying in their bunks, still fully clothed in their Fleet uniforms, including their boots. Their hands were pressed together on their stomachs and their heads were positioned neatly in the center of their pillows. It was like they had been placed in a death posture inside a coffin, ready for funeral guests to pay their respects. Sterling's attention was then drawn to the two Sa'Nerran devices attached to the bunks, close to each crew member's head.

"Crow, what do you make of those?" asked Sterling, beckoning his chief engineer over.

Crow hustled up to the door, placed his tool case down outside then removed a PDA from its holder on the engineer's left hip. While Crow scanned the alien devices, Sterling glanced across to Shade and the other commandos. They had moved up to the port-side docking hatch, which was already open, leading inside the Sa'Nerran shipyard.

"It's almost certainly an adaption of the Sa'Nerran neural device that we're already familiar with," Crow said, snapping Sterling's attention back to his engineer. "I'd have to study one in greater detail to know more."

Crow then reached out to grab one of the devices from the frame of the bunk, but Banks caught the engineer's hand. Crow winced, as if a bear-trap had just snapped shut around his wrist.

"We don't know what will happen if we remove that," said Banks, releasing Crow's hand, though her eyes still held him in a tight grip. "That device is not why we're here," Banks continued.

"Stick to the mission, Commander," said Sterling, agreeing with his first-officer that caution was required. "If there's time, we'll grab one of the devices on the way out. But we don't want to wake these sleeping beauties before we have what we came for."

Crow nodded, still shaking his throbbing wrist. "Aye, Captain," he said, shuffling past Banks, while also shooting her what could only be described as a dirty look. Banks returned the glare with even greater intensity and Crow quickly retreated. Sterling then moved out of the cabin and waited for Banks to exit before closing door. He then moved to an auxiliary access panel on the wall and used his command override to seal all the crew cabins on the ship.

"Just in case there are more of them hibernating in

here," Sterling said to Banks, who was observing him with interest as he worked.

"This place gives me the creeps," said Banks, checking along the corridor. "It's like a damn morgue in here. Even the temperature feels colder than it should be."

"The Sa'Nerra like it cold," said Sterling, moving ahead and following Shade and the commandos out into the docking section of the Sa'Nerran shipyard. It resembled a spaceport waiting lounge, except there was no-one waiting inside it.

"The room is clear, Captain," said Lieutenant Shade through the neural link. "There are only two exits from this room and we have them both covered."

Sterling nodded; an instinctive and pointless gesture, since Shade was ten meters ahead with her back turned to him.

"You're up, Commander Crow," Sterling then said out loud, meeting the eyes of his ever-curious engineer. "Remember what I said. Get in, grab whatever encrypted data you can then get out."

"Yes, Captain," answered Crow, hurrying deeper into the docking area then dropping to his knees at the base of a Sa'Nerran computer console.

Sterling and Banks followed, watching the engineer attempt to prize off the front panel of the console without success.

"Need a hand, Lieutenant Commander?" said Banks, as the engineer continued to struggle.

Crow glanced up at Banks, his furrowed brow

highlighting the fact that the engineer apparently hadn't forgiven the Commander for manhandling him earlier.

"Be my guest, Commander," Crow replied, offering Banks the tool he'd been using.

Sterling could see that Crow's passive-aggressive response had not gone unnoticed by his first-officer, though this time Banks let it slide. Refusing the tool, Banks then gripped the edges of the panel beneath the computer console and tore it away as effortlessly as ripping cardboard.

"You're now on the clock," Banks said, resting the mangled panel against the wall. "I suggest you hurry."

Crow set to work, cracking open his tool case and plugging an assortment of devices into the Sa'Nerran computer. Banks and Sterling stepped away from the engineer to allow him space to work. As he did so, Sterling glanced back toward the docking hatch that led inside the Imperium, covering it with his plasma pistol. The sight of the Fleet crew members, entombed in their bunks, was still bothering him.

"Turned humans are strong, but there's no way they're breaking down cabin doors," said Banks, seeming to sense Sterling's unease. "The Imperium's crew are not getting out."

"Let's hope they never turn you," replied Sterling, continuing to aim his pistol inside the Imperium. "Amped up even more than you already are, you could probably tear a hole in the hull with just your bare hands."

"How do you know I can't already do that now?" quipped Banks, dropping to a crouch and covering her captain's back. Then she glanced up at Sterling, brow scrunched into a frown. "Hey, how do you know that Sa'Nerrans prefer the cold?" she asked, out of the blue.

Sterling was amused that Banks had picked up on his earlier, off-hand comment. There wasn't much that slipped past his first officer unnoticed. It was one of the traits he respected about her.

"Over lunch a few months ago, I had the pleasure of Graves detailing one of the many experiments he'd conducted on the aliens, before Griffin recruited him," replied Sterling. "Fifty-five degrees is their optimal room temperature, apparently. But they die within a couple of minutes at one sixty in dry air."

Banks frowned up at Sterling. "How the hell did he find that out?"

"He locked twenty Sa'Nerran prisoners in a sauna, one after the other, and timed how long it took them to die," replied Sterling.

Banks snort-laughed, but then she appeared to realize that Sterling was completely straight-faced.

"You're serious?" said Banks.

Sterling smiled at her. "And you wonder why it freaks me out when he sits down to eat at our table?"

Suddenly, Sterling heard Shade's voice in his mind. It cut through him like a foghorn being sounded in a tunnel.

"Captain, I'm detecting movement coming this way," his weapons officer said through the neural link.

Sterling and Banks swiftly moved into cover as Shade and the commandos fell back.

"I can't get a clear reading, sir," Shade went on. "Ten contacts, maybe more, one hundred meters out."

Sterling focused on Crow, who was still engrossed in his work. "Commander, we're going to have company very soon. Save what you have and pull back, now."

"Just give me one more minute, Captain, I'm recovering some fascinating data," replied Crow.

Sterling cursed under his breath then crouch-ran up beside the engineer. "Crow, disconnect now, that's an order!" he barked into the officer's ear.

Sterling's sudden arrival and forceful order snapped Crow to attention. "Yes, sir, disconnecting now," the engineer said, beginning the process of shutting down his devices and disconnecting the wires.

"They're right on us, Captain," Sterling heard Shade call out in his mind.

Sterling nodded to Banks and they both took up positions, ready to attack whoever was about to walk through the doors.

"Ensign, get ready to punch it as soon as I give the order," Sterling said to his helmsman through the open neural link. "Don't wait till I'm back on the bridge. Just haul-ass, as planned."

"Aye, Captain," came the prompt and confident reply from his pilot.

"Five seconds..." said Shade.

Sterling hunkered down and slipped his finger onto the trigger of his pistol. The doors at the far end of the docking space then slid open and two Sa'Nerran warriors marched through. A millisecond later, plasma weapons fire erupted toward the aliens and the two warriors fell. More Sa'Nerrans then charged though the opening to replace the fallen combatants, but they were hit and killed just as quickly. Then plasma fire began flying back through the opening toward them. One commando caught a blast head-on and was killed instantly, his entire face melted away like wax on a candle.

"Any time now, Crow..." said Sterling, aiming and firing at the advancing wave of warriors. The expressions on the leathery faces of the yellow-eyed aliens were as unreadable as ever. If Sterling's crew had caught the Sa'Nerrans by surprise, or of the aliens had known they were waiting, he had no way to tell.

"Almost there..." Crow replied, still frantically dislodging cables and devices.

More aliens moved through and another commando was hit. In his mind, Sterling heard Shade order the remaining commandos to fall back. The smell of burned Sa'Nerran and human flesh now clouded the room and filled Sterling's nostrils. It was a familiar smell. A terrible smell. The smell of war. It drove Sterling on harder than ever.

"Now, damn it," snapped Sterling, grabbing Crow and hauling him up while continuing to fire at the advancing warriors. He took a hit to his side, but it glanced off his combat armor, which then bubbled and fizzed from the energy of the plasma blast. Sterling continued to fire, wounding another two Sa'Nerra, but the power cell in his pistol was already nearly depleted. He went to release it and slap in another when Crow yanked a data device clear of the computer console and held it up like a trophy.

"Transfer complete, I have the data!" cried Crow. The engineer then drew his own pistol and added to the torrent of plasma blasts that were flying towards the Sa'Nerran attackers. "I'll cover you, Captain, now go!"

Sterling withdrew, expecting his engineer to follow close behind him, but as he reached Commander Banks, he saw that Crow was still firing at the enemy.

"Crow, get over here!" Sterling called out as he and Banks continued to fall back, laying down covering fire. However, Crow was now pinned down behind the computer console. Another commando was hit and killed, but the Sa'Nerran ranks had thinned too. Through the haze of burning flesh and material, Sterling could now count only six warriors. Then a voice cut through him like a scalpel.

"Lucas, hold your fire, it's me!"

The Sa'Nerran plasma blasts ceased and through the smoke Sterling saw the face of Captain Lana McQueen.

CAPTAIN LANA McQUEEN barged her way through the center of the six remaining Sa'Nerran warriors and stood in front of them. The warriors did not react to her presence or her actions. They simply resumed their prior formation, rifles held at port arms like an honor guard. Lieutenant Shade and the two surviving commandos used the lull in fighting to withdraw into safety. However, Commander Crow was still ducked down behind the computer console, between Sterling and the Sa'Nerran warriors.

"Lucas, hold fire, I'm here to talk," said McQueen. Her voice was different somehow, Sterling realized. It was unmistakably the voice of Lana McQueen, but she was speaking as if they were strangers. The familiarity and camaraderie between them was gone. The Omega Captain was also out of uniform. Instead, she was wearing Sa'Nerran armor, though it had clearly been custom-made for her more slender and taller human frame. "Tell your commandos to stand down," McQueen continued. "We have much to discuss."

"You're here to talk?" replied Sterling, his tone a mixture of shock and disgust. "Just who the hell are you speaking on behalf of, Lana?"

McQueen smiled and stretched out her arms, indicating to the warriors that were standing behind her. "Things are different now, Lucas. Soon, you'll understand."

"All I understand is that they've turned you, and the rest of your crew," Sterling hit back. He then glanced across to Crow and tried to get his attention. However, the engineer only managed to take a single step out from behind the computer console before McQueen's voice echoed through the room.

"Stay where you are, Lieutenant Commander Crow!" McQueen barked, her voice suddenly becoming as hard as her new alien armor. Crow immediately froze like a mime artist pretending to be a statue. "You have something that doesn't belong to you," McQueen continued.

Crow slowly withdrew and ducked back into cover as one of the Sa'Nerran warriors aimed its rifle at the engineer. Apparently satisfied that Crow had got her message, McQueen then focused her attention back onto Sterling.

"Come on, Lucas, don't be a fool, there's no escape from here," McQueen continued, offering Sterling an artificial smile. "There are thousands of Sa'Nerran warriors on this installation alone, and an entire taskforce that's on the way to intercept your little ship, hidden in the planetary rings."

Sterling gritted his teeth and tightened his grip on his pistol. He tried hard to not let his face give away his feelings, but it appeared that McQueen could still read his expressions. He then glanced down at the power indicator on the weapon. The pistol's cell was already nearly depleted, but he had at least one good shot left.

"I admit, you got further than I expected you to," McQueen continued, still smiling at Sterling. "Surging inside the ring system was a bold move, worthy of an Omega Captain." Then her expression hardened again. "But this is where your Omega Directive ends, Lucas. Give yourself up. Make it easier on yourself and your crew."

Sterling shook his head. "We managed to get into this system and we can get out again too," he hit back. It wasn't just talk; Sterling trusted the abilities of his ship and his crew. He slowly raised the pistol and aimed it at McQueen, causing all six warriors to immediately focus their weapons on him.

"Hold!" McQueen yelled, raising a clenched fist. To Sterling's astonishment the warriors obeyed her order. "You really don't understand what's happening here, do you Lucas?" the captain of the Imperium said in a tone that was both bitter and derisive. "I haven't been turned by the Sa'Nerra. I've been educated by them and joined them by choice. We all have." The words hit Sterling like a plasma bolt to the head. "Everything makes sense now, Lucas. I understand the Sa'Nerra's point of view, and they have accepted me as the voice that will speak on their behalf. The Sa'Nerra would prefer that humanity simply yields and accepts its new place in the order of the galaxy. But make no mistake, if you resist, we will annihilate you, and your world."

"If you think I'm going to surrender then your traitorous, addled brain has forgotten who it's talking to," hissed Sterling.

McQueen lowered her clenched fist and cocked her head to one side. "You won't shoot me, Lucas," she began, with a cockiness and arrogance that the real Lana McQueen never displayed. You and I are the same," McQueen went on. She then held out her hand, reaching into the space between them. "One way or another, you're going to join me. You can either stand by my side, and play a key role in the new order. Or you can just be another drone in the Sa'Nerra's human army."

Sterling laughed then returned McQueen's fake, insincere smile. "Or I can just do this," said Sterling, pulling the trigger.

The plasma blast flashed across the room and struck McQueen in the chest. She fell, and was pulled back into safety by her troop of alien warriors. Seconds later the room was again filled with weapons fire.

"Crow, move!" Sterling shouted, feeling the heat from a blast of plasma fizz past his ear.

Lieutenant Commander Crow darted out from cover but was hit in the back and knocked flat on his face. The device that he'd used to retrieve the encrypted Sa'Nerran data spun across the floor and stopped several meters in front of Sterling. It was achingly close, but still out of reach.

"Cover me!" Sterling yelled while rushing out to retrieve the vital intelligence, but the weapons fire was intense and he was struck to the shoulder and knocked down. He growled, pressing his gloved hand to the melted armor, the heat from which was now burning his flesh. Banks dragged Sterling back and through the docking hatch as more plasma blasts flashed past. "No, we need that device!" Sterling shouted, unable to overcome Banks' raw strength.

Lieutenant Shade then darted past him, moving so fast she was almost a blur. Plasma rippled through the air, missing the weapons officer by millimeters. Sterling and the others continued to return fire at the Sa'Nerra as Shade scooped up the device then wall-flipped off a support pillar in the center of the room. Landing cleanly on the deck, Shade raced toward cover but was struck in the back by a blast of plasma. Sterling caught her in an act of pure reflex before his officer fell face first into the metal decking.

"Get back to your stations," Sterling called out, as two of Shade's commandos hauled the officer up and helped her along the docking tunnel. Then he saw Lieutenant Commander Crow on the deck, hand stretched out toward him.

"Captain!" the engineer croaked, smoke from the plasma burn to the armor on his back still wisping upward. "Captain, please!"

Sterling cursed. Crow was too far away to risk a rescue, but he'd be damned if he would allow another Fleet officer to become part of McQueen's servant army. Raising his pistol, Sterling squeezed the trigger and shot Clinton Crow in the head. The engineer collapsed to the deck, more smoke rising from the charred skin on his scalp. Then Sterling slammed the button to close the hatch and ran like hell.

STERLING RACED through the corridors of the Fleet Marauder Imperium as plasma blasts hammered into the docking hatch to his rear. Ahead, he saw Commander Banks waiting for him, her brow furrowed and muscles taut.

"Where's Crow?" said Banks, glancing back toward the hatch leading into the alien shipyard.

"He didn't make it," replied Sterling, reloading his now fully-depleted plasma pistol while the two of them hustled through the Imperium's narrow corridors. "But I have the data device, so assuming Keller can get us out of here, we can still salvage something from all this."

Sterling then tapped his neural interface and reached out to his helmsman. "Ensign, Commander Banks and I are making our way back to the ship now. As soon as you see the docking seal turn green, execute maneuver 'breakout'."

"Aye, sir, standing by," Keller replied, smartly.

Sterling was about to severe the link when another voice invaded his thoughts.

"Lucas, you can't get away," hissed Lana McQueen inside his mind.

Each word caused a shooting pain to rush through Sterling's temples. His vision suddenly darkened and he felt his body thump into the deck. When his eyes cleared again, he was lying on the floor, his body held in Banks' arms. He could see her lips moving, but the only words he could understand were the ones inside his head.

"Join me, Lucas," McQueen continued, sounding wispy and ethereal. "Let us begin this new Sa'Nerran era together."

Sterling fought to push the voice from his mind, using the same force of will that he so often employed to bury his darker thoughts and emotions. He reached up and tapped his neural interface and the sounds of the ship raced into his ears.

"Captain? Can you hear me?" cried Banks, helping him to his feet.

"It was McQueen," Sterling replied, cutting to the chase. "She's still alive."

Banks' mouth fell open, but before any words came out the lights in the corridor went dead. A red glow then bled up from the alert lights at waist level and a series of solid thumps thudded along the walls. Sterling and Banks stood back-to-back. Then the doors to the crew quarters slid open and the turned crew of the Invictus darted out, like crazed zombies thirsting for flesh.

"Go!" Sterling cried out, though his shout was barely audible over the fizz of his and Banks' plasma pistols.

Crew member after crew member fell, filling the cramped hallways with the familiar smell of burning flesh. Sterling glanced ahead to the docking hatch leading into the umbilical that connected the Imperium to his own ship. His heart skipped a beat as he realized it was closing.

"Mercedes, get the hatch door!" Sterling called out, peeling the plasma pistol from Banks grasp. Banks' head snapped toward the hatch, then she ran, ploughing through two more turned crew members like a bulldozer. Plasma blasts flashed from the pistol in each of Sterling's hands, but still the crew of the Imperium came on. They were emerging from stairwells and pulling themselves out of crawlspaces, across the smoldering bodies of their fallen comrades.

"Blast the hinges!" Banks cried. Her hands were wrapped around the hatch door, which creaked and groaned as the motors fought against the inhuman strength of the officer.

Sterling turned one of his pistols toward the door, still shooting at the advancing horde with the other, and opened fire. The metal of the hinges cracked and then grew hot until the plasma pistol's cell ran dry.

"That's all I've got," shouted Sterling, kicking one of the turned crew in the chest then blasting him through the neck at point blank range. There was an earsplitting howl from behind him. It was a scream of raw, primal effort, louder and more aggressive than any sound Sterling had heard before. It was followed by the grind and wail of fractured metal. Sterling glanced back to see Commander Banks, holding the docking hatch above her head, his first-officer's face red and eyes burning with rage.

"Get back!" Banks yelled.

Sterling pressed himself to the wall as Banks launched the slab of metal toward the approaching crew members. It tore through them, smashing bone and crushing muscle so that the flesh of the turned crew popped like ripe tomatoes. Teeth gritted, Banks advanced, but Sterling caught her arm, feeling the swollen, rock hard muscle through her tunic. Banks glared at him, and not for the first time, the sight of his enraged first officer struck fear into his soul.

"Mercedes, that's enough!" he yelled, but Sterling could see in Banks' eyes that he hadn't reached her. Tapping his neural interface, he tried again as his first-officer pulled her arm free of his grasp with ease. "Mercedes, snap out of it and get on board, that's an order!" Sterling yelled. Suddenly, the raw brutality left her eyes, but still Banks did not move. "NOW, Commander!" Sterling added, screaming through his mind.

Finally, Banks shook her head and her jaw unclenched. "Aye, Captain," she said, appearing embarrassed. She then spun on her heels and waited for Sterling to move ahead.

More turned crewmembers clambered over the broken docking hatch and the bodies crushed beneath it, but Sterling was already through the tunnel and back on-board the Invictus. He hit the button to close the hatch even before Banks had fully made it through. Gears whirred and the slab of metal slid shut, but the turned crew of the Imperium were relentless. Running into the hatch at full speed, several of the turned humans slid their fingers through the gap between the door and the frame. However, despite the enhancement to their metabolism caused by the Sa'Nerran neural weapon, the turned crew lacked the primal, animal strength of Commander Mercedes Banks. Unable to overcome the motors driving the hatch to close, the door crushed the fingers and hands of the turned crew, leaving bloody, pulpy smears behind. The hatch light then turned green and a moment later the Invictus powered away from the Sa'Nerran ship yard.

Sterling was thrown to the deck from the sudden burst of acceleration, but Banks reacted with lightning instincts. His first-officer held onto his chest armor, sparing Sterling from being slammed into the bulkhead like a rag doll. Grasping a hand hold on the wall to steady himself, Sterling saw the Imperium slip away behind them. Then the exhaust trails of two torpedoes snaked out from the Invictus and their sister ship was incinerated in a ball of fury and flame.

STERLING FELT the thump of rock and ice hammering against the Invictus' hull as solidly as if it were his own chest that had borne the impact. He had barely any time to recover before the ship then veered hard to port and Sterling was slammed against the corridor wall. He'd lost count of the number of times he'd been tossed around the cramped interior of the Invictus during his short journey from the docking hatch to the bridge. His shoulders were bruised and his hands were cut and bloodied from repeated falls. Yet his resolve was not weakened. Nothing short of being blown out into space through a breach in the hull was going to stop him from reaching his post.

"Report!" Sterling called out as the door to the bridge whooshed open and he staggered inside.

"We're on course through the ring system," Commander Graves called back, while practically falling off the command platform to allow Sterling through. "The shipyard has launched twenty Wasps, and they are pursuing us with haste. There is no sign yet of the Sa'Nerran strike force."

"They're out there," said Sterling, grasping the sides of his captain's console and smearing his own blood along the metal panels in the process.

Through the viewscreen, Sterling could see clusters of rock and ice the size of houses flashing past the ship like gigantic cannonballs. Then he peered down at his console and brought up a reverse camera view of the pursuing Wasps. This was the moniker that Fleet personnel had given to the single-seater Sa'Nerran fighter craft that were on their tail. It was on account of the fact the ships were annoying and able to deliver a painful sting, but were rarely lethal. However, twenty Wasps was enough to take down a ship like the Invictus. Sterling knew that if the Sa'Nerran fighters concentrated their attacks on the Invictus' engines, their ability to escape would erode as quickly as their armor plating. Then the much more powerful strike force, led by MAUL, would be free to close in for the kill.

Sterling glanced over to Keller, intending to ask his helmsman how much longer they had to go before they broke out of the ring system. However, the young officer was in an almost trance-like state of concentration. The last thing the pilot needed was his captain barking at him for an update, Sterling reasoned. And in truth, he didn't need to be apprised of the situation. There were really only two possible outcomes. They either made it out in one piece or were smashed into oblivion against a hunk of rock and ice. Sterling considered that the chances of the latter occurring were far greater if he distracted his talented ensign than if he did not.

"Thank you, Commander, you'd better get back to the med bay," said Sterling, turning back to Graves. "We have wounded, and we'll have more before this is over."

"Aye Captain," said Commander Graves, calmly stepping away from the command platform. "I shall prepare my butcher's knives in readiness for the inevitable influx."

"You do that, Doc," replied Sterling, a little taken aback. He then cocked an eyebrow in the direction of Commander Banks, who had also now managed to drag herself to her station. She tapped her neural interface and opened a private link to Sterling.

"The scariest part is that I don't think he's joking," said Banks, watching the medical officer depart with the unruffled calm of a surgeon.

"I don't think Graves and humor are compatible," replied Sterling before closing their link and adjusting his gaze to the viewscreen.

More thuds hammered the hull of the Invictus, but the volume and timbre of the sound had changed.

"Damn it, those aren't rocks hitting us," he said out loud. "We're being shot at."

Sterling hurriedly checked his console and saw that the Wasps were gaining, pushing their single engines to their limits in order to charge the Invictus down. Two of the compact fighters had already been obliterated by flying rock and ice. However, Sterling couldn't rely on the billions of fragments that made up the planet's ring system to take care of the pursuing ships. Turning to the weapons console, he expected to see Shade's night-shift relief officer in the post, given that Shade had taken a plasma blast to the back during their retreat from the shipyard. However, the lieutenant was standing tall at her station, as if she'd never left it.

"Lieutenant Shade, you should be in the med bay," said Sterling. He made sure to come across with the appropriate level of authority and firmness, though in truth he admired the young woman for remaining on duty.

"I'm fine, Captain. I wish to continue my duties," replied Shade, in a manner that was bordering on rude. Sterling often forgot the officer's troubled history, given that it had never interfered with her work. Shade then seemed to recognize that her tone had perhaps been a little rebellious. "With your permission, of course, sir," she added.

Sterling cast his eyes down to the wound on the weapon's officer's back. A dinner plate-sized section of her armor had been melted through and some of the damaged fibers had fused with her burned flesh. However, she wasn't bleeding, and her eyes and responses were still as sharp as ever.

"Permission granted, Lieutenant," replied Sterling, opting to trust Shade's judgment of her own condition. "Though if you die at your post, I'm going to be pissed," he added. It wasn't a joke, and Shade didn't laugh, not that she ever did. "Now get those Wasps off our ass."

"Aye Captain," replied Shade, smartly. "I've already got something in mind, but I'll need Ensign Keller's help."

"Go ahead, Lieutenant," said Sterling, as four more of the pursuing fighters blinked off his screen. Some had been destroyed by the Invictus' plasma turrets, but the mass of rocky obstacles in the ship's wake was also starting to take a heavier toll on the enemy's numbers.

"Ensign, steer us close to that large moonlet up ahead," said Shade. "Fly past it as close as you can get."

Keller uttered a crisp response, but kept his eyes focused on the helm. Plasma blasts from the pursuing Wasps flashed past, but an increasing number were also landing true.

"Whatever you're going to do, do it fast," said Sterling, alternating his focus from the viewscreen to the damage control readout. The ship was taking a pounding, and as tough as it was, Sterling knew that everything had its limit.

"Hold her steady..." continued Shade as the Invictus practically skimmed the surface of the moonlet like a skipping stone. "Just a few more seconds..." she added, while hovering her finger over her console.

Sterling watched on, unable to do anything other than wait. He fixed his eyes onto Shade's hand, waiting for it to hit the console and fire their weapons. It was an agonizing few seconds that felt like an eternity.

"Firing!" Shade called out.

Sterling turned to the viewscreen and saw four torpedoes snake out from the Invictus' aft launchers. The weapons sped toward the moonlet, and disappeared inside an inky black crater.

"Brace for impact," Shade called out, gripping her

console more tightly, and prompting Sterling to do the same.

The torpedoes detonated, fracturing the moonlet into a cloud of smaller rocks and dust that expanded and enveloped the pursuing Wasps. Moments later, the Invictus was hit by a shockwave that propagated through the higher-density environment inside the ring system. However, compared to the near constant barrage of rock and ice already bouncing off the hull, the blast felt relatively tame.

"There are only four Wasps left, Captain," said Shade, as the dust-cloud dissipated. "And they're pulling back."

"Well done, Lieutenant," replied Sterling, triumphantly thumping his fist against his console and smearing more blood onto it in the process.

"Emerging from the ring system now, Captain," called out Ensign Keller.

Suddenly, the Invictus penetrated the barrier of stellar material inside the ring system and burst into empty space, like a dolphin leaping out of the ocean. Sterling's console lit up like a Christmas tree, though he didn't need to assess the readings to know why. Lurking just beyond weapons range was the Sa'Nerran strike force, led by the warship they knew as MAUL.

"Ensign Keller, tell me those ships are where we expected them to be," said Sterling.

Freed from the constant need to adjust their course through the ring system, Keller turned back to face Sterling. His face was flushed and beaded with sweat.

"They're closer than we projected, sir," replied Keller.

The pilot looked on the verge of collapse, as if he'd just run a marathon and had been asked to run another. "MAUL is too smart to expect we'd just head out through the ring system on a direct course for the aperture. It looks like he's positioned the strike force around the ring system, covering different points of exit."

"It's a ship, ensign, not a 'he'," Sterling hit back. "MAUL is nothing more a hunk of metal with a crew, just like this one. Except this crew is better."

"Aye, sir," said Keller, wiping the sweat from his eyes.

"To make a run for the aperture, we're going to have to go through one of those destroyers," said Banks, looking up from her console. "We can avoid MAUL and likely outrun the Skirmishers. But there's no getting past that ship without a fight."

Sterling nodded. "Then let's give it a fight," he said, turning to Lieutenant Shade. "Shore up the armor and point defense guns, Lieutenant. We hit that destroyer with everything we have, point blank range."

"Aye, sir," replied Shade, crisply.

Despite the situation and the searing pain she must have been experiencing, the expression on his weapon's officer's face had not altered. Sometimes Sterling wondered if the woman even experienced pain in the same way as everyone else. Sterling then turned to Ensign Keller, who was already looking at him, knowing that his role in what came next would be just as pivotal as Shade's was. However, there were no specific instructions he could give the young helmsman. The Invictus wasn't a World War One bi-plane that they could throw around the skies of Europe, maneuvering in an instant. All they could do was go hard at the destroyer and make their approach as unpredictable as possible using thrusters to alter their angle and position. Their point defense guns could handle torpedoes and mass projectiles, but plasma weapons were harder to evade. Sterling knew that all they could do was make themselves as hard to hit as possible, and hope their state-of-the-art regenerative armor was up to the job.

"Fly as fast and as crazy as you can, Ensign," said Sterling. "Then once we're through, run like hell for that aperture."

Ensign Keller acknowledged the order then Sterling finally turned to Commander Banks. However, she was already a step ahead of him.

"Electronic jamming is focused in on the destroyer," said Banks, leaning on her console a little more heavily than usual. The exertion of physically tearing a docking hatch off its hinges had clearly taken its toll, even on his near super-human first-officer. "They'll struggle to get a solid lock through all the EM soup we're putting out. One of the warriors on board would have to practically lean out of a window to get a clean shot."

Sterling's console chimed several alerts and he glanced down at it, puffing out his cheeks. "No such trouble for those other ships, unfortunately," he said, looking at the twenty torpedoes that the other Sa'Nerran warships in the strike force had already launched at them.

"I'm not worried about the torps," said Banks. "It's the pot-shots they're taking at us with their plasma rail guns that bother me. A couple have already given us a pretty close shave."

Sterling nodded then focused ahead. They'd done all they could. No matter how well he planned, and no matter how ballsy their tactics, anyone could get a lucky shot. The pieces were all in play. All they could do now was let the match unfold and see who came out on top.

"Thirty seconds..." said Shade, hand poised over her console, waiting till the last moment to fire.

Through the deck plating, Sterling could feel the machine-gun like rattle of their point defense cannons firing. The guns had created a shield against the torpedoes and physical shells that the Sa'Nerran destroyer was throwing at them with relentless fury. The entire ship was now shaking, not only from the intense thruster maneuvers that Keller was performing in order to throw off the destroyer's aim, but from the impact of the plasma blasts and projectiles that were sneaking through their defensive barrier. Sterling again focused on the damage control panel, seeing patches of regenerative armor darken and turn red. A series of powerful vibrations then rippled through the deck. Sterling knew every shake, shimmy and sound the Invictus made, and he knew the hull had been breached.

"Hull breaches, deck two, three and four. Emergency bulkheads in place," Banks called out, as more vibrations and thuds rocked the bridge.

"Hold your course," Sterling called out. It was unnecessary to say, since they no longer had a choice, but the crew hearing his voice and hearing the conviction in it was enough.

"Firing," Shade called out, her voice still remarkably composed.

Sterling gripped the sides of his console and watched the plasma blasts tear out into space ahead of them, striking the destroyer cleanly on the port bow. There was a flash of light and the viewscreen briefly went white, until the external feeds compensated for the intense glare of the warship's violent detonation.

"Direct hit, enemy destroyed," Shade confirmed, announcing the victory with a touch more gusto than Sterling was used to hearing from her. However, it made sense that the only thing that could move his weapons officer to joy was the delivery of violence and death, Sterling realized.

Ensign Keller, however, was far more vocal, shaking his fist and whooping as if his team had scored in the dying seconds to win the championship. Commander Banks joined in the cheers, but Sterling was still focused down on his console, staring at one blinking indicator in particular. They had made it past the destroyer, and now had a clear run to the aperture. The other ships would not be able to catch them in time – not even the heavily modified and augmented MAUL. And the torpedoes that sailed through space after them would not penetrate the barrier created by their point-defense guns. However, they had not come through unscathed. Commander Graves had already reported fourteen dead and seven wounded, two critically. Yet, as cold as it may have seemed to any outside observer, Sterling did not lament the dead. This was war, and in war soldiers died. He would honor them in time, and in his own way, but in order to do that they had to make it back to Fleet space. Sterling stared at the blinking indicator again and cursed under his breath. During the firefight with the Sa'Nerran destroyer, their reserve fuel tank had been hit, causing the ship to automatically eject their fuel into space. One of the shimmies that Sterling had felt was the blast of the fuel store detonating in the darkness behind them. Their internal fuel store was still intact, but their high-energy maneuvers had depleted them to ten percent. They had enough to reach the aperture and to surge, but not enough to get back into Fleet territory.

"You look particularly miserable for someone who just played chicken with a ship twice its size and lived to tell the tale," said Banks.

From the quizzical expression on her face, Sterling guessed she'd been watching him for some time. He sighed and pointed down at his console. Banks frowned and stepped beside him, looking at the blinking indicator that had transfixed Sterling for the last few seconds.

"Ah, crap," muttered Banks, closing her eyes and gently shaking her head.

"My thoughts exactly," replied Sterling. "We're not out of this yet."

STERLING PEERED out through the viewscreen at a sea of lush green trees that seemed never ending. It was a stark contrast to the darkness and emptiness of space, but also a welcome sight for a battle-weary spacefarer. However, as much as he would have enjoyed to simply soar over the planet's surface for a few more minutes, Sterling had other more pressing priorities to attend to.

"There, how about that spot?" Sterling said, pointing at the viewscreen. He then jumped down from his command platform and moved beside Ensign Keller so that his helmsman could better see what he was indicating.

"There's enough tree cover to shield us from view, though it's a good couple of miles from the settlement," Keller replied, slowing the Invictus to a hover.

"That'll be fine, Ensign, we can use our ground rovers to head into town," Sterling replied, giving Keller a reassuring pat on the shoulder.

"We'll need to scuff them up a bit, so it doesn't look

obvious that we're from Fleet," Commander Banks chipped in. "Same goes for our clothes. We obviously can't wear our uniforms. These settlers are as likely to want to kill us as the Sa'Nerrans are."

"Given how Fleet abandoned them, I'd say they're probably more likely to want to gut us," Sterling replied, stepping back onto his command platform.

Both Sterling and Banks had referred to the settlers' likely desire to murder them in a lighthearted manner, though in truth it was no joking matter. All of the former UG planetary colonies that ended up inside the Void after the start of the Sa'Nerran war held a deep resentment against the Fleet. This was no less true of the planet they had managed to limp to after surging through the aperture to escape the Sa'Nerran strike force. Its name – or at least the designation the United Governments had given it – was Colony Hera 4ML. It hardly tripped off the tongue, Sterling thought to himself, idly. The planet was relatively deep inside the Void, and had so far been left alone by the Sa'Nerra. Though with the development of the new neural weapon, Sterling wondered how long it would be before Hera 4ML, and others like it, were harvested for bodies to form part of the aliens' turned workforce.

"Set us down, Ensign, and give us as much cover as you can," Sterling said, turning his attention back to the matter at hand. "If you have to do a little bit of woodcutting then so be it."

Keller responded with a brisk, "Aye, sir," then set about burrowing the Invictus inside the dense forest, using its hundred-meter-tall trees to shield the battle-scarred Fleet

Marauder from view. Even with the ship's reactor reduced to minimal power and its engines disabled, Sterling knew that the Invictus could never be fully hidden from the scanners of an orbiting Sa'Nerran vessel. However, the extreme use of cover was not to hide them from the probing yellow eyes of the alien warriors, should they come looking at Hera 4ML, but from the colonists themselves. If he was to get the resources he needed to repair and refuel the ship before the Sa'Nerra discovered them, he needed the colonists' co-operation. Though, if it came down to it, he'd take what he needed by force. That prospect didn't excite him, but it didn't faze him either. There was more at stake than the lives of a few backwater colonists.

Sterling winced as tree after tree was felled by the descending mass of the Invictus. He guessed that many of the trees had likely taken centuries to reach the imposing heights they had achieved. In contrast, tearing them down had taken mere seconds. It was a brutish destruction of natural life for an entirely self-serving reason, yet this was exactly what the Invictus had been built to do. Whether turned humans, Sa'Nerran warriors, or simple trees made no difference to him; their mission was destruction. Their job was to cut away the corrupted flesh then eradicate the disease, so that what remained of humanity could survive.

Sterling was roused from his thoughts by a weighty thump that resonated through the deck. Then the familiar thrum of the Invictus' engines began to diminish.

"We're on the ground. Thrusters and engines powered down, sir," said Ensign Keller.

"Understood, Ensign," replied Sterling, as one of the

giant trees they snapped like a twig toppled past the viewscreen and bounced off the hull on its way to the forest floor. "Keep the key in the ignition, we may need to get out of here in a hurry," he added.

Sterling was about to head off the bridge when an alert chimed on Banks' console. He stopped and threw his head back, as if looking skyward to the gods for help. "Tell me that's not a Sa'Nerran warship entering orbit," he groaned, casting a weary glance at his first officer.

"Well, it is a Sa'Nerran warship, but it appears to be a phase one Skirmisher," Commander Banks replied.

This time Sterling let his head fall forward, as if he'd lost all the strength in the muscles in his neck. "A Marshall?" he asked, though he already knew the answer.

"Aye, sir, looks like it," replied Banks.

"And I suppose it's heading to the same town we are?" Sterling asked, holding on to the slim hope that the ship might be en route to one of the other towns on Hera 4ML.

"Right again, Captain," said Banks, suddenly sounding as weary as Sterling felt.

Sterling puffed out his cheeks and blew out a sigh before noticing that Ensign Keller had spun his chair around to face them and had his hand held up.

"This isn't school, Ensign, you don't need to raise your hand," said Sterling, allowing his irritation to spill out.

Banks smirked, though not cruelly. Keller's occasional greenness was endearing, but only because when it mattered most their young helmsmen never let them down, as he'd already demonstrated several times that day. Keller sheepishly withdrew his raised hand and tried to nonchalantly rest it on his thigh.

"Sorry, Captain, but I was just wondering what a Marshall is?" the helmsman asked, again showing his lack of experience in the Void.

"Marshalls are a bit like a cross between mercenaries and Wild West lawmen," said Sterling. "Besides Fleet and the Sa'Nerra, they're just about the only ones out in the Void that can traverse the apertures. They travel from colony to colony, settling disputes, usually violently, and getting paid handsomely for their services."

"So, these Marshalls are human?" Keller asked, clearly intrigued yet also still confused. "But Commander Banks said the ship was a phase one Skirmisher. Those ships haven't been active for decades."

This time Banks answered. "In the early part of the war, the Void was littered with the remains of defeated warships," she began, seeming to enjoy giving the young ensign a history lesson. "Some of the traders who were cut off in the Void pieced these ships back together from the wreckage. Most have been destroyed in the years since then, but a handful of the strongest captains survived, and carved out a niche for themselves in the Void. Those are the ones we now call the Marshalls."

"But how can they fly a Sa'Nerran Skirmisher?" Keller replied, now leaning forward. He was fully invested in the story of these frontier adventurers. "I thought no one could comprehend the Sa'Nerran language?"

"The Marshalls don't understand the language any better than we do," replied Banks, shrugging. "They figured out the basics through a process of trial and error. Mechanically, there isn't much difference between Fleet and Sa'Nerran tech."

"As fascinating as this little discourse is, can I remind you all that we have a ship to repair and refuel?" said Sterling.

The sharpness in his voice caused the ensign to snap back into his seat and spin around to face the viewscreen again. The mention of repairs then reminded Sterling that he was currently without a chief engineer. This, he admitted to himself, was his fault alone, considering he was the one who'd shot Crow in the head to prevent him from being captured.

"Unfortunately, repairing the Invictus isn't going to be straightforward, since we no longer have Crow on board," Sterling added, shaking his head.

"Lieutenant Sullivan is now in charge down in engineering," said Banks. "She's capable and dependable. She'll get the job done."

Sterling nodded. "Then bring her along. I want to make sure we barter everything we need from these colonists."

"And what about the Marshall?" Banks asked.

Sterling cursed. He'd already forgotten about that particular complication. "If he gets in the way then we'll deal with him," he replied. Then he had a thought. "Though his arrival might actually be a blessing in disguise."

"How so?" Banks wondered, folding her powerful arms and looking at Sterling through narrowed eyes. Marshalls had a reputation for causing problems with the Fleet, rather than fixing them.

"The Marshalls need to trade and resupply too," reasoned Sterling. "It's likely this Marshall has some of the parts we need on his ship."

Then another voice joined the discussion.

"Or we could just take the fuel from the Marshall's ship, along with anything else we need." Sterling spun around to see Lieutenant Shade staring at him. She was slightly hunched over and had one hand wrapped around her side, pressed to the wound on her back. Shade shrugged. "Just a thought, sir," she added, nonchalantly.

"I like her plan better," said Banks, with a wicked smile.

"So do I," replied Sterling, though unlike Banks, he wasn't smiling. He was deadly serious. "If it comes to that, then I have no problem taking what we need. But let's hope it doesn't come to that," he added, somberly. "The last thing we need right now is another fight."

Sterling then set off for the exit, aiming a finger in the direction of Shade while he walked. "Lieutenant, go and see Graves and get that wound tended to right away. That's an order."

Lieutenant Shade appeared taken aback by the order then immediately jumped down from her station and hustled after Sterling. She was clearly struggling from her injuries, though from the flat, emotionless look on her face, it was impossible to tell the weapons officer was in excruciating pain.

"You'll need me out there," snapped Shade, blocking Sterling's path. She then appeared to recognize the impertinence of her statement and actions and quickly corrected herself. "What I mean to say is, as your weapons officer, I should be at your side, sir," she added, forcing herself to adopt the stiff-sounding military manner in which Fleet officers were supposed to talk.

Sterling stopped and locked eyes with Shade. She held his gaze for a couple of seconds – which was at least one second longer than the officer could normally manage to look anyone in the eye – before awkwardly looking away.

"I didn't say you weren't coming, Lieutenant," said Sterling, irritated that Shade had stood in his way. "I just ordered you to get your wounds tended to. Right now, you could barely fight off a couple of kittens, never mind an irate colonist, not to mention a Marshall or Sa'Nerran warrior."

"Aye, sir," replied Shade, stepping aside. Her eyes were still cast down to the deck.

"We meet in the cargo hold in one hour," Sterling called out, resuming his route to the exit. "No uniforms, and concealed weapons only. Again, we'll need to scuff them up so it's not obvious who we are. As far as anyone on this forsaken rock is concerned, we're colonists, just like them. Understood?"

There was a chorus of, "Aye, sir," from the officers on the bridge. Sterling set off again, then felt a familiar neural connection forming in his mind.

"Are you serious about taking what we need from the Marshall?" asked Banks, speaking through their private neural link.

Sterling stepped into the elevator and waited for Banks

to enter too. "I don't mean that we kill him, necessarily," he replied in his mind. "These colonists aren't our enemies, and we kill enough of our own kind as it is." Then he shrugged and added. "We just need to appropriate the fuel without the Marshall realizing it."

"'Appropriate...' said Banks, smiling. "That's a fancy word for steal." Then her expression hardened. "And what if we can't 'appropriate' what we need? How far are you willing to go?"

Sterling cast a sideways glance at Banks. "It won't come to that, Mercedes. But if it does the simple fact is, we need that fuel more than they do," he replied, coolly. "So, no matter what happens, we aren't leaving this rock without it." He paused for a second to meet Banks' eyes fully. "Do you have a problem with that, Commander?".

Banks stood by his side, hands pressed to the small of her back, and simply shook her head. "No, sir. Not at all."

THE MAIN COLONY town on Vega 4ML was called Hope Rises. Sterling had no idea whether this was the town's original name, or something its inhabitants had chosen for it, after being stranded in the Void. However, as their ground rover trundled down the pockmarked main street of the town toward the trading district, the only thing Sterling could see rising into the air was smoke. From the appearance of the town, hope had left it a long time ago.

Turning the rover onto a stretch of smoother road, Sterling took the opportunity to glance over his shoulder and check on Lieutenant Shade, who was in the rear. Incredibly, his weapons officer was no longer showing any signs of discomfort from her plasma injury. Sterling knew that his chief medical officer was fond of advanced, experimental and often outlawed forms of treatment, but even so Shade's recovery was remarkable. Sterling then glanced at Commander Banks. She was in the passenger seat, staring out at the colonists through the rover's windows like a tourist on a Jeep safari. The only member of the bridge crew missing from the rover was Ensign Keller. Despite requesting to come along for the ride, Sterling had ordered his helmsman to remain on the bridge in the event that a speedy getaway was required.

"Stop looking at them," said Sterling, as his first-officer continued to peer at the inhabitants of Hope Rises like they were exhibits in a zoo.

"But they're looking at us," replied Commander Banks, from the passenger seat.

"They're looking at us because we're strangers," said Sterling. "Just act normal, like we're travelers from another town, as we agreed."

"I don't know how to act normal in these clothes," said Banks, clawing at the civilian outfit she'd cobbled together from items in the crew stores. Like the rover, which they'd hammered and scuffed up, the garments they all wore had been intentionally damaged to give them a suitably tattered appearance. "All I've worn for the last five years is my Fleet uniform. This stuff feels weird against my skin."

Sterling scowled at Banks, running over a pothole as he did so, which jolted the rover and almost gave him whiplash.

"Seriously? You haven't worn anything other than a Fleet uniform for five years?" asked Sterling, keeping one eye on the road and the other on his first officer.

"Have you seen me in anything else in all the time we've served together?" replied Banks.

Sterling thought for a moment, but couldn't recall a single occasion, even when they were off duty.

"Is that dedication to the Fleet, or just a lack of imagination?" he smiled.

"It's just practical," said Banks, choosing neither of the two options Sterling had presented. "Besides, the fibers used in Fleet uniforms are as tough as old boots, and resistant to slashes, chemicals and fire. Considering my unique metabolism, I tend to rip normal clothes pretty easily."

Sterling laughed. *"Unique metabolism,"* he said, enjoying the casual way that Banks had framed her gift of freakish strength. "Let's just hope you don't tear a hole in your pants while we're out here then."

"If I do, then it will be because you just jinxed me," replied Banks, smiling warmly.

"The trading district is just ahead," said Lieutenant Shade. Sterling looked at his weapons officer in the rear-view display. She had the appearance of a grumpy teenager who was being forced to endure her parents' incessant banter on a long road trip.

"Thank you, Lieutenant," Sterling replied, not that he'd needed Shade to point it out. "Is your squad in place?"

Shade checked the computer that was wrapped around her left wrist, like a giant sweatband. "They're in position, sir," Shade replied, pulling the sleeve of her jacket back down to cover the device.

Sterling nodded. "Okay then, let's go and meet the locals," he said, pulling the freshly beaten-up rover into a parking spot and switching off the motor. There was a sudden thumping sound coming from outside the rover and Sterling's hand immediately closed around the grip of his pistol. He glanced left, ready to draw the weapon should it be required, then saw the face of a kid staring at him. The boy was perhaps no more than five or six and had his mouth pressed to the glass of a truck parked to their side. He was blowing out his cheeks and forming a seal against the glass with his lips, like some kind of sucker fish.

"There you go," said Banks, jumping out of the rover. "Say hello to the natives."

Sterling got out of the rover then thumped his fist against the glass, causing the kid to jolt back. The boy then hurled a string of what Sterling assumed to be local curses at him, while also giving him the middle finger.

"I think when we finally beat the Sa'Nerra, we leave these colonies in the Void," said Sterling. "It's like society out here has regressed by centuries in only the last fifty years."

Lieutenant Shade then jumped out of the rover, landing beside the truck window where the kid was still flipping the middle finger to Sterling. The boy saw Shade's face, peering in at him with her cold, emotionless eyes, like some sort of ghoul, and immediately sat facing the front.

"Do you normally have that effect on children, Lieutenant?" asked Sterling, though he was grateful for her unexpected intervention. The kid was beginning to piss him off.

"I have that effect on everyone, sir," Shade replied. Coming from anyone else, it might have been a joke at her own expense. However, though Sterling knew little about Opal Shade, he knew for sure that she didn't tell jokes.

Sterling approached the main entrance of the trading post, which was a sprawling complex that incorporated not only the trading center, but a hotel, several eateries and a huge bar. A man in a wide-brimmed hat, perhaps in his late seventies, sat in a rusted metal chair outside. A half-drunk bottle of dark, frothy liquid sat on the arm of the chair, and he was smoking a hand-rolled cigarette. The old man sucked on the cigarette then smoke that was blacker than oil billowed from his nose. It smelled like burned herbs, cinnamon and sweat, though Sterling figured the pungent bodily odor was more likely to be rising off the old man's damp, mud-brown shirt instead. However, whatever the actual composition of the smoke was, it stung Sterling eyes like soapy water.

"I'm looking for the Marshall," said Sterling, standing in front of the man. Another plume of smoke forced to him to wipe water from his eyes.

"You ain't from these parts, kid, that be right?" replied the old man, in a guttural dialect that was as thick as the smoke escaping from his nostrils.

"No, we're from a town a few hundred miles south of here," replied Sterling. "Our rovers are damaged, so we're looking to trade for parts."

"You a funny talker, mister. All folks talk this funny from south town, that be right?" the man replied, sucking in another long draw from the cigarette. The tip burned brightly and the man's eyes narrowed as he sucked in the acrid smoke.

Sterling opened his mouth to answer, but then sighed and shut it again. He turned to Banks, hoping she might understand the strange pidgin language the man was using. However, she just shrugged and shook her head.

"What about the Marshall?" Sterling asked, trying a different line of attack. "Do you know where he is?"

The old man's eyes suddenly looked beyond Sterling then he shriveled into his chair and bowed his head low, covering his eyes with the brim of his hat.

"Did I hear my name?"

Sterling turned to see a man in a black frock coat, flanked by two associates in short, leather jackets. They had all just pushed through a side door and appeared to be on their way out of the trading post.

"Are you the Marshall?" asked Sterling, looking the man over. The coat wouldn't have looked out of place on his namesake from the eighteenth century, Sterling thought. However, the rest of the man's outfit was far more modern. Beneath his coat, Sterling could see a combat vest, similar to the sort used by the Fleet a decade ago. His pants had been modified with armor plating that was clearly taken from a Sa'Nerran warrior.

"You in need of my services, kid?" the Marshall replied, stepping closer and probing Sterling with his keen, narrow eyes.

Sterling scowled back at him. The man was perhaps only in his early-forties, though he had the face of someone who enjoyed a hard life and hard drinking. Even so, it barely made the Marshall ten years Sterling's senior and calling him "kid" just rubbed him up the wrong way.

"I need some specific parts and supplies," Sterling continued, trying to remain civil despite taking an instant dislike to the man. "The sort of thing that a travelling man such as yourself might be in possession of. Or could perhaps source."

"That's not what I do, kid," the Marshall replied, tossing a coin into the lap of the old man, who still hadn't looked up from beneath his hat. "If you want to trade, go to the trading post."

The Marshall turned and started walking in the direction of the spaceport. Sterling felt his pulse quicken. Their entire plan relied on keeping the man distracted long enough for Shade's commando team to steal the fuel from his ship. If he was heading back to it now then they'd have to quickly switch to plan B. And while Sterling didn't have a problem with killing the Marshall if it came to it, the chances were high that others would get caught in the crossfire if a fight started. And the colonists of Hera 4ML had suffered enough at the hands of the Fleet.

"How's your man doing today?" asked Lieutenant Shade.

The Marshall stopped and turned on his heels, the thick soles of his boots grinding the stony floor to dust. "He's undefeated. As usual." The Marshall took a couple of steps toward them, though this time he was focused on Shade. "Why? You looking to make a bet, or to challenge?"

Sterling quietly observed the exchange, intrigued at what his weapons officer had in mind. Then he felt a neural link form and heard Banks in his head.

"Do you know what she's doing?" Banks asked.

"Not nearly as often as I'd like," Sterling replied, watching the Marshall and Lieutenant Shade square off.

"I challenge," said Shade, coolly. "If I win and beat your man then you get us the parts we need."

The corner of the Marshall's mouth curled up. "And if my guy wins, little lady? What do I get?" The Marshall's eyes washed over Shade in a way that make Sterling's skin crawl and his stomach churn.

"You don't get *that*, asshole," Shade replied, though the spirited manner of her reply only seemed to encourage the Marshall. "But if your guy beats me then I will join your crew. Willingly."

The Marshall's eyes lit up. "Quite an offer, little lady." Then he gestured to the two men behind him. "But as you can see, I already have a crew. And as pretty as you are, I can't see what use I'd have for you, besides the one you already denied me."

Shade then grabbed the bottle of liquid from the arm of the old man's chair and hurled it at one of the Marshall's men. It struck the man on the bridge of his nose, shattering both bone and glass. Before the man had even begun to fall, Shade had launched herself at the second associate. This man reached inside his coat, and Sterling saw the flash of metal from a blade that had been concealed there. However, the deputy didn't get a chance to use it. Shade landed blow after blow in a stunningly fluid and ferocious combination that was as elegant as it was devastating. The second man landed hard on the stony floor, blood pouring from his nose, mumbling curses and threats. Shade pressed the sole of her boot across the man's throat and choked him into silence.

The Marshall laughed heartily then began clapping. "Okay, little lady," he said, flashing his eyes at Shade once again. "You just got yourself a deal."

STERLING REACHED the bottom of a long flight of narrow, dimly-lit stairs and waited for Banks and Shade to catch him up. With each step further into the belly of the trading post at Hope Rises, the roar of a crowd grew louder. It was a roar that Sterling had heard many times before, sometimes even coming out of his own mouth. It was the primal scream a person uttered when they were clamoring for blood.

"I applaud your quick thinking, Lieutenant, but do you know what you've gotten yourself in to here?" Sterling asked. He was speaking to his weapons officer through a neural connection so they couldn't be overhead.

"Aye, sir, these underground fighting rackets exist on many of the Void worlds," replied Shade, who was limbering up her arms and legs while waiting for the Marshall to gain them entry. "I'm familiar with the rules, such as they are."

A burly seven-foot-tall monster of a man stood guarding

the entrance to the fighting arena. Sterling scowled at the man, hoping that the competitors on the other side of the door were lesser in stature.

"That's not what I mean," said Sterling, shuffling closer to the entrance. "These places aren't for sparring. The fights only end when one of the two fighters can't continue." Sterling then forced Shade to meet his eyes. "People die in these rings, Lieutenant."

Shade did not flinch at Sterling's statement. "I know Captain," she replied, coolly. For once she had managed to hold his eyes for more than a few seconds. "I know what I'm getting into, sir."

The Marshall and his two goons, both of whom were looking at Shade with murderous glares, then removed weapons from inside their coats and placed them into a metal storage box. The Marshall's weapon was a conventional firearm that had been discontinued from use by the Fleet a century ago.

"Crap, that means we're going to have to surrender our weapons too," said Commander Banks. She was standing beside Sterling, her powerful arms folded tightly across her chest, with a pissed-off look on her face.

"Don't worry, we still have you, Commander," said Sterling. "You're a walking weapon, more dangerous than anything we're likely to put in that metal box."

Banks was not amused. "Are you sure I can't take your place, Lieutenant?" she said, flicking her eyes across to Shade.

"I made the challenge, Commander, so it has to be me

who steps into the ring," said Shade. "Those are the rules in these places."

The Marshall appeared to be studying them more closely, perhaps wondering why they were all silent, yet still looking at one another. The practice of implanting neural technology at birth had steadily died out in the Void colonies, largely due to the lack of specialist medical equipment. However, even those who possessed neural implants, which included the Marshall, tended not to use them. There were many conspiracy theories concerning how neural communication had been devised by the United Governments as a means of monitoring people's thoughts. As a result, most of the Void colonies snubbed the practice of neural conversation. Sterling had once thought this notion to be nonsense, but after having seen Admiral Griffin employ a now-banned neural scanning device, he wasn't so sure.

"Everything okay, Marshall?" Sterling asked out loud, if only as a way to break the silence and stop the suspicious Marshall from glaring at him.

"You'll need to check your weapons, if you're carrying any," the Marshall said out loud.

Shade slipped her plasma pistol into a second metal box without complaint, then Sterling did the same. Banks unfolded her arms and pulled her pistol out from inside her jacket. Staring up at the seven-foot doorman she dropped the weapon into the box with a loud crash. The doorman simply peered down at her, his face every bit as surly as Lieutenant Shade's expressions on a bad day.

"I'll be wanting that back," Banks said, backing away.

However, the giant man just closed the box and handed it to a woman who was waiting behind a cubby hole to his rear.

"Nice collection of shooters you have there," said the Marshall, as the box was taken into the cubby hole. "Fleet issue? New models too, by the looks of it. How did you come by them?"

"There are plenty of dead Fleet personnel in the Void," replied Sterling, shrugging off the Marshall's probing question. However, the lawman continued to peer at him with narrow, suspicious eyes. "You're not the only one flying around the Void, picking up salvage," Sterling added, sensing that he needed to give the Marshall something more. "I bought them from another trader. He didn't tell me how he got them, and I didn't ask."

"I see," said the Marshall, in a way that suggested he hadn't bought into Sterling's answer one bit. Then the lawman smiled and gestured to the door. "We're all good to enter now. I'm going to enjoy seeing my guy whoop this little lady's ass." Then he paused and appeared to reconsider his statement. "Though not too badly, of course. I want her pretty little face to still be pretty when she starts working on my ship."

"I'd worry about the face of your man, instead," said Banks, sticking up for Shade, whose ice-cold demeanor had meant she hadn't risen to the bait. Banks, on the other hand, was far quicker to anger.

"Oh, my guy can't really get any uglier," replied the Marshall, chuckling. The lawman's deputies were also smirking, thought the mirthful expressions were more of a struggle for them on account of the damage Shade had done to their faces.

Sterling was about to ask the Marshall what he'd meant by his statement when the door opened and the answer became apparent. Inside a caged ring across a narrow sea of baying fight fans was a Sa'Nerran warrior. The alien was pummeling a thick-set, three-hundred-pound brawler with its leathery fists, as if it were merely toying with its opponent. Each hard strike generated a roar from the crowd, which was chanting for it to hit harder and faster. However, as Sterling drew closer, it became obvious that this was no ordinary alien warrior. The Sa'Nerran was wearing what looked like gladiatorial armor from the times of ancient Rome. It had been decked out in a red tunic with leather shoulder pauldrons, although its mottled, barrel-shaped gray chest was bare. A spiked helmet sat on top of the warrior's round head, which only seemed to accentuate its egg-shaped, yellow eyes. And, like the sizeable hulk that was manning the door to the arena, the Sa'Nerran was at least a foot taller than any warrior Sterling had seen before.

"What the hell is that?" said Banks out loud, scowling at the alien. "It looks like some sort of beast from Greek Mythology."

"I found it inside a Sa'Nerran shipwreck that had drifted into orbit around New Gibraltar," said the Marshall, with more than a hint of pride in his voice. "The thing was half-dead, and I almost put it out of its misery. Then I thought to myself, a Sa'Nerran cage fighter could be one hell of a thing." The Marshall laughed and smiled. "I guess I was right. Fifty-two straight wins, so far." He flashed his eyes at Shade. "Soon to be fifty-three."

Sterling turned to Lieutenant Shade, but his weapons officer had pre-empted his question. She scratched the side of her head, tapping her neural interface in the process.

"I know their weaknesses, Captain. I can take it." Shade said, the confidence in her voice filling Sterling's mind. "The commando squad are almost done. I only need to keep them distracted for a few more minutes."

Sterling turned back to the caged ring just as the Sa'Nerran brute stomped its huge foot down across its opponent's jaw, dislocating it savagely. There was a wave of "ooohs" from the crowd, many of whom recoiled, grasping their own jaws in sympathy. A referee, who had been officiating from way over the other side of the ring, called for the bell. However, this didn't stop the Sa'Nerran from continuing to punish the thick set man, who was now either unconscious or dead.

"This one is next!" The Marshall shouted out, grasping Shade's wrist and thrusting her hand into the air alongside his.

Shade tugged her arm free, glowering at the Marshall in the process. Opal Shade only had two expressions – blank or angry. The crowd turned and began to laugh and jeer, throwing beer cans and papers cups at Shade as she made her way to the ring, pushing through the baying mob. One man stood in her way, brown liquid from the bottle in his hand dribbling down his chin.

"I'll go a few rounds with yer, missy!" the drunk slurred, making a thrusting motion with his pelvis. The crowd roared with laughter and continued to roar as Shade punted the man in the groin then stepped over him to continue her path to the ring. The door to the cage had been opened to allow her in, and also to allow the body of the Sa'Nerran barbarian's last victim to be dragged out.

"I'm beginning to think we should have just seized the Marshall's ship by force, and taken the fuel that way," said Commander Banks, as they all took up prime positions in the crowd to watch the fight.

"It would have required us to commit more of the crew, and likely just have started a riot," Sterling replied, through their neural link. "Our numbers are thinned out as it is, and I need every able body out there fixing the Invictus."

"I just hope Shade can handle this monster," said Banks, turning back to the caged ring. "She might be a little morose, but she's damn good at her job. I'd hate to have to find another weapons officer."

Sterling thought back to when the subject of Opal Shade had come up during a call with Admiral Griffin. Griffin had said that Shade could be trusted, without revealing why, as was typical of the guarded flag officer. The fact she had been recruited straight out of Grimaldi Military Prison and had not undergone the rigors of an Omega Directive test had always given Sterling pause. Yet Shade had never let him down, and he believed she wouldn't let him down now.

"She can handle it," said Sterling, confidently answering Banks despite the lingering questions in his own mind. "And if she can't, she'll be dead anyway."

"Just another to add to the butcher's bill," sighed Banks,

resting forward against the railings that separated the Marshall's private viewing area from the throng below.

The door to the cage was then shut and locked and the official, himself splattered in blood from the fights that had come before, indicated for the bell to be rung. The sound resonated around the dank, sweaty cellar room with a darkly sinister quality. It was like the sound that marked the beginning of a two-minute silence. However, the somber resonance of the note was soon drowned out by the rising clamor of the crowd, as Opal Shade and the Sa'Nerran warrior raised their guards.

A LEATHERY FIST thumped into the back of Lieutenant Shade, sending her tumbling across the blood-stained mat. The crowd roared and Sterling winced, his hands tightening around the cold, rusted metal of the hand rail.

"Come on, damn it," Sterling urged, as Shade scrambled to her feet. The weapons officer then narrowly avoided being kicked in the head by the alien warrior, which had followed up its strike with frighting speed. Had the blow landed, Sterling knew the fight would have been over. Instead, the alien's heel slammed into the cage, rattling it like an angry gorilla at a zoo.

"It's okay, she's doing well," said Banks, though it sounded more like she was trying to reassure herself than Sterling. His first officer also had a tight hold on the handrail, though because of her strength the metal had begun to bend.

Shade ducked under another powerful swing and countered with a hard combination of shots to the alien's ribs, forcing it to retreat. Banks shook her fist and joined in with the rest of the baying crowd, roaring in appreciation of Shade's spirited fightback.

"You're enjoying this, aren't you?" asked Sterling. It wasn't said in an accusatory manner, but he could see the fire in his first officer's eyes. It wasn't as bright or as hot as the times when Banks lost control and turned into a monstrous killing machine in her own right, but clearly the commander liked a good fight.

"If there's time, I might even have a turn myself," said Banks, who then recoiled and let out an "ooh", as the Sa'Nerran warrior caught Shade with a glancing blow.

"I think just one of my officers fighting to the death is quite enough for today," replied Sterling, wincing again as Shade was thrown against the cage by the brutish alien. Shade slipped aside just in time to avoid the warrior's fist, which slammed into the scaffolding in the corner, making a ringing sound almost as resonant as the match bell itself.

"The Marshall has been smart, I'll give him that," said Banks, glancing across to the lawman, who was whooping and hollering a few meters from them. "They've protected the weak spot at the back of the alien's neck with that helmet."

Sterling nodded. He'd quickly understood that the purpose of the alien's armor wasn't just theatrical. However, the knees were still unprotected, though considering the tree-trunk like size of the alien's limbs, he wondered whether the warrior had any weaknesses at all. Banks roared again as Shade dodged then landed a hard kick to the alien's leg, causing it to buckle and stagger back.

However, the Sa'Nerran recovered quickly and the advantage was lost.

Banks then suddenly froze, hands gripping the railings, and Sterling realized she was receiving a neural communication. He glanced across to the Marshall to make sure he hadn't noticed, but the lawman was too busy hollering at his fighter to finish the job. Spittle was erupting from the Marshall's mouth as the man bawled instructions.

"The commando squad has the fuel loaded into the rover," said Banks, stepping closer to Sterling and speaking out loud, ironically to avoid suspicion. "They're en route back to the ship now."

Sterling acknowledged Banks then turned his back to the Marshall and rubbed the side of his face, brushing against his neural implant as he did so.

"Ensign Keller, how's it looking over there?" he asked, reaching out to his helmsman through the link.

"Repairs are about seventy percent complete, sir," Keller replied. The ensign's voice came through strongly despite the riotous noise surrounding Sterling. "We're in a fit shape to leave."

"Understood, Ensign, stand ready to depart," Sterling answered. "The commando squad is en route back to you now with the fuel. Get it into the tanks without delay."

"Aye, Captain," Keller replied then the link went dead.

Sterling turned back to face the cage, but caught the Marshall's suspicious eyes looking at him again.

"Aren't you enjoying the fight, mister?" said the Marshall, shouting over the roar of the crowd, which had just erupted on account of Shade getting thrown into the corner. "It just seems that you aren't paying much attention."

"I've seen her fight before, I'm not concerned for the outcome," replied Sterling, trying to sound as nonchalant and dismissive as possible. The Marshall's reservations about him were clearly growing.

"We'll see," the Marshall hollered back, shooting Sterling a wide, toothy grin before turning back to the action.

Sterling waited for the Marshall to become fully immersed in the fight again then casually brushed past his neural interface for a second time.

"Lieutenant, we have the fuel," said Sterling. However, the sudden invasion of Shade's mind distracted her, and she ate a shot to the jaw. Sterling winced again, and watched as the alien pressed its advantage, landing another shot to the ribs before Shade managed to dance away.

"Understood..." was the single word reply from his weapon's officer. However, despite the brevity of her response, Shade's answer had revealed much about her state of mind. Neural communication conveyed more than merely words. It also allowed those linked together to feel one another's emotions. It took training and focus to be able to keep those emotions in check, but in times of stress they bled through the link more freely. Sterling had expected to feel Shade's anxiety and fear, and even her doubts, but all he felt was an impatient, burning rage. "Get ready. This will be over soon," she added, holding her ribs and sidestepping around the ring.

The link went dead, not that Sterling intended to

respond to Shade for fear of distracting her again. However, as it turned out, he needn't have been concerned. Shade had clearly just been playing for time. Stepping up several gears, she set to work on the Sa'Nerran warrior's legs, darting in and landing swift, sharp kicks then retreating before the warrior could react. The alien soon lost patience with this tactic and tried to muscle Shade against the cage, but she broke the hold then snapped a ferocious kick to the side of the alien's knee, causing it to hiss and drop to a crouch, unable to stand. Shade followed up with a front pushing kick that drove the Sa'Nerran head-first into the bars. The gladiator-style helmet became trapped and the alien's waspish sounds grew louder and more aggressive. It finally pulled its round head clear of the helmet and pushed itself up, charging at Shade like a maddened animal. For a split-second, Sterling though that Shade was going to be driven so hard into the cage that she'd be cut into slices. However, at the last moment Shade made her move, tripping the alien and sending it crashing into the blood-stained mat. A perfectly-executed heel strike to the back of the alien's neck then swiftly finished the job.

The audience gasped and an eerie silence fell over the arena. It lasted only for a few seconds before the crowd again began to roar, though this time for a mixture of reasons. Some marveled at what they had just witnessed, while the many who had lost money simply threw beer bottles or punches at whomever was closest. The bell rang and the official, who once again had stayed well clear of the action, raised Opal Shade's hand in victory. Banks' victory cries rose above those of anyone around her, and her grip became so tight on the hand-rail that she snapped the metal clean in half. Sterling shook his fist also, as much from relief as from exhilaration. On a purely selfish level, the victory meant he didn't have to recruit a new weapons officer. He then turned to the Marshall, a smile beaming across his face, intending to rub the man's nose in his victory. However, instead of the lawman's demoralized face what he saw was a pistol being pointed at his heart.

Sterling nudged Commander Banks, who was still lost in the moment, drinking in the roar from the crowd as if it were fine champagne. His first-officer finally turned, throwing a congratulatory arm around Sterling's shoulder before she too saw the pistol. Banks face fell and her arm dropped back to her side, fist clenched.

"I should have explained to you that I'm a sore loser," said the Marshall. He was backed up by his two deputies, who were doing their best to shield the lawman's pistol from view. "So, I'll be taking your companion with me, anyway. She'll be a mighty fine asset to my crew. In addition to just being mighty fine." The Marshall laughed heartily and his goons joined in on cue.

Sterling took a step forward, intentionally shielding Commander Banks from the weapon aimed at his chest. This wasn't some chivalrous act in order to protect her, and he knew Banks well enough to know she wouldn't assume as much. However, while the Marshall had somehow managed to sneak a weapon inside the arena, the lawman was unaware that Sterling had done too. The difference was that Sterling's weapon was not a pistol, but a near super-human woman. Sterling wanted to be sure that the Marshall's attention was focused solely on him, so that Banks was free to make a move when needed.

"A deal is a deal, Marshall," said Sterling, facing down the armed man without fear. "Don't make the mistake of crossing me."

The Marshall laughed again, though this time it was scornful, and his deputies did not join in. "Do you think I survived all this time as a lawman without learning how to recognize when someone is keeping secrets?" the man said. Sterling felt his stomach tighten into a knot, but he held his ground and maintained his posture. "I don't know who you are, or why you're at Hope Rises, but it sure as hell ain't to trade." Then the Marshall's chin dipped and he looked at Sterling over the top of his eyes. "I assure you, mister, you will tell me everything. And then you will be judged."

Sterling glanced down at a fold-up chair that was positioned between himself and the Marshall. He steeled himself, ready to kick it at the man and launch his attack. However, before he could make the move, the door to the arena burst open and a man darted inside, shouting at the top of his voice.

"Sa'Nerra!" the man shouted, banging what looked like a wooden chair leg against the metal hand-rail. "It's a raid! The Sa'Nerra are coming!"

The crowd immediately charged toward the exit, pushing past one other and trampling over any that were unlucky enough to fall. Suddenly a group of people barged between the Marshall and his deputies and the Marshall's weapon fired, causing more chaos and panic. Sterling wasted no time, rushing forward and grabbing the Marshall's wrist, pushing the barrel up the ceiling. The Marshall roared and thumped a fist into Sterling's jaw. He tasted blood and smashed his own fist into the lawman's face, landing a harder and cleaner blow that stunned the man. The Marshall's deputies were soon on him, trying to wrestle Sterling's hand away from their employer. Then Banks appeared, throwing members of the passing throng aside like they were helium-filled balloons. She grabbed the two deputies by the throat and lifted them so that the toes of their boots danced across the sticky floor, like inept ballet dancers. Her eyes were fierce, but Sterling could see that Banks was still in control. Smashing the heads of the two goons together, she then tossed them over the railings, crushing more of the escaping crowd below.

The stunned Marshall let go of his weapon, allowing Sterling to strip it from his grasp, and held up his hands in surrender.

"Okay, kid, you got me this time," the Marshall said, showing his broad, toothy smile again. He backed away from Sterling, but only succeeded in walking into the mass of hyper-dense muscle that was Mercedes Banks. The lawman cowered from Banks, as if her five-feet nine-inch diamond-cut physique was even more threatening than that of the monstrous Sa'Nerran cage fighter. "We'll just call it quits. How's that?" he said, still holding his hands up.

Any other Fleet officer would have accepted the man's

mewling apology. However, Sterling had also survived in the Void for long enough to know that the promises of men such as the Marshall meant nothing. He also knew that prideful, humiliated men held grudges. Sterling had enough trouble to deal with as it was, without a vengeful lawman on his tail.

"Here's my judgement," said Sterling, aiming the compact pistol at the man's heart and squeezing the trigger. The Marshall flinched then stared down at the blood oozing from his chest. He looked up at Sterling, mouth agape, but all that came out was a guttural croak, followed by a trickle of blood. Then he slumped forward and fell face-first onto the floor.

"I'm glad you're on my side," said Banks, staring down at the body, wide-eyed.

"Come on, we need to get moving," said Sterling, brushing off Banks' comment. He looked over to the cage and saw Lieutenant Shade making her way across the rapidly thinning sea of spectators. Even under the dim lighting of the arena, Sterling could see that she was pretty beaten up, though her movements were still strong and confident. He jumped down from their private viewing area and met her in the ringside section, which was now mostly clear of people, bar those who had been trampled underfoot.

"Well done, Lieutenant," said Sterling, stepping over the unconscious, bloodied body of a fight fan. "But we're not out of this yet. The Sa'Nerra are apparently on their way."

"The commando team reports that they're back at the

ship, and that the fuel is loaded," said Shade, wiping blood onto her bare shoulder from the corner of her mouth. "Shall I have them re-group and head back here?"

The distant sound of plasma weapons fire was now filtering down the stairwell beyond the entrance. Shouts and screams were mixed in with the blasts.

"No, have them remain on standby in the lower hold," said Sterling. "We'll bring the commandoes to us."

Sterling, Shade and Banks continued to push on through what remained of the crowd, which had bottlenecked at the narrow door. Sterling fired the compact weapon he'd taken from the Marshall twice into the air, causing the crowd to part and let him through. Holding the weapon high so that the colonists could clearly see it, he moved ahead then tapped his neural interface to connect to Ensign Keller.

"Ensign, report," said Sterling, stopping in front of the man mountain who had wordlessly demanded they hand over their weapons before entering the arena.

"One phase-three Sa'Nerran Skirmisher is hovering just south of Hope Rises, Captain," said Ensign Keller. "They dropped a ground assault squad of twelve warriors and appear to be scouting the colony. There is no indication they have detected us."

"It's time to change that, Ensign," said Sterling. "Launch and take care of that enemy vessel. Then set down at our location and open the lower hold. The commandos can deal with whatever is left of the ground assault squad." The ensign responded briskly and the link went dead. Sterling then turned to the enormous doorman, who appeared to be the only one in the entire arena besides themselves who wasn't panicking.

"I'm going to need our weapons back," said Sterling, standing tall, although the top of his head barely reached the level of the doorman's Adam's apple. The man peered down at Sterling, but remained unmoved. "Please," Sterling added, as an afterthought. Sometimes he forgot that not everyone he met was under his command.

The enormous man slowly turned to the side and rapped his enormous knuckles against the hatch of the cubby hole. A couple of seconds later it opened and the face of the woman who had taken the metal boxes appeared. She saw Sterling, rolled her eyes and disappeared inside the room again. Sterling smiled up at the doorman as they waited; the behemoth stared back at him blankly. The woman then returned and slid two metal boxes out onto the shelf.

"You may as well have these too," she said, unlocking both boxes, one of which contained the weapons that had belonged to the Marshall and his deputies. She then slammed the hatch shut without another word.

Sterling handed out the weapons then picked up the conventional firearm that had belonged to the Marshall and held it out to the doorman. "You might need this," he said, offering the man the weapon. The doorman shook his head slowly from side to side. "Suit yourself," Sterling said, shoving the weapon down the back of his pants.

Sterling stepped away from the doorman and moved to the bottom of the stairwell with Banks and Shade close behind. He'd only managed to place one foot on the sticky steps before the sonorous rumble of a voice behind him caused him to stop. He turned back to the doorman, though the man mountain was now looking at Lieutenant Shade.

"Good fight," the doorman said, his voice so low and loud that it rattled Sterling's chest like a nightclub subwoofer. "Good to see you again," he continued, rattling Sterling's chest some more.

Shade nodded respectfully toward the doorman then turned and waited for Sterling to lead the way. A dozen questions immediately leapt into his mind, but as intriguing as they all were, he knew that now was not the time to ask them. Running up the stairs, weapon raised, Sterling made his way to the main exit of the trading post. There was already heavy fighting outside, and dozens of bodies littered the stony ground. Plasma blasts flashed past the windows, along with terrified colonists.

"What's your ETA, Ensign?" Sterling asked his helmsman through a neural link.

"Overhead in ten, sir," replied Keller, his voice again brisk and efficient.

Sterling closed the link then nodded to Banks and Shade. "I don't know about you two, but I've had enough of this town," he said.

"No argument from me, sir," said Banks.

"I'll miss the fights," said Shade, surprising Sterling not for the first time that day.

"On three," said Sterling, turning the power setting of his plasma pistol to maximum. He counted down in his head and burst out in the street.

Plasma blasts flashed from their pistols and two Sa'Nerran warriors fell, kicking up dirt and stones as their lifeless bodies crashed to the ground. Running up beside the truck where the rude kid had flipped him the bird earlier, Sterling and the others took cover from the plasma fire that was returned in their direction. Glancing inside the truck, he saw the kid, hunkered down in the footwell. Plasma blasts were ripping into the side of the vehicle and already several holes had been punched through the thin metal doors.

"Hold them off," cried Sterling, handing his pistol to his first officer. Banks took the weapon without question and continued to shoot at the advancing warriors. Sterling then peered skyward and spotted the predatory shape of the Invictus on the horizon, heading toward them fast. Yanking the door of the truck open, he saw the Sa'Nerran Skirmisher through the smashed window of the vehicle. It was heading their way and was only a few hundred meters behind the alien ground troops.

"Kid, come on," said Sterling reaching inside the truck. The other side of the vehicle was already almost destroyed, leaving barely any cover for the boy. The kid reached for Sterling's hand and he pulled him out of the cab, turning his back to the warriors as he did so. He felt the thump and burn of plasma blasts strike his body armor, and grimaced against the pain.

"They've got a ship!" the boy cried as Sterling placed the kid inside the back of his rover, which was still parked next to the truck. Unlike the vehicle he'd rescued the boy from, the rover was hardened against plasma blasts and conventional firearms. "Their ship is coming! We're going to die!" the boy cried.

Sterling pushed the kid's head below the door then leaned inside. "These alien assholes aren't the only ones with a ship, kid," he said, casting his eyes up to the sky. The boy followed the line of Sterling's gaze, then the Invictus roared overhead. Moments later the air was split by the piercing, shrieking wail of six plasma rail guns all firing in unison. The flash of light was blinding, and was followed a moment later by another eruption of light and flame as the Sa'Nerran Skirmisher was utterly obliterated. The Invictus descended; the pressure from its thrusters blowing people across the gravel like litter. The lower hold opened and the squad of commandos piled out, making short work of the remaining Sa'Nerran warriors on the ground.

Sterling lowered his weapon and turned back to his officers. Shade had now switched from her angry face to her blank, emotionless expression, which signified to Sterling that everything was under control. However, Commander Banks looked like someone had just shot her dog.

"What's wrong, Commander?" asked Sterling. Out of everyone, he expected Banks to be the one celebrating. Unexpectedly, Banks then turned to Sterling and raised her arms, showing rips in the sleeves of her shirt and down the thighs of her pants.

"I told you this damned civvy clothing is a bunch of crap," she said, sliding her fingers into the various holes and tears. "I can't wait to get my uniform back on."

A whoop from behind him gave Sterling a fright, and

he spun around to see the boy standing on the back of the rover, hands in the air.

"Holy shit, that was so cool!" the boy cried, leaping up and down on the back of the rover like it was a trampoline. Parts of the destroyed Skirmisher were still falling from the sky like fireworks.

Sterling snorted a laugh then glanced across to his ship, which had now set down and was awaiting their return. It looked majestic under the late evening light of the planet's star, like a bird of prey, surveying its hunting ground.

"You're not wrong there, kid," he said, smiling.

STERLING GRASPED the sides of his captain's console, putting a little more weight onto it than usual, due to the pain that still throbbed in his back from the Sa'Nerran plasma blast. He'd briefly allowed Graves to administer first-aid to the wound. However, Sterling was in too much of a hurry to get back to the bridge for the doctor's ministrations to have had much effect. Lieutenant Shade had also allowed Graves to quickly treat the worst of her injuries before insisting that she return to her post. Under normal circumstances, Sterling would have ordered that Shade remain in the medical bay to be treated fully for the numerous injuries she'd sustained during the cage fight with the alien warrior. However, their circumstances were rarely ordinary and their current predicament was no exception.

"The Sa'Nerran strike force has spotted us, Captain," said Commander Banks from her station beside him. She was still wearing her torn civilian clothing, and together with Sterling and Shade, it looked like a group of vagabonds had commandeered the Invictus. "The remaining five Skirmishers are all out of position, searching the other planets and moons in the system. But the three Destroyers and MAUL remained in a group."

Sterling tapped his console and brought up a long-range image of the main strike force on the viewscreen. Even from their current, safe distance, the looming presence of MAUL was unsettling. He quickly calculated the projected course of the various enemy vessels, while rubbing the tired muscles in the back of his neck. All courses eventually intersected with their own. The only variable was the time it would take the ships to intercept the Invictus.

"So, it's a race then," said Sterling, glancing across to Banks.

His first officer simply raised her eyebrows and nodded. "It certainly looks that way," she sighed.

MAUL was leading the destroyers directly to the aperture. Its objective was to cut Sterling off before he could surge into the Fleet side of the Void. The Skirmishers, on the other hand, were coming straight at them, all from different angles. Sterling could already see torpedoes on his scanner readout, launched from the five smaller ships. Soon the Skirmishers would be taking long-range pot-shots with their cannons too, in the hope of striking a lucky hit. Distance wasn't really a factor in space. Accuracy was what mattered.

The Sa'Nerra would know that a ship as advanced as the Invictus would be able to take out the torpedoes long before they were a threat. However, taking pot shots at them would force Sterling to expend power making small adjustments to their velocity and orientation. This was the only way to avoid the long-range attacks, though success was by no means certain, even with a pilot as skilled as Ensign Keller. The real purpose to all the attacks, however, was to slow the Invictus down. Each time they expended power to adjust their velocity, MAUL would gain ground. And if the strike force reached the aperture before they did, it would be game over. Sterling knew it, and so did MAUL.

Sterling sucked in several deep breaths and steeled himself, ready to make an announcement to the crew. It was one of his least favorite duties, but he knew it was important. If the captain was confident then the crew would all draw from that strength. Tapping his neural interface, he then opened a wide link, allowing everyone on board to monitor.

"All hands, this is the captain," Sterling began. "The Sa'Nerran strike force is still in pursuit, but they don't know who they're dealing with. We've beaten them before and we'll do it again." Sterling could feel the energy of the crew through the neural link. It was like electricity pulsing down his spine. "Prepare to operate in low power mode. And put on your jackets. It's going to get cold in here." Sterling closed the link then nodded to Banks, who began to execute the order.

"Reducing life support systems to minimum power," said Banks, as non-essential consoles on the bridge started to power down. "All non-combat functions going offline in ten seconds. Reducing gravity fields by twenty percent."

She continued to work for a few seconds longer then turned to Sterling. "All available power routed to the main engines, Captain. We're as ready as we're ever going to be."

Sterling sucked in another deep lungful of air, which already tasted colder than it had a moment ago, then turned to Ensign Keller. The young officer was watching him, eagerly awaiting his order.

"Are you a betting man, Ensign Keller?" said Sterling, feeling goosebumps tingle across his skin from the rapidly reducing temperature on the bridge.

"I like a flutter every now and again, sir," Keller replied. The helmsman smiled and glanced across to Lieutenant Shade. "If we're talking about fights, then I know who to put my money on," he added.

Sterling smiled, though Shade, naturally, did not. "This time we're trying to avoid a fight, Ensign," he continued. "This is a race. The winner gets to go home. The loser gets blown into atoms. Who is your money on, Ensign?"

"MAUL is a beast, Captain, but there's nothing in the galaxy faster than the Invictus. Not with me at the helm." The young officer's confidence was bordering on bravado, but it was also exactly what Sterling needed to hear.

"Then get us to that aperture, Ensign Keller," said Sterling, standing tall, his hot breath fogging the air above his console. "Give her everything you've got. And then push her some more."

"Aye, sir," Keller answered, the young man's own breath hanging in the air long after he'd turned back to his helm controls. The ship began to accelerate hard.

Sterling closed his eyes, listening to the pulse of the

reactor, the thrum of the engines and the rattle of the deck plating beneath his feet. He knew just by the feel of the ship when the engines had reached their peak, and he knew the exact point at which the powerful drive system had exceeded its design specifications too. All engineers built in tolerances, he told himself. Like human beings, machines could be pushed beyond their limits, some more than others. However, the Invictus was no ordinary warship. It was an Omega Taskforce warship; the only one. Like its unique crew, Sterling had confidence that the vessel could supply what he demanded of it. And if it couldn't, they were dead anyway.

"Point defense cannons are engaging the torpedoes," said Lieutenant Shade, the glow of her console mixing with the low-level red alert lights to cast dark shadows across her face. "But the computer is having difficulty tracking all of the plasma blasts."

Sterling nodded to Shade, acknowledging her update, then addressed Keller again.

"Do what you can to avoid the incoming fire, Ensign," said Sterling. His fingers were already becoming numb from the cold. He considered fetching a jacket, but he felt rooted to the spot, as if his boots had already frozen to the metal deck plates. He glanced across to Banks, Shade and Keller, seeing puffs of vapor come from their mouths, and recognized the look on each of their faces. None of his bridge crew would leave their posts, not until they surged or MAUL blasted them out of the cosmos.

Suddenly an alert rang out on Banks' console, but Sterling didn't need his first officer to explain the cause;

the unique alert tone told him that there was a hull breach.

"Hull breach, deck one, cargo hold!" cried Banks, having to raise her voice to be heard over the near-calamitous roar of the ship's engines. "Emergency seals in place. Integrity stabilizing."

"How long until we reach the aperture, Ensign?" Sterling called over to his helmsman. He could have spoken to him through a neural link, but everyone was amped up and also near frozen. If there was a chance to exercise any muscle, even the ones in his jaw, he would take it.

"We're approaching the deceleration point now, sir," replied Keller. Then he glanced back at Sterling, mist billowing from his mouth like a steam train. "Just how fast do you want me to surge, Captain?"

"Just how fast can do you do it, Ensign?" replied Sterling, throwing the question right back at the pilot.

"We've taken some damage, sir," Keller replied, making some rapid calculations on his helm console. "We know the ship can handle double the regulation surge velocity. I can maybe push it to one hundred and ten percent."

"Enter the aperture at one hundred and fifty percent of the regulation surge velocity, Ensign," said Sterling. His announcement caused the young officer's breath to quicken even further, but the young man didn't argue. Sterling had given his order and Keller would carry it out.

"Aye, sir," replied Keller. "Preparing deceleration for surge at one-fifty standard velocity."

Sterling then turned to Banks. "MAUL will briefly gain on us while we're decelerating. That's when it will try to hit us hardest," he said, thinking ahead to the next step. "Once we have the power back from the engines, dump all you can into the regenerative armor and RCS thrusters."

"Aye, Captain," replied Banks, briskly.

Sterling then turned to Shade. "The point defense guns won't do anything against their plasma cannons, but do whatever you can to keep those ships busy. I don't care if you have to take your boot off and throw it at them. Torpedoes, cannons, turrets, I don't care. Give them everything until there's nothing left to give."

"Aye, sir," replied Shade, her face still partially hidden in shadow so that she looked even more menacing than usual.

"Did our message get through the aperture relay?" Sterling said, turning back to Banks.

"The strike force is throwing out so much interference it's hard to know," said Banks, shrugging. "But we'll find out soon enough."

Sterling nodded then turned back to face the viewscreen. Despite the temperature on the bridge having dropped below forty-five degrees, he no longer felt cold.

"Prepare for hard deceleration in ten," called out Ensign Keller.

Sterling tapped his neural interface and connected to the entire crew. "All hands, brace, brace!" he called out in his mind, then closed the link and grasped onto the sides of his console, digging his heels into the deck. The ship's inertial negation systems, which allowed them to accelerate and decelerate without the forces liquefying their skeletal structures, were not fully effective when pushing the engines well over standard. At best, their deceleration maneuver would feel like trying to hang on to a spinning merry-go-round. At worst, Sterling would end up pancaked to the rear bulkhead, like some sort of macabre work of art. As it turned out, the reality was somewhere in the middle.

"Ensign!" Sterling called out in his mind, feeling his feet lift off the deck. His numb fingers were already struggling to keep hold of his console.

"Just a few more seconds!" Keller called back, the young officer's voice so loud in Sterling's mind that his brain hurt.

Sterling could feel the strength in his fingers fading. Then, slowly and painfully, his left hand slipped off the console. He gritted his teeth and bit down hard, trying to hang on with his remaining hand, but it was no use. Speeding away from the console toward the rear wall of the bridge, Sterling suddenly jerked to a stop, suspended in mid-air. He felt something wrapped around his wrist, the grip so tight it was excruciating, and looked up to see Commander Banks holding on to him.

"Five seconds!" Ensign Keller called out to Sterling in his mind.

For each of those five seconds it felt like Sterling was having his hand surgically removed, but Banks held firm. Suddenly, the gravity system stabilized and he dropped to the deck, landing hard. Banks pulled him up and thrust him back onto the command platform. There were no words of concern. No, "Are you okay, sir?" There wasn't time for concern. There was only time for action.

"All weapons, firing!" Shade called out.

"Regenerative armor at two hundred percent," shouted Banks. "Incoming fire... Brace for impact!"

Sterling gritted his teeth again and glowered out at MAUL through the viewscreen. Torpedoes, plasma cannons and every single point defense cannon on the Invictus had fired all at once. MAUL slid in behind one of its escort destroyers, which took the brunt of the assault and exploded in a fiery mass. To their sides, two Skirmishers had failed to take down the torpedoes Shade had fired, and both erupted in unison. Then the Invictus was hit. Sterling was thrown against his console, his head hitting the cold metal surface hard. The next thing he knew Banks was again hauling him to his feet. Blood coated her hands, though he didn't know whether it was his or hers. The ship was rocked again and Sterling heard the dreaded alarm tone indicating they'd suffered new hull breaches. However, there was nothing more he could do. The Invictus would either take the beating and survive or it wouldn't. Sterling spat blood onto the deck and stared out at the blinking beacons of the aperture.

"Come on, damn it, surge!" he called out, spitting blood onto his chin as he growled the words. "Surge!"

Then the ship fell through the aperture and time stood still. The sparks of electricity, crackles of flame and whine of alarms all vanished. All that remained was his own thoughts, and the knowledge that their battle was far from over yet.

THE INVICTUS CRASHED through the aperture and exploded back into the universe in an instant. The calming absence of normal reality that existed in the space between apertures was gone and now all Sterling felt was pain. For several seconds he had no idea where he was, then his eyes adjusted to the light and he found himself staring up at the ceiling of the bridge. His head and back throbbed and his ears were ringing. It felt like he'd been hit by a truck.

"Report," Sterling croaked, but all he could hear was ringing in his ears. He tried to call out again, but despite feeling the vibration of his voice resonate through his chest, he was still deaf to his own cries. Fighting the intense pain in his body, Sterling pushed himself up to a crouch and was immediately hit with a wave of nausea. It threatened to overwhelm him and he had to clamp his jaw shut for fear of throwing up. To his left he could see Commander Banks flat out on the deck, her arms and legs slowly moving, though without any coordination or purpose. Lieutenant Shade was slumped over her console, though she too was showing signs of life. Sterling waited for the nausea to ease then slowly rose to his feet and staggered back to his captain's console, using it as a crutch. What he saw on the viewscreen quickly caused his nausea to return with a vengeance. The Invictus was spiraling out of control, causing the stars to whirl in a chaotic kaleidoscope of light and darkness.

Sterling turned his eyes away from the dizzying scene on the viewscreen and stared down at his console. However, the array of flashing alert panels and status indictors was just as stomach-churning. Cursing, he turned to the helm control station then realized Ensign Keller was no longer seated there. He cursed again, spotting his helmsman sprawled out on the deck behind his station. A ribbon of crimson red blood was leaking out onto the cold metal plates from a deep cut to his head. However, there was no time to tend to the pilot. For all he knew, the strike force was already on their way through the aperture to finish the job they'd so nearly completed at Hope Rises on Colony Hera 4ML.

"Something on this damned ship must still work," Sterling growled, again peering down at his captain's console. The screens were blinking and pulsating like a set of malfunctioning fairy lights on a Christmas tree. He hammered his fist against the console, resorting to the age-old technique of fixing technology with brute force. Whether from the effects of his blows or, more likely

Sterling realized, from sheer coincidence the console stabilized. He skimmed through the condition report, but it made for grim reading.

"What's the damage?"

Sterling glanced left, the sudden movement of his head again bringing on a wave of nausea. Commander Banks was back at her console, looking like she'd just woken up from a heavy night of drinking.

"Main power is down; we're running on reserve cells," Sterling began, skimming through the list. Banks also conducted maintenance on her console by slapping it with her palm. The force of the impact nearly snapped the unit off its pedestal. "We have no helm control, or helmsman," Sterling added, gesturing to Ensign Keller on the deck. "Scanners are also down. We're out of control and as blind as a bat."

"I'll try to reach Lieutenant Sullivan in engineering and focus on getting power back online," replied Banks, hovering her hand over her neural implant ready to make the connection. "Power, helm and defensive systems need to be the priority. Those Sa'Nerran bastards could surge through the aperture at any moment."

Sterling nodded, the slight movement of his head causing more shooting pain to rush through his temples.

"Weapons are down, but armor integrity is holding at forty percent."

Sterling glanced right, taking care to move more gingerly this time, and saw Lieutenant Shade back at her post. Considering she'd only recently finished a cage fight with a Sa'Nerran warrior larger than any Sterling had ever seen, she somehow looked in better shape than he felt.

"Focus on the regenerative armor, Lieutenant," replied Sterling. "If that strike force does come after us, we won't last more than a few seconds in a shooting match."

"Aye, sir," Shade replied, a little less briskly than usual, but still with an impressive degree of vigor.

The door to the bridge then slid open and Commander Graves staggered inside, holding his medical kit.

"What's the butcher's bill so far, doctor?" asked Sterling as Graves made his way onto the command platform.

"Nine dead, twenty-eight wounded," replied Graves, glancing down at a medical computer wrapped around his left forearm. "Thirty-two wounded if I count everyone on the bridge."

"Don't be so quick to update your tally, commander," replied Sterling, allowing Graves to inject a concoction of drugs into his neck.

Graves scowled then noticed Ensign Keller lying on the deck. "Or perhaps it's ten dead?" he added, with the cold detachment that could only come from an Omega officer.

Sterling grabbed the medical injector out of Graves' hand then ushered the doctor in the direction of Ensign Keller. "Assuming this ship isn't crippled, the one man I will need is a helmsman," he said. "I don't care if he's dead already, Commander. Bring him back. That's an order."

Graves appeared slightly affronted by the command. "I am not a necromancer, Captain," the medical officer said, staggering toward the unconscious ensign and dropping to his knees at the helmsman's side.

"Today you are, Commander," Sterling hit back. He didn't care if he was asking the impossible, he was the Captain and could ask what he damned well liked.

"Lieutenant Sullivan reports that main power will be back online momentarily," Commander Banks said, stepping beside Sterling and updating the condition report on his console. "We'll have partial scanners and thruster controls too, though the main engines need a full restart. Needless to say, I've made that her priority."

Sterling felt and heard the thrum of energy surging through the power conduits that ran throughout the ship. The condition report on his console updated again to show that partial helm control had been restored.

"Take the helm while Graves resurrects our pilot," said Sterling, turning back to Banks. "I'm sick of spinning through space like a damn shuriken star."

"Aye, Captain," Banks replied, darting across the bridge and sliding into the seat at the helm controls.

"Scanners coming back online, sir, but they will take a couple of minutes to calibrate," announced Lieutenant Shade.

"Can you see if there's anything else out there," Lieutenant?" asked Sterling, focusing his own efforts on distributing what power they had to the critical systems.

"No, sir, not yet," Shade replied.

With the inertial negation system still on minimum power, Sterling felt the kick of the thrusters begin to correct their uncontrolled spin. Then as the ship came under control, his own nausea began to diminish too.

"Point us at the aperture, Commander," said Sterling,

tapping his finger against the side of his console. "If our scanners can't tell us who is out there then hopefully our eyes can."

Banks acknowledged the order then worked the helm controls. Steadily the RCS thrusters oriented the Invictus so that it was facing the aperture they'd punched through at a ludicrously unsafe velocity. The viewscreen flickered as Sterling zoomed in on the interstellar gateway. Then he breathed a sigh of relief as all that was visible were the blinking lights of the beacons that marked the boundary of the aperture.

"Well, unless they're hiding right behind us, MAUL and his friends haven't arrived yet," said Sterling.

Ensign Keller then got to his feet, using the side of the helm control station for support. Sterling could see that the wound to his head, in addition to several other wounds that he'd hadn't noticed before, had been tended to by Graves.

"How's the patient, Commander?" Sterling asked his medical officer.

"He was actually dead for a time, but as ordered, Captain, I have revived him," Graves replied, dryly.

"I'm ready to take my station, sir," said Ensign Keller, who looked remarkably well for someone who had been dead only a minute earlier.

"He should be in the medical bay, Captain," Commander Graves cut in, though there was little conviction in his statement. Graves clearly knew that Sterling was not about to allow anyone to begin their convalescence just yet.

"Unless he's going to die again in the next few hours, I need my helmsman at the helm," Sterling hit back.

"He will not die of his current wounds," Graves replied, closing his medical kit and heading toward the exit. "Though of course we all may still die in the next couple of hours," Graves added, darkly.

"Thanks for the vote of confidence, doctor," said Sterling, as Ensign Keller replaced Commander Banks at the helm control station.

"Permission to return to medical, sir," Graves asked, halting by the side of the captain's console.

"Granted, Commander," Sterling replied, meeting the physician's strangely dead eyes. He was reminded of Graves' assertion that the doctor was not a necromancer, but at that moment he wasn't sure.

Turning back to the viewscreen and the blinking lights of the beacons, Sterling tapped his neural interface and connected to his temporary chief engineer. "Lieutenant Sullivan, what's the eta on our main engines?"

"Give me ten minutes, Captain," Sullivan replied. "Even without being able to see her, Sterling could tell that his engineer was bustling around the engine room like a furious wasp. "We'll only have about fifty percent thrust, but it will get us home."

Sterling was about to respond when the aperture flashed like a pulsar. Then his mouth went dry as a Sa'Nerran warship burst into existence, bearing the distinctive scars of countless battles.

"MAUL..." said Sterling, out loud.

The aperture flashed again and the two remaining

phase four destroyers appeared, followed closely after by three Skirmishers. Sterling cursed then focused back on his neural link to Lieutenant Sullivan.

"We're going to need those engines now, Lieutenant," said Sterling, his tone calm but urgent. "Or we're all dead."

IN THE SPACE of only a few minutes, the bridge crew of the Fleet Marauder Invictus had gone from comatose to being more alert and alive than Sterling had ever seen them. A Sa'Nerran strike force led by a warship that had racked up more individual kills than any other was bearing down on them, and Sterling knew there was no hope of defeating it. Their engines and scanners were down, power was sporadic and they were still a long way from Fleet space. It seemed hopeless, but Sterling had faced tough odds before and beat them. An ordinary ship and crew would be finished, but the Invictus was far from ordinary.

"Sullivan, any time now for those engines…" said Sterling, through a neural link to his temporary chief engineer. He had opened the link to allow his bridge officers to monitor.

"I can give you fifty percent capacity in thirty seconds, captain," Sullivan called back. "But there's a chance we'll just blow the fusion power distributors to hell trying."

"I'll take that chance, Lieutenant," replied Sterling, thumping his fist onto his console. In truth, he'd expected them to be dead in the water for longer. "Notify Ensign Keller directly when the engines are online."

Sullivan responded then Sterling closed the link. He peered out at MAUL for a few moments on the viewscreen, studying the scars on the ravaged hulk of metal for any areas of potential weakness. However, he knew it was folly to hope that MAUL was vulnerable. The vessel wore its damage proudly on the surface, like badges of honor, but underneath the battered hull was a killing machine in pristine fighting condition.

"Keller, set a course away from that wolfpack and aim us at the nearest aperture back to Fleet space," Sterling ordered.

Keller spun around; his face flustered. "Sir, without scanners, I can't get a fix on the aperture."

Sterling rushed over to his helmsman's side and quickly entered a sequence of commands into his console. "Before we sailed the stars, Ensign, we used to navigate by them," Sterling said, as the viewscreen switched to show empty space. A collection of stellar objects was then highlighted on the screen, ranging from distant nebulae and galaxies to clusters of stars. "There, head for the nebula that looks like a bull's head," said Sterling pointing to the highlighted phenomenon on the screen. From our current position, the portal is in that direction." We can fix the destination point exactly when the scanners come back online."

Keller nodded and made the adjustments on his console. "Course laid in to the bull's head nebula, sir."

Sterling jumped back onto this command platform and slid around the side of his console.

"Prepare to engage the engines with everything we've got," he called over to Keller, while resetting the viewscreen to show a magnified view of the strike force.

"Standing by, Captain," said Keller, fingers poised over the helm controls, waiting for Lieutenant Sullivan to notify him that engines were restored.

Sterling's console chimed in tandem with that of Commander Banks' station. He peered down at the system status readouts, waiting for the engine section to turn from red to green. *Come on, damn it...* Sterling thought, trying to will the ship into action with only the power of his mind. The status readout blinked then flashed between red and green before the color finally solidified and held steady.

"Engaging engines now!" Keller called out.

The heavy kick of the main engines engaging almost threw Sterling off his command platform, but he just managed to hold on to his console with the tips of his fingers.

"See if you can divert more power to inertial negation," Sterling called out, as the strength in his fingers began to wane. "There's no point in us escaping if we're just stains on the bulkhead."

"Aye, Captain," Banks replied, managing to work comfortably while holding on to her console with only one hand. Sterling often envied his first-officer's inhuman strength, but he did so now more than ever.

The forces on his body began to lessen and Sterling tried to relax his grip, though every muscle he had remained taught. He glanced at the viewscreen, seeing the relative velocity between the Invictus and the strike force decrease. The Invictus may have been wounded, but the Marauder-class destroyer was still one of the fastest ships ever built. *Hopefully, fast enough...* Sterling thought.

Suddenly the bridge was rocked hard, as if they'd collided with a comet or another ship. The lights on the bridge consoles flickered chaotically and Sterling detected that the pulsing thrum of the engines was gone.

"Reactor one has failed, sir!" Sullivan called out to Sterling through a neural link. "It's contained, but main engines have automatically shut down. It will be an hour before I can get them back, and even then, we won't have enough power to outrun the Sa'Nerra."

Sterling's hand clenched into a fist. "Do whatever you can, Lieutenant," he said. "I'll find us another option."

Sterling had again allowed the rest of the bridge crew to monitor his conversation. He wanted them to hear that he hadn't given up, and that there was still hope. Yet, the truth of it was he was out of ideas. Then out of nowhere, he felt a searing pain inside his head, like a migraine that suddenly switched on at full intensity. The pain was so concentrated he almost passed out.

"Captain, are you okay?" asked Banks. Sterling realized she was at his side, holding onto his arm.

"It's just a headache," said Sterling, as the pain began to subside. As it did so, he felt something else. Something familiar. Banks' console chimed an alert, but his first officer remained by Sterling's side and read the information on the captain's console instead.

"We're receiving an incoming communication," said Banks, brow scrunched into a frown. "It's coming from MAUL."

Ensign Keller and Lieutenant Shade both turned to face the captain's console. In all the decades that the Sa'Nerra had terrorized and waged war on the Fleet, never once had they attempted to communicate. Sterling was initially also confused, but then he understood the reason for the familiar feeling he'd experienced moments earlier.

"Put it on the viewscreen," said Sterling, meeting Banks' perplexed and doubtful eyes. "Trust me, Mercedes," he added, in a softer tone. "I think I know what's going on here."

Banks nodded then returned to her station. "Putting them through now, sir," she said, executing the command.

The image of MAUL and the Sa'Nerran strike force gave way to a figure dressed in Sa'Nerran warrior's armor. However, the figure itself was not a Sa'Nerran. It was Captain Lana McQueen.

Captain McQueen appeared in the center of the
bridge, presiding over the Sa'Nerran crew like a monarch.
To see his former friend and colleague seemingly in
command of MAUL - the Sa'Nerran fleet's top gun – was
both bizarre and unsettling. McQueen's armor was
identical to the armor Sterling was familiar with except for
its color. Instead of shades of darkness, McQueen's armor
had a golden luster, somewhere between bronze and brass.
Had it not been for the fact she was the only human aboard
an alien warship, the armor alone would have set her apart.
To McQueen's side, set one step back was a Sa'Nerran
warrior that was nearly as battle-scarred as the infamous
ship was. Its yellow eyes were locked onto Sterling's
through the viewscreen. He could hear the waspish hiss of
its breathing. The rest of the bridge was shrouded in
darkness, as if there was a stage spotlight focused on
McQueen and the alien at her side. Sterling had seen a lot

of strange things in his career, but he had to admit that the scene before him was tough to beat.

"Quite the run around you've given us, Captain," said McQueen, breaking the awkward silence that had followed since her appearance on the viewscreen. "Though I suppose I should have expected nothing less from the great 'Captain Lucas Sterling'," she added, bitterness seeping into her words. Then her eyes hardened. "I offered you a chance to join us, and in return you tried to kill me," she continued, forcing the words out through gritted teeth. The former Fleet captain then rapped her knuckles against her new Sa'Nerran armor, above the location where Sterling had shot her. "A shot to my heart, Lucas. How poetic, and also pathetic."

"My answer is the same, Lana, or whatever we're supposed to call you now," Sterling hit back. "You can play dress-up in that fancy armor and pretend you're one of them, but you're not. We'll never surrender, and neither will the Fleet. If there's anything of the real Lana McQueen still in there, she'd know that."

McQueen smiled, though there was none of the impishness that Sterling was used to seeing from the headstrong captain. This was a malevolent smile; the smile of someone who basked in cruelty and the misery of others.

"Surrender is such a noble-sounding word, don't you think?" McQueen finally answered. "An agreement between two honorable forces that one has bested the other. A very human word, and one the Sa'Nerra could never interpret, even through me." She placed her hands at the small of her back and raised her chin, instantly appearing to grow by two inches. "Submit, on the other hand, is a word the Sa'Nerra knows." She shrugged. "Or at least they understand its meaning. Submit, succumb, yield, expire, perish, die..." McQueen went on, her tone becoming sharper with each new word that escaped her lips. "The Sa'Nerra are not interested in your surrender, Captain. They merely crave your demise."

Sterling glanced down at his console, noting that their propulsion systems were still down. However, he could see that power was being re-routed and that engine controls were being diverted through secondary backups. Sullivan was busy, he realized. He had to believe she would come through.

"Then why 'join' them?" Sterling asked, resolving to keep McQueen talking for as long as possible. "If the Sa'Nerra simply want to extinguish humanity, all you're doing is assisting in your own murder."

"This is what you don't understand, Lucas," replied McQueen, shaking her head at him. "If you knew what I knew, and could feel what I feel, you'd know that it is the Sa'Nerra that deserve to prevail. There can be no peaceful coexistence between two species who were both born to conquer and rule. There can be only war, until one remains." McQueen's eyes softened a fraction then she drew her arms out from behind her back, reaching toward Sterling as if asking for him to take her hand. "I offer you again the chance to join me, Lucas. Join me in ending this war and the Sa'Nerra will ensure humanity does not suffer needlessly." McQueen then squeezed her open hand into a fist. "Resist and we will inflict suffering upon your colonies and worlds like nothing you could ever imagine."

The two sides of McQueen's temperament seemed to be constantly in flux. There were brief flashes of the Lana McQueen that Sterling remembered, but these were subordinate to a new, more dominant personality. And it was a persona that was darker and colder even than the heart of an Omega Captain.

"Partial scanners back online," Lieutenant Shade said to Sterling, communicating through a neural link. Sterling glanced down at his console, seeing the Sa'Nerran strike force closing in. However, the scanners were detecting something else too. An energy build-up from the vicinity of the aperture in the direction of the bull's head nebula.

Sterling glanced across to Banks, who had apparently also observed the build-up and was working frantically at her console. Her brow was furrowed and her jaw clenched shut. Then she thumped the side of her console, almost snapping it clean off its pedestal, and looked at Sterling. However, this time her expression had lifted, almost to the point of joy. Sterling glanced at his own console again then understood why. There was only one thing he knew of that could cause such a large build-up of energy that close to an aperture.

"You can take a message back to your Sa'Nerran masters from me," Sterling said, finally responding to McQueen's demand. "You can tell them Fleet will never submit, succumb or yield, and neither will I. If you want a fight to the death, so be it."

McQueen pulled her fist back to her chest and Sterling could see that it was shaking with rage.

"So be it, Captain Sterling," the former Fleet officer spat in reply. "The extermination of the human race begins now, starting with you." The viewscreen then faded back to the image of MAUL and the strike force.

"The Sa'Nerran vessels are getting ready to fire," said Lieutenant Shade, with urgency but without fear. "Wait, I'm detecting a surge. Whatever it is, it's big."

"There's nothing bigger, Lieutenant," replied Sterling, standing tall and peering out through the viewscreen expectantly.

Suddenly the Invictus was rocked by a powerful shock wave, but this time it wasn't a fusion reactor overloading. This was the result of a massive spatial distortion. Sterling's console flashed up an alert then what remained of the ship's scanners managed to update the reading. However, Sterling didn't need to look at his console to know the cause of the alert. He could already see it on the viewscreen.

"The Fleet Dreadnaught Hammer has just surged in," said Commander Banks, grinning up at the massive capital ship as its titanic hull dominated the viewscreen. Two more distortions then rocked the ship, though this time with less force. "Heavy Cruisers Javelin and Gladius just came onto the board too."

"It's about damn time!" said Sterling, thumping his console. His overriding feeling was not one of relief, but determination. Now they were more than a match for the strike force, even with MAUL in the mix. A sudden rush of adrenalin had set his pulse racing and his heart thumping.

It was time to stop running. It was time to take the fight back to the Sa'Nerra and its new mouthpiece, Lana McQueen.

"We're receiving a transmission," Banks added, glancing across at her captain.

"Put him through, Commander," said Sterling.

Captain Oscar Blake appeared inset on the viewscreen. "Need any help, Captain Sterling?" said Blake, not even bothering to disguise the smug look on his face. However, Sterling couldn't begrudge his former commanding officer a moment to gloat. He had arrived literally in the nick of time.

"If you insist, Captain," replied Sterling, with matching bravado. "We'll try to leave some of them for you."

The corner of Blake's mouth curled up then his image vanished from the viewscreen. Sterling could already see that the strike force had split up, with the Skirmishers forming a separate attack wing. The Sa'Nerran destroyers were heading for the Javelin and the Gladius, while MAUL, as usual, was less easy to predict. However, it looked like the Sa'Nerra's most decorated warship was angling to take on the Hammer.

"McQueen has some balls to take on a dreadnaught without her two escorts," said Banks, sounding like she almost admired the gutsiness of the move. Sterling, however, wasn't so sure. MAUL hadn't racked up the number of kills it had made by being reckless.

"Partial engines back online," Ensign Keller called out. "Controls are responding."

"Main power is stabilizing," Shade's voice called out, adding to the mix. "Regenerative armor is online."

"What about weapons, Lieutenant?" asked Sterling.

Sterling was sure he caught the flicker of a smile curl the lips of his stoical weapons officer, though he passed it off as a trick of the light.

"I can give you a few shots, sir," Shade replied, patiently waiting for Sterling to give the order he knew she wanted him to give.

"Then take us in," said Sterling, grasping the side of his console. "Use the Hammer for cover and pick off those Skirmishers. This time, we'll let the big guns handle MAUL and those Sa'Nerran destroyers."

A chorus of "aye, sir," rang out on the bridge then the Invictus accelerated in pursuit of the Fleet's mighty flagship. Plasma weapons-fire and high-explosive cannon rounds were already lighting up the space ahead of them.

"Stay clear of the Hammer's point defense perimeter," said Sterling, watching as a cloud of explosive shells erupted around the dreadnaught, taking out the slew of torpedoes that had been launched at the massive ship. The vivid flash of plasma rail guns then rippled across the hull of the Hammer and two Skirmishers exploded in flames. Sterling targeted one of the remaining Skirmishers on his console. It was maneuvering hard to avoid the Hammer's defensive perimeter, and had flown straight in front of them.

"All yours, Lieutenant," said Sterling, looking across to his weapons officer.

The flash of plasma weapons lit up the space ahead of

the Invictus then the Skirmisher was hit square in the middle of the vessel's broad back. The shots blasted a hole though the ship, leaving it on fire and spiraling out of control. Then the familiar thump of weapons fire impacting on their hull shook Sterling off balance. Another Skirmisher had turned to attack, but Sterling had barely opened his mouth to order Shade to engage, when a barrage from the Hammer reduced the enemy vessel to atoms.

"That brute is spoiling our fun," said Banks, though Sterling could tell that she was enjoying the fireworks show.

Sterling also allowed himself to smile, though he knew they weren't out of danger yet. Peering down at the readout from their partially functioning sensors, he looked for the famous heavy destroyer, but couldn't see it.

"Where the hell is MAUL?" Sterling said out loud. The scanner display flickered and he saw the vessel. The heavy destroyer had turned and burned hard away from the Hammer while it was occupied with the Skirmishers. MAUL's escorts had managed to separate the Javelin and Gladius from the protection of the capital ship, and now the two Fleet cruisers were trapped between the jaws of the Sa'Nerran strike force. More flashes lit up the darkness and the final Skirmisher disappeared off Sterling's scanner readout.

"Stay with the Hammer," Sterling called out to Ensign Keller, realizing that the cruisers were in danger. Turning to Shade, he added, "and throw everything we have left into one more volley from the main rail guns."

The Invictus drove on through the Void in the shadow

of the Fleet's monstrous capital ship. Sterling's fingers were tapping rapidly against the side of his console, urging them to go faster, but deep down he knew MAUL had outplayed them this time. Plasma fire flashed out from the alien heavy destroyer, and for a moment it looked like the entire ship was just one enormous weapon. The Javelin was struck first and obliterated. The Gladius tried to run, returning fire against MAUL, but the Sa'Nerran destroyers quickly reduced the Fleet cruisers engines to rubble and smoke. MAUL opened fire again and the Gladius was gone.

"Target that damn ship!" Sterling called out, feeling anger swell inside him.

His thoughts at that moment were not for the hundreds of lost souls aboard the cruisers, but for the woman who had turned her back on them all. He wanted Lana McQueen dead. However, the Sa'Nerra's new ambassador wasn't done fighting yet. MAUL and the Sa'Nerran Destroyers unleased a ferocious barrage at the Hammer, and Sterling saw explosions ripple across its hull. Sterling knew the dreadnaught well enough to know that McQueen had targeted it plasma guns on the starboard bow. The Hammer would need to turn its starboard beam toward the remainder of the Sa'Nerran fleet in order to get off another shot, and this would give MAUL another opportunity to strike.

"Weapons locked, Captain," Shade called out. "Charged to one-fifty percent."

"That'll melt the accelerator coils and render the whole weapons system useless," said Commander Banks.

However, Sterling was on the same page as his weapons

officer. They only had one shot, so they may as well make it a good one.

"Fire at will, Lieutenant," said Sterling. "We're going need a major refit anyway, so what does one more system matter?"

"Aye, sir," replied Shade, as the Hammer continued to turn. "Firing..."

The intense flash of plasma blasts on the viewscreen did nothing to ease Sterling's already aching head. Nor did the scream of alarms that followed as the damage control readout lit up, showing the catastrophic failure of their plasma weapons system. However, Sterling was focused only on the effect of their last-gasp attempt to rid the galaxy of their most deadly adversary. The plasma blasts tore through space and Sterling held his breath as they rippled through the wing of the battle-scarred heavy destroyer. Banks let out a victory cry, but Sterling knew they'd missed the killing blow by the narrowest of margins. Nothing but a direct hit would do. MAUL was not that easy to take down.

"MAUL has taken heavy damage, but their hull integrity is intact," Shade called out. Her fingers worked frantically at her weapons console, but then she shook her head. "But our weapons systems are gone. We have nothing left, sir."

"It's up to the Hammer now," said Sterling, willing the behemoth to turn faster. MAUL was already running for the aperture, leaving its two destroyer escorts to face down the Hammer instead. It was a suicide move, but like all good games of chess, a sacrifice was never made lightly.

"What the hell are they doing?" said Commander

Banks, watching the destroyers maneuver into an attack posture.

"They're sacrificing themselves," said Sterling, folding his arms. "They've moved into the line of fire so that the Hammer can't get another shot off at MAUL."

Banks huffed a laugh then shook her head. "That's damned cold. I've never seen the Sa'Nerra do that before."

"They've never had an Omega Captain on the bridge of a warship before," replied Sterling, glancing across to his first-officer. "She's playing us at our own game."

Sterling turned back to the viewscreen, just as the Hammer unleashed a full broadside, obliterating the two Sa'Nerran destroyers. However, it had taken heavy fire from the enemy vessels too. He knew Captain Blake well enough to know that he wouldn't risk the Fleet's flagship by pursuing MAUL deeper into the Void. The battle was over. McQueen had gotten away. Yet he knew in his bones that it would not be the last time they crossed paths.

Sterling tapped his neural interface and opened a link to Lieutenant Sullivan. "Good work, Lieutenant," he called out to his temporary chief engineer. "We're in the clear now, so ease down before we blow any other systems," he added. Half of his mind was distracted by the sight of MAUL and McQueen slipping away and it took him a few seconds to realize that Sullivan hadn't answered. "Lieutenant Sullivan, respond," Sterling said, attempting for a second time to make contact. However, the link appeared to be inactive. Cursing, he opened the link to everyone on the ship. "Lieutenant Sullivan, respond," he said again, growing more frustrated by the second. There was another pause then Commander Graves voice entered Sterling's head.

"Lieutenant Sullivan is dead, Captain," Graves said, matter-of-factly. "She was caught in a blast when the plasma weapons system overloaded. Five more dead, in all, sir."

Sterling sighed and shook his head. "Thank you, Commander. Sterling out," he said, closing the link.

Instead of sorrow at the loss of another crew member, Sterling's first thought had been how they would now patch-up the Invictus in order to limp back to F-COP. He again considered whether this made him a bad person, but then he reminded himself that this was war. Sullivan was the most recent to die, but she wouldn't be the last. That was the truth of it, as cold as it sounded. He couldn't afford to become mawkish or sentimental. All he could do was mourn the dead in his own way and ensure that their sacrifices – and the sacrifices of those still to come – were not for nothing.

CAPTAIN LUCAS STERLING leaned across the railings of the observation level in Hangar B of the Fleet Dreadnaught Hammer. Given the sorry state of the Invictus, it had been decided that they should dock and allow the Hammer to return them to F-COP. Admiral Griffin would no doubt be anxiously awaiting his report, and although he'd spent the last two hours going through everything that had happened in his mind, he still didn't know where to start. The major threat was, of course, the titanic vessel that the Sa'Nerra had been building inside the Void. That it appeared capable of somehow dematerializing small moons was worrying enough. However, somehow, he felt that the true threat was actually Lana McQueen. The Sa'Nerran ship was just metal and components. Ships could be destroyed - the only difference was the size of the boom when they exploded. Lana McQueen, however, was another matter. As a Fleet captain, she was a walking encyclopedia of Fleet knowledge, tactics and strategies, all of which were now in the hands of the enemy. However, more than this, she was an Omega Captain, just like Sterling. One of only two in the Fleet. She was cold, calculating and capable of anything, just like Sterling was. The Sa'Nerra had always been single-minded, efficient killers, but they were never callous. At least not in the way that McQueen could be. What his fellow Omega Captain's role was, and how much influence she had, were both big unknowns. However, her appearance on the bridge of the Sa'Nerran Fleet's most lethal vessel suggested she was more than a mere puppet.

"Tough little ship."

Sterling had been so lost in his own thoughts that suddenly hearing a voice behind him almost caused him to fall over the railings. He jerked around and saw Fleet Admiral Griffin standing to his rear.

"Admiral, I didn't realize you were on board," said Sterling, pushing away from the railings and straightening his back.

"I wasn't," said Griffin, stepping closer and leaning on the railings, as Sterling had just been doing. "I commandeered the Viking when your message was relayed to me. I was in E-sector at the time, with the third fleet."

"Looking for more recruits, eh?" said Sterling, taking the Admiral's cue and resting on the railings again.

"What I was or was not doing is not your concern, Captain," Admiral Griffin hit back. Sterling suppressed a smile. It hadn't taken long for the snippy flag officer to assert herself. Then Griffin surprised him by opening up a little. "With word of the enhanced neural control weapon spreading throughout the admiralty, the 'Void Recon Unit' is coming under tighter scrutiny," she continued, sounding even more aggravated than usual. "And then there's this super weapon to contend with. These two factors combined are leading to increased pressure by the United Governments for a diplomatic solution."

Sterling nodded, remembering his run-in with Captain Wessel and the veiled threats the irksome man made about the Void Recon Unit. He realized he hadn't had an opportunity to mention this to the admiral, but now didn't seem like the right time. Lana McQueen was still front and center of his mind.

"Who else knows about McQueen?" Sterling asked. He'd already sent a brief encoded report to the Admiral, using the secure communications chip Griffin had given him on F-COP.

"No-one but you, your bridge team and myself," Griffin replied, for once replying without making a point of chastising Sterling for prying. "The Hammer arrived too late to monitor McQueen's transmission, and obviously the Javelin and Gladius were lost, thanks to MAUL." Then Griffin appeared more wistful. "But it's only a matter of time. If you're right and McQueen is now acting as some sort of spokesperson for the damned enemy, we can expect her to make her presence known soon enough."

Sterling rubbed the back of his neck, feeling suddenly weary. He couldn't remember the last time he'd either slept or ate.

"McQueen is like us," Sterling eventually replied, watching the engineering crews inside the cavernous hangar deck below scurry around his ship. "She's devious and knows how to play the system. She'll use the UG's desire for peace as a way to coerce the war council into scaling back military operations further."

"Your analysis is unfortunately accurate, Captain, but it's actually worse than that," replied Griffin, looking even more pissed off than when she had arrived. "The knowledge that anyone could potentially be a turned agent for the Sa'Nerra will ripple throughout the Fleet like an earthquake. On one side of the fault line with be those who suspect their fellow crew, and on the other will be those who are under suspicion. The Sa'Nerra won't need to destroy us. We'll tear ourselves apart."

Sterling cursed under his breath. Then he realized that his knuckles had gone white from the pressure of gripping the railings and he had to force himself to relax his hold.

"This is why the Omega Taskforce is needed, now more than ever, Captain," Griffin continued. She then pushed away from the railings and locked her intense, clever eyes onto Sterling. Instinctively, he straitened to attention, again surprised by the almost supernatural power the Admiral held over him. "However, I'm afraid that for the time being, you're a taskforce of one. Until the dust has settled, there's little chance of me getting a replacement for the Imperium out of space dock any time soon."

Sterling hooked a thumb toward his own ship. "It's barely even a taskforce of one, Admiral. There's not much left of the Invictus as it is."

Griffin glanced over at the Marauder, nestled inside the belly of the Hammer, though she appeared unperturbed by its disheveled state. "That ship has proven itself, Captain, as have your crew," Griffin said before again locking eyes with Sterling. "As have you, Captain." This last sentence was said with pride, and despite himself, Sterling felt his chest swell. "We'll rebuild the Invictus, even stronger than before," Griffin added, turning back to the hangar bay, like a noble surveying her estate.

"The sooner the better," replied Sterling, also turning his attention back to his damaged ship. Griffin was right – it had taken a pounding, but it had come through when it mattered the most. "We need to find out more about this Sa'Nerran super ship, and the new neural weapon."

"Patience, Captain, you'll be back out there soon enough," said Griffin, her confidence betraying the fact she was clearly hatching plans in both of these areas. "As for the super-weapon, long range probes have already reported back. It's gone, though where we don't yet know. These are questions for another time, however. First, let's get you back into the fight."

Admiral Griffin turned to leave and Sterling straightened again as she stepped away. However, the flag officer made it only a few paces before stopping and glancing back at him.

"I already have a replacement chief engineer for you," Griffin said, seeming to have just remembered this fact. "She's only a senior lieutenant, and to be honest I only just promoted her to that rank," she added, being uncharacteristically forthcoming. "She comes with some baggage, but she'll keep you flying and that's all that matters."

"What's her name?" Sterling asked, intrigued by the admiral's colorful description of his new engineer.

"Lieutenant Razor. Katreena Razor," Griffin replied. "I'll have her report to you once we reach F-COP."

Admiral Griffin again turned away, but Sterling's curiosity, combined with his precociousness and talent for extracting information from the admiral spurred him on to ask another question.

"What did she do to merit the status of Omega officer?" Sterling asked. Such information would typically be in the new officer's file, but he couldn't guarantee this and didn't want to lose the opportunity to grill Griffin for answers.

Admiral Griffin's eyes narrowed and she folded her arms, apparently deliberating whether to answer Sterling's question.

"She sealed eight crew members inside a failing reactor chamber then ejected the core, along with all eight people inside," Griffin eventually replied. "It saved the ship. That ship then won the battle."

Sterling frowned. "That's a hard call, but I'd expect any hard-ass fleet engineer to make that same choice," he replied, a little disappointed by Griffin's explanation. "It doesn't sound like much of an Omega Directive test."

Griffin smiled, which was an expression that did not suit her war-weary face. "That wasn't intended to be part of the Omega Directive test, at least not one that I set up," Griffin replied. "The situation occurred by genuine accident, but the result was probably the toughest test anyone has faced."

This got Sterling's attention. He wanted to know what

was tougher than his own test, which had forced him to blast the head off his friend and fellow officer on the bridge of the Fleet Dreadnaught Hammer.

"Okay, you've piqued my interest," replied Sterling.

"One of the crew that she was forced to eject into space was her brother," Griffin said. "He was her twin, and the only family she had left in the universe."

Griffin then waited and observed Sterling's suitably stunned face for a moment before again turning to leave. Sterling considered responding, but in truth there was nothing to say. Griffin had answered his question. Besides, if the hardcore fleet admiral trusted Razor, he knew he could too.

"You were right about Shade, by the way," Sterling called out as the admiral strolled away. Opal Shade remained the only member of Sterling's crew that he knew barely anything about, since Griffin had remained oddly tight-lipped about her. "We wouldn't have survived without her." Sterling noticed that the admiral had stopped, but not turned back to look at him. He hoped that her current chattiness might encourage her to reveal something more about his mysterious weapons officer.

"That's good to hear, Captain," Admiral Griffin replied, her eyes still focused ahead. Then without another word, she marched away. However, to Sterling's perceptive eyes, the admiral appeared to be walking just a little taller than she had been before.

STERLING PUSHED a meatball around his meal tray, rolling it through the marinara sauce one way then another with his fork. Commander Mercedes Banks sat opposite him in the wardroom with an empty tray at her side. She had her elbows on the table and her chin resting on the backs of her hands, which were knitted together to form a cradle.

"If you're not going to eat that, slide it my way," Banks said. She had been greedily eyeing Sterling's meal tray for the last couple of minutes. "Twenty-two is a good one, so it's best not to let it go to waste."

Sterling skewered the meatball then held it up as if to taunt her with it. "Don't be polite, just get yourself another tray," he said. Then he waved the meatball in a circular motion, looking at the empty tables to their sides. "We're the only ones in here anyway. Everyone else is on F-COP while they conduct the repairs to the Invictus."

Bank shrugged then slid off her chair as Sterling shoved

the meatball into his mouth. It was already cold and he immediately regretted doing so.

"How come you didn't want to eat on F-COP?" Banks said, sliding over the serving counter and sifting through the different meal trays to find one she liked.

"I'm not in the mood for company," Sterling replied, tossing down his fork and nibbling on the selection of cheese crackers instead.

"If you want to be alone, I can go," said Banks, though she hadn't sounded affronted, and it came across as a genuine offer.

"No, I don't mean you, Mercedes," Sterling said, realizing his gaff and twisting around in his chair to look at her. "You're different."

Banks slid a meal tray into the processor then scowled back at Sterling. "Different, as in I'm not company?" she asked.

"Different, as in you're not like everyone else," said Sterling, realizing he was now digging himself further into a hole. "Different in a good way."

Banks shrugged again, seeming to accept Sterling's nonsensical response. "I guess we're all a little bit different on this ship."

Sterling tossed a handful of cheese crackers into his mouth then peered around the compact wardroom in the Invictus. Like much of the rest of the ship, it had not escaped unscathed. Some of the lights were out and sections of wall were twisted, torn open, blackened and scorched from power distribution nodes that had blown during their many battles. However, the food processors still worked, as did the TV screen that hung on the wall opposite Sterling's table. It was switched on, but muted, and was showing one of the numerous Fleet-run entertainment channels.

"We're more than a little bit different," Sterling said, turning back to Banks, who had slid the new meal tray out of the processor. Steam was billowing out from under its cover. "We're unique. The only Omega Taskforce ship left in the fleet. Maybe the only one there'll ever be."

Banks tore the protective film off the meal tray and shoved it into the recycler, then grabbed a clean fork and hopped over the counter again. Sliding the tray onto the table next to Sterling, she drew up a chair and sat beside him, instead of opposite.

"Do you want to talk about it?" Banks said, making a start on the food. Sterling noticed she'd also selected number twenty-two this time. Clearly, him taunting her with a cold meatball had tempted Banks into trying the tray for herself.

"Talk about what?" said Sterling, finishing off the last of the crackers on his tray.

"McQueen," said Banks, while skewering a couple of meatballs. "I know you two had a thing."

Sterling slid his chair around so that it was angled slightly toward Banks and regarded her with quizzical eyes. "I thought we already discussed us talking about my personal relationships," he said, surprised by the brazenness of the question.

"Apologies, Captain," Banks replied. "I didn't mean to be impertinent." She then fixed her gaze ahead and went back to devouring the meal.

Sterling sighed then slumped back into his chair, staring up at the TV screen. It was showing the latest episode of a popular game show, though even with the signal being passed through aperture relays, there was a significant lag compared to those closer to earth. However, he wasn't paying attention to the show. Banks had read his mood expertly. Lana McQueen had been pre-occupying his thoughts since he'd first seen her on the Sa'Nerran shipyard. However, the reason the turned captain was on his mind wasn't because they'd 'had a thing', as Banks had put it. It was because he couldn't shake the feeling that something major was about to happen, and that McQueen would be at the heart of it.

"Let's get one thing straight," Sterling said, glancing back to Banks, who had a fork halfway to her mouth. "I couldn't give a damn about Lana McQueen," Sterling continued, tapping his finger on the desk. "The only thing we had is sex." This statement shocked Banks like a slap to the face, causing her to choke on a meatball. It took several thumps of her chest to dislodge the chunk of processed, lab-grown meat, and several more seconds before she was able to breath properly again. "McQueen is bad news. She knows too much, and she's too much like us."

Suddenly, Banks' eyes narrowed and Sterling saw that she was looking up at the TV screen. He turned his attention to it and realized why. The quiz show had been interrupted by a news broadcast. Front and center on the

TV screen was Lana McQueen, dressed in her golden Sa'Nerran armor. A ticker underneath read, "Sa'Nerra Make Contact."

"Speak of the devil..." said Banks, folding her arms.

"Computer, turn up the volume on the TV," Sterling said, sitting bolt upright in his chair. The sound of Captain Lana McQueen's voice then filled the wardroom.

"The United Governments Fleet are the aggressors. The Sa'Nerra want only peace, but your warmongering military masters simply want to conquer us," said McQueen, in what appeared to be a pre-recorded statement. "As a former Fleet officer, I have joined with the Sa'Nerra to act as emissary," she continued, offering the viewer a warm smile that made Sterling want to spit blood. "I urge the people of Earth and the United Governments territories to speak to your leaders to seek a peaceful resolution to this bloody conflict." The camera then pulled in tighter on McQueen's face. "But be warned. The Sa'Nerran desire for war is not the only lie Fleet has been telling you. Ask them about the Omega Directive. Ask them why Fleet ships are sent to hunt and kill your own people. Once you know the truth, I am confident that you too will join with me in fighting for peace."

The image then pulled back to a wider-angle shot, but this time there was someone else standing beside McQueen. Sterling leaned closer to the screen, his eyes scrunched up, scarcely able to believe what he was seeing.

"Wait, is that Lieutenant Commander Crow?" said Banks, also leaning closer.

Sterling massaged his temples, which were suddenly throbbing with pain.

"Yes, it is..." Sterling said, staring at his former engineer on the screen. A large metal plate covered the left side of his head, from his forehead above his left eye to the base of his skull.

"What the hell have they done to his head?" asked Banks.

"I shot him, instead of allowing him to be captured," replied Sterling, candidly. "I didn't want another command-level officer being turned like McQueen."

To most people, Sterling's admission would have been shocking, perhaps even disturbing. However, Banks was an Omega officer. She knew that sometimes in war, you had to do terrible things.

"We obviously need better guns," said Banks, shaking her head at the duo of turned Fleet officers. "I'll see what I can arrange."

The faces of McQueen and Crow then faded to black and were replaced with the words, "Best Wishes from Your Sa'Nerran Emissaries for Peace."

Sterling barked a laugh at the screen as the bulletin then switched back to a reporter, who was beginning an analysis of the breaking news. "Computer, turn that damn thing off," Sterling barked, hurling his fork at the device. It missed and bounced off the wall just below the screen before clattering onto the metal deck.

"We have to kill her," said Banks. Sterling noticed that the fork in her right hand had been mangled under the pressure of her grip. Her left hand was clamped around the table. Four finger-shaped indentations were now pressed into the surface. "We have to kill them both."

"The damage is already done," sighed Sterling, flopping back into his chair and meeting his first-officer's eyes. "Fleet will move fast to deny everything, and put a spin on it, but enough people will still believe. Things will be different now, for us most of all."

Banks pushed her tray into the center of the table and sat back in her chair alongside Sterling. Neither of them spoke; there didn't seem to be anything more to say. Then the computer chimed an alert – the equivalent of a polite cough in order to get someone's attention – and Sterling waited for the inevitable summons.

"Captain Sterling, Fleet Admiral Griffin has requested that you, 'get your ass into her office right now'." The computer announced, cheerfully.

"Sounds like Griffin caught the news too," said Banks.

Sterling pushed out his chair and stood up. Given the emotional and physical ups and downs he'd experienced in the last few days, he was surprised he wasn't still dizzy from the ride. However, he also knew that the roller coaster they were on had just begun, and was only going to get worse.

"Come on, let's go and see the Admiral," said Sterling, holding out a hand to Banks, who was still slumped in her chair like a bored teenager in class.

"You want me to come?" Banks replied, snapping her body upright.

"We're in this together, whether you like it or not," said

Sterling, still with his hand stretched out. "It's me and you, Mercedes. Me and you against the whole damned galaxy. If the Fleet wasn't suspicious of us before, they're going to hate us now." Then he frowned and pulled his hand away. "Unless you want out?"

Banks stood up, seeming to rise to a height that was even taller than Sterling, despite the fact she was three inches shorter. "I don't want out. I want to get further in," she said, holding out her hand. "I'm in this till the end."

Sterling smiled and went to take Banks hand, but as he reached out, she drew it back. "Unless you're just going to end up shooting me in the head, like Crow," Banks added, cocking her head in the direction of the TV screen.

Sterling knew it was meant in jest – a bit of lighthearted fun to break the tension – but all he could see at that moment was the face of Ariel Gunn. It had been Admiral Griffin who had put him in the position of having to shoot his friend – an act that had landed him command of the Invictus. He hadn't wanted to do it. He didn't want to be in a position where he might have to do something similar again. Yet he also knew that if the situation arose where killing one of his own officers was necessary in order to save the ship or even win the war then he wouldn't hesitate. And he needed Banks to know that.

"If it comes to it, Mercedes, and you get turned, then you need to know that I will kill you," said Sterling, with the cold, factual delivery of an Omega Captain. "And if it comes to it, I need you to do the same to me."

Banks eyes narrowed. "It won't come to that, Lucas,"

she said, her muscles becoming tauter. Sterling could see a glimmer of the wild Mercedes Banks in her eyes. The Mercedes Banks that could lose control.

"But if it does. Swear to me you'll do it," said Sterling, still with his hand outstretched.

Bank clasped her hand around Sterling's, gripping so tightly that he heard his knuckles crack.

"If it comes to it, I swear I will kill you, rather than let you be turned," said Banks.

The tone of her voice was firm and unwavering. Sterling knew in his bones that she meant what she had said. He nodded and tightened his own grip on Banks' hand, though it felt like squeezing a block of solid metal.

"Let's just hope it doesn't come to that," Sterling said, releasing Banks' hand. "Now, let's go and see the Admiral. We have work to do."

Commander Mercedes Banks stepped alongside Captain Lucas Sterling and together they left the wardroom of the Fleet Marauder Invictus. Like them, the ship had been through a war. And like them, it had not escaped without scars. The Omega Taskforce may have been reduced to one, and Sterling knew that McQueen's statement would only make it harder for them to operate. Yet, he was undeterred. His ship and his crew had proven themselves in battle. They'd do so again. The war was about to take a sharp turn for the worse, but Sterling was unafraid. Desperate times called for desperate measures. The rest of the Fleet may not like who they were and what they stood for, but they didn't have to. Sterling and the crew of the Fleet Marauder Invictus would take the fight to the enemy, in ways the others could not. And maybe – just maybe – that would be enough to tip the balance back in their favor. It had to be, because if they failed, the war was lost. And Captain Lucas Sterling didn't like to lose.

The end (to be continued).

CONTINUE THE JOURNEY

Continue the journey with Omega Taskforce Book Two: Void Recon. Available from Amazon.

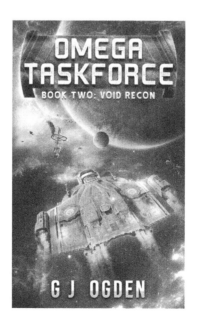

At school, I was asked to write down the jobs I wanted to do as a "grown up". Number one was astronaut and number two was a PC games journalist. I only managed to achieve one of those goals (I'll let you guess which), but these two very different career options still neatly sum up my lifelong interests in science, space, and the unknown.

School also steered me in the direction of a science-focused education over literature and writing, which influenced my decision to study physics at Manchester University. What this degree taught me is that I didn't like studying physics and instead enjoyed writing, which is why you're reading this book! The lesson? School can't tell you who you are.

When not writing, I enjoy spending time with my family, walking in the British countryside, and indulging in as much Sci-Fi as possible.

Subscribe to my newsletter:
http://subscribe.ogdenmedia.net

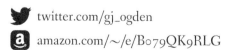

twitter.com/gj_ogden
amazon.com/~/e/B079QK9RLG